THE MAN WHO WOULDN'T DIE

THE MAN WHO WHO WOULDN'T DIE

A NOVEL

A. B. JEWELL

WILLIAM MORROW
An Imprint of HarperCollins*Publishers*

HarperCollins books may be purchased for educational, business, or sales promotional use. For information, please email the Special Markets Department at SPsales@harpercollins.com.

FIRST EDITION

Designed by Diahann Sturge

Front matter art © agsandrew/Shutterstock, Inc.

Library of Congress Cataloging-in-Publication Data

Names: Jewell, A. B., author.
Title: The man who wouldn't die / A.B. Jewell.
Description: First edition. | New York, NY : William Morrow, [2019]
Identifiers: LCCN 2018037121 | ISBN 9780062201201 (paperback)
Subjects: | BISAC: FICTION / Thrillers. | GSAFD: Noir fiction.
Classification: LCC PS3618.I36 F67 2019 | DDC 813/.6--dc23 LC record
   available at https://lccn.loc.gov/2018037121

ISBN 978-0-06-220120-1

19 20 21 22 23 LSC 10 9 8 7 6 5 4 3 2 1

TO UNCLE MORT

AS FAR AS POSSIBLE WITHOUT SURRENDER, BE ON GOOD TERMS WITH ALL PERSONS.

—MAX EHRMANN,
"DESIDERATA: A POEM FOR A WAY OF LIFE"

STRIKE WITH KINDNESS. IF THAT GOES SOUTH, THE THUMPER.

—FITCH

THE MAN WHO
WOULDN'T DIE

ONE

MY FACE WAS buried in an expense report when the office door swung open. A woman in a silk blouse moving like a blue streak didn't stop until she reached the front of the desk.

"You've got to help me."

"Clyde . . ." I muttered. I looked through my half-open door to see why my receptionist had failed, once again, to stop an interloper. By the time I turned back to the woman, she was already midsentence. ". . . Captain Don, I'm sure you heard. It was no accident. I have proof."

"Slow down, Ms. . . ."

"Donogue. Tess."

"Clyde!"

Nothing fried me like doing expenses, since it was one of the handful of things I expected of Clyde, along with answering the phone and keeping people from barging in. It had already been one of those mornings. I nearly missed the subway thanks to the flash mob outside the Apple store. Bunch of Phippies—hippies who protest phone-related injustice.

What do we want?
Extended store hours.
When do we want it?
Sundays and holidays.

"Do you have an appointment, Ms. Donogue?"

"Please, Mr. Fitch—"

"Fitch."

"Fitch." She crossed her arms. This one wasn't used to hearing no. With a slender finger she curled sandy-blond hair behind one ear. She looked at the license hung crookedly in a bare space on the wall. I half expected her to put me in my place by pulling out her degree from the Stanford Graduate School of Business.

"I hear you're the best. I'll do anything," she said. She flashed a smile but her heart wasn't in it. Exhaustion tugged the skin under her eyes. She'd been attractive in her day, and commanding, and that day wasn't so long ago. In this town, I've heard a term used for someone like her: TELF, Tech Executive I'd Like to Fund.

"Look," she said, "I can get you friends and family shares."

I clenched my teeth. Early on a Monday, I thought, for this kind of desperation. A guy had come in a few weeks earlier and tried to weasel out of his bill by offering me solar panels for my car. Since the second boom started and the techies came north, I figured I'd heard it all.

I held up my left hand, flashed the ring finger. "I'm all filled up with friends and family."

"I thought you guys were all lone wolves."

"State your business, Ms. Donogue." The famous last name swelled in my mouth. Tasted like the entire month's nut. Made it tough to toss her on her keister. "You busted in past Clyde and I'm knee-deep in figuring monthly expenses."

"I'm sorry. That was presumptuous. I'm trying to get your attention."

I scratched my face. I should've shaved.

"Your dad died. Cycling Skyline. I'm sorry, but accidents happen."

I'd read it in the paper—it made all the news. Donald Donogue, Captain Don, technology industrialist and garden-variety eccentric, flipped over the handlebars and face-planted not long after fueling up at Alice's. It happened two weeks earlier, then a big memorial with mucho heart rending about Captain Don's world-changing ideas. After making his money on this thing and that, he became obsessed with using singularity to achieve immortality, some sort of far-fetched nonsense to use computers to create eternal life.

"It wasn't an accident," Ms. Donogue said. She spread her palms open, flat, like: *Don't you see?*

"So you said. Respectfully, that's why we've got police, Ms. Donogue."

"*Mrs.*"

"Excuse me?"

"Mrs. When I got married, I kept my maiden name but took the Mrs."

I must've shaken my head because she explained: "Helps balance tradition and independence. Tradipedence, for short, maybe. The community is still crowdsourcing the nomenclature."

I didn't bother to ask what community.

"Listen, Mrs. Donogue . . ."

"Technically . . ."

"I've got a day job."

After doing the expense reports, I'd planned to help work on a nothing-fancy case for a landlord who was paying to prove his suspicion that his renter in the Outer Richmond was involved in unlawful behavior.

"Technically, I'm still married, but we're separated. It's ugly. It's all so ugly . . . I went to the police. They didn't exactly laugh me out of the place, but what could they do? My dad flipped over his . . . He hit his head . . ." This seemed genuinely painful. "A witness saw it. So the police don't see why they should go beyond that. I need a detective. Like I said, I hear you're good. The best."

"I'm very sorry to hear about your father. The thing is, I'm booked. I wish I could . . ." I paused. "What makes you think it wasn't an accident?" Nearly hated myself for letting that one through the filter. And I was positive I'd still hate myself for it later.

"I got a message," she said insistently. She reached into her bag. It was one of those newfangled deals that were all the rage, part purse, part briefcase, backpack, computer bag, low-energy refrigeration device. What Bond would wear if he needed quick access to a detachable, Bluetooth keyboard—at Davos. She pulled out a piece of paper and unfolded it. Glanced at the paper but didn't show me.

"It says Daddy was murdered."

"I'll play along. What's it say, exactly?"

She hesitated. She turned away from me and sat in Old Leather, the recliner opposite my desk that my better half, Terry, got me when I opened up the place. My visitor kept her face down in the paper and I took a breath and added up the last three minutes: woman barges in, starts yammering like she's pitching a VC in an elevator—dead guy, mysterious circumstances, nowhere to turn. Only thing about it that made sense was that she'd flown past Clyde. Not so tough, since he tended to think of his day job as trading gossip on the Hollywood Stock Exchange.

While I waited for her to choose her words carefully, I couldn't help wondering who would refer this trustafarian to an ill-tempered dick with a basement office just off Church, below the old Pasta Primadora, where they now hold the AA meetings at lunch.

"He says it was no accident," she said. She'd started quivering.

"Who does?"

"My father. Captain Don."

"Come on now. Make some sense."

"The message is from my dad. It says: 'No accident. They got me. I hope you' . . ." She stopped and looked up. "That's where it stops. 'I hope you' . . . Maybe he ran out of characters, but I think otherwise."

"Your dad sent you an e-mail warning he was going to be murdered? Why didn't you say something before the . . . before he died?"

She looks down. "I didn't *get* it before he died."

"C'mon, just say whatever it is you're saying." I finally lost it. This kook needed to go back to wherever she came from.

"I got it yesterday!"

"You got an e-mail yesterday from your dad." Unsaid: *who died two weeks ago.*

"A tweep, actually, but yes . . ."

Now my prospective yawn turned into a prospective eye roll.

"Listen." I tried for sympathetic. "Some huckster is messing with you."

"No!"

I leaned back.

"No," she repeated, more softly. "He used my private account and my . . . my private name. He sent this himself. Yesterday."

"How do you figure?"

"You know what Daddy was into—singularity, plus."

I'd had some vague idea. Singularity, the idea that computers will someday think for themselves. Sentience. Donogue was one of those nuts who said the real end game of all this technology is eternal life, through electronic union with our gadgets. Equal parts engineering, neuroscience, and witchcraft. Even more nonsense than Faceburg turning a profit or video games as education tools. But it attracted some big-time followers.

"This tweep, Mr. Fitch . . ."

"Fitch. What about it?"

"He sent it from beyond."

TWO

THE DOOR BURST open, giving way to a whir of pageantry. Clyde had tied purple bows around the bottoms of his dreads. Looked like Medusa got a makeover.

"I told you. I told you . . ." he started. Six feet and 145 pounds of broken blender motor, Clyde moved and talked in whirs and jerks.

"Clyde . . ."

"I told you Jolie and Pitt would adopt again! I knew it. Apart and still building that beautiful family. Boom!"

"Clyde."

"From Ethiopia. Anywhere from East Africa pays six to one! Who's this?" Clyde looked at the damsel in the leather chair. Then at me. "Oh, you had a visitor earlier."

"Clyde, this is Mrs. Donogue. She walked right past you earlier. *She's* the visitor."

"Right, makes sense. Did you offer her coffee?" he asked me, then blinked. "Donogue?"

"That one."

"Oh." Clyde did a singsong thing with his head, back and

forth. His tasseled dreads swayed. He was orienting, which usually took him some time. I'd gotten used to the idea that Clyde's neurochemicals ebbed and flowed. Terry said he should be long gone, but I had a soft spot, having known a few addicts in my day, some in my own family. Irish Catholic and all that. Anyhow, aside from the fact that he was terrible at his job, Clyde's . . . well, there's not really an anyhow. He was terrible at his job. Period.

"I'm going to the noon meeting."

"Was there a reason you came in here other than to tell me you made money on Brangelina?"

"Um . . ."

"What's in your hand, Clyde?"

"Oh yeah, Lieutenant Gaberson called."

He walked forward and put a note on my desk, from an old-school phone pad available only online or at Office Depot. I had a rule: nothing in e-mail. Never dies. That edict went through my mind as I glanced at the note from Clyde. Never dies. Like my visitor's father. Give me a break.

"Says it's important," Clyde said.

Lieutenant Gaberson was my best contact in the SFPD. Knew him during a brief stint with the ATF; we parted ways after he decided to join a local department and I decided to take the option of resigning gracefully rather than being fired for a gentle haymaker I gave a meth dealer to stop him, in real time, from beating the shit out of the kid who turned him in. In the private sector, haymakers aren't verboten, but they do cost extra.

"Thanks, Clyde. Can *you* offer Mrs. Donogue coffee?"

"I'm working on the expense reports."

"You were trading gossip. I'm doing the expense reports."

"No wonder I couldn't find them. Go for it, if you'd prefer." He looked as if he might leave but instead stepped back and eye-balled our visitor. Whatever else you could say about Clyde, he'd experienced enough in his day to see right through people.

"Your dad was a serious kook," Clyde said to Mrs. Donogue. I almost reprimanded him but his tone was reverent, and if you knew Clyde, the word itself—"kook"—was reverent too. He meant to say the old man, now presumed dead, walked to the beat of his own drum.

"Thanks, I think." She turned to me. "So you'll take the case?"

"What case?" asked Clyde.

"Don't be late for your meeting." I tried to dismiss him. But he didn't move.

"What, Clyde?"

"I'm going to the afternoon meeting too." He looked at our visitor, studied her. "My name is Clyde and I'm an addict."

"Hello, Clyde."

This lady seemed pretty together for someone getting e-mails from the grave. I turned to Clyde as he was hopping foot to foot. On the edge again. Two meetings was a bad sign.

"Take the afternoon off, Clyde."

"'Preciate it." He whirred away.

"So you'll take the case?" Mrs. Donogue turned back to me.

"No." No sooner had the word sprung out than I sensed the lie. Who was I kidding? I wasn't saying no, not yet. I was negotiating. Even the Snipchap people turned down $3 billion the first time around. Then doubled their money. Besides, Terry wanted to go on a fall cruise somewhere warm and, for the backyard, wanted low-thirst-plant landscaping, seeing as how we've not had rain in months. Money for succulents doesn't grow on trees.

"Please, Fitch."

"Respectfully, do you hear yourself? You're telling me that your father sent you an e-mail after he died."

"Tweep. I know how it sounds. I'm just asking you to look into it. Can I show you something?" She rummaged in one of the nine zippered side pockets of her brief-pack. She pulled out a picture, which she placed on my desk. I leaned over, catching sight of the expense reports in my peripheral vision.

The picture looked printed from one of those clunky full-color ink-jets. It showed the old man himself, standing over his bicycle next to another lean old-timer on a bicycle. Smiling, leathery men, sweat trickling from their helmets. Arms around each other's shoulders.

"Do you know who that is next to Daddy?"

I shook my head even though the guy looked familiar.

"Alan Klipper," she said.

Klipper the Shipper.

"Yeah," like she was confirming my thoughts. "The guy with the boats." Understatement of the year; Klipper's yachts ran to the dimensions of the Sears Tower, the one christened *Speak Freely* used only for sensitive TED Talks held in international waters. His submarine, they said, could go toe to stern with the Russian navy, what hadn't been sold off for parts.

"What am I supposed to be looking at?"

"These two, the pair of them, they *are* singularity meets immortality. In the last weeks, they were together all the time. They were doing something, *on*to something. I'm telling you. All the secrecy and chatting and all that reminded me of when Daddy met with Jobs before the Apple TV launch."

"Wasn't that a dud?"

"Just ahead of its time."

I smirked. "Not my kind of job."

"I can get you in the front door with Klipper."

I pretended to consider her offer. "I'm not an MBA." But I took her point: I couldn't even begin to guess how many entrepreneurs would give the family egg donor for five minutes with the big investor.

"His grandson, my estranged . . ." She choked on it. "I can get you in to see Danny Donogue too. He worshipped his grandfather. My son is the future."

Danny Donogue, that name rang a bell too, but I couldn't place it beyond his position in the zeitgeist.

"Look, I know what you think when you look at me. Socialite, the kind of woman who gets what she wants, strong and beautiful."

"Um . . ."

"It's not just that. I'm a good person. A decent person. In each of the last few years, I've raised money and traveled with students from Palo Alto high schools to see some of the InEfs."

"I'm not familiar."

"It refers to parts of the world, other places, that aren't flourishing, that aren't as efficient as Silicon Valley. Most of them are overseas. But some are in our own backyard, in the United States."

"You've got to be kidding me."

"I know. In *America*. It really opens up these kids' eyes to understand that there are entire communities, right here, that aren't maximizing. It's not their fault, obviously. It's about resources and culture." She had totally missed my meaning. "Anyhow, Mr. Fitch, my point is, I'm not all about the money."

"Fitch."

"But I know it's important. And I assume it's important to you. Or, I assume you do like money—or, at least, need it."

Boom. Just like that, it was end-of-flirtation time, the moment I've been waiting for. We were at the point when I got to hear how much it was worth to this woman for me to go ghost hunting.

"You've got a standard rate," she said.

Sure, $550 a day plus expenses, I didn't say. "Doesn't apply to grave digging."

"Fitch, I am telling you that something very strange is going on. Someone killed my father, or tried to. I'm sure of it."

"Tried t—"

I took her meaning just as she interrupted me. "He's out there." She grandiosely swept her hand across the air.

I sucked in a deep breath. "A grand a day plus a two-thousand-dollar signing bonus, nonrefundable. I don't get off my ass, I keep it."

"That's ridiculous. Do I look like the federal government?"

I held my tongue. When had the biggest whipping boy in the world become the people who paved the roads? I didn't like it any more than the next guy, but, Christ, everyone in the Valley thought they could "change the world," one app at a time, while the government played the role of just another customer.

"That's my price."

"When can you start?"

I almost laughed at her quick embrace of my price. I looked at the mug Terry got me that read *Big Daddy's* and thought I should replace it with one that read *World's Worst Negotiator*. This woman spoke in *B*s, billions, and I'd just low-balled her with the price of an appetizer at the French Laundry.

"And expenses." I eked out some self-respect.

"Of course. I've got a list of a few people . . ."

"Stop."

She looked up at me as I stood for the first time since she'd tsunamied in here. She seemed off balance.

"You're a large person," she said.

Six-four when I'm crouching, two-fifty when I'm benching. A gut, sure, but Terry always said it was more to love. "I can handle myself." I winced when I wasted this truth on her. "This is the part where you stop telling me what to do."

"Of course." She lowered her blue eyes. Raised them again. "How can I help?"

"I'll think on that."

She stood as well. She patted the picture.

"And the e-mail," I said.

"Tweep." She paused. She unfolded the piece of paper, put it next to the picture.

"Mrs. Donogue, I'll be honest with you. There is no way that your father wrote an e-mail—tweep—from the grave. Maybe he wrote it before he died. Maybe someone else wrote it. Maybe you made the whole thing up."

She looked me dead in the eye. "People doubted my father for years. They doubted when he said there would be dumb terminals, doubted his investment in mobile, the motion-sensor stuff, Big Data. So I don't blame you for being a skeptic."

"Fancy boxes with wires are one thing, eternal life is altogether different."

"Most of his stuff was wireless."

"You take my point."

"I don't actually. The human brain is a computer. It computes and stores data. It uses an electrical system."

"Okay, so?"

"So my father figured out how to keep the brain on ice. How to keep it alive, plugged in. How to connect it to the data stream even after the body was . . ." Her voice trailed off.

"Go on." I was at a remarkable crossroads between intrigued and incredulous, like watching a reality TV show when the host yells "surprise!" 'cause everyone's been eating kitten.

"He called it the Spirit Box." She said it softly again, incredulous herself, or embarrassed. "Immortality of our minds, our selves, the brain. I think Daddy figured it out. He solved it. I think someone killed him for it."

I'd had enough. "Leave me your down payment, phone number, and a way to reach this Klipper. I'll report back in a few days."

She reached into her purse-back-case. "You take Bitcoin?"

"No."

She shrugged. "Virtual currency has the upside of equity."

"Cash."

"Have it your way."

I finally said it: "For someone whose dad just died, you're pretty on the ball."

"My dad would've hated the idea that just because he died, er, died-ish . . . I'd suddenly stopped trying to be efficient. I want to solve his murder and I want you to help me."

She laid money and contact information on the desk and started walking to the door. Just before she walked out, she ran a hand along the back of her blue skirt to smooth it down. She peeked over her shoulder, suggestion made.

"I'll be in touch." But I'm not sure she heard me as she disappeared the way she came in.

I looked down at the photo, then the urgent message from Lieutenant Gaberson. Then the expense reports. I thought: there's no amount of caffeine in the whole goddamn world . . .

THREE

LIEUTENANT GABERSON AND I had a monthly standing coffee date at Lindy's. Literally standing. Turned out, the research showed, it was bad for some reason to go from a standing desk to a sitting coffee. There's a metric showing that it throws off parking karma or some ridiculous nonsense, but you argued with Big Data at your own risk. For years, Gaberson and I had come to Lindy's and then it turned standing-room-only, as advertised, even when it was mostly empty. Which it was not on this cloudy midmorning.

Just as I arrived, there was a scuffle in the long line out front. Gaberson explained that they'd just gotten new beans in from Argentina, some family-owned plot that produced two pounds every six years, and Lindy's had won the lottery for half a pound. The line had been building for days. Some guy near the front wasn't scent-free and everything unraveled from there.

"Let's go to Starbacks," Gaberson muttered.

This, whether intended or not, quelled the in-person, Insta-charm flame war over who deserved the rare beans. They all had a new common enemy: us and our gutter tastes in coffee.

Ten minutes later, we'd perched in a green booth on Market near Van Ness. Gaberson was carrying a brick-size black case, looked like something you'd use to store snow chains. He set it at his feet, under the booth. He didn't explain and I didn't ask.

The place was empty except for three middle-aged men, sitting separately but each wearing a hoodie graced on the front with the word "Fresno," the latest city whose name inexplicably had begun to label all clothing.

"Lieutenant, to what do I owe the pleasure?"

He twirled his super-petit chai. I'm a big fan of Gaberson. It wasn't easy working with the PD and their shrinking resources and ever-changing demands. A year earlier, he was right in the middle of their new community policing test for which, over the course of a day, he had to ask people in a twelve-square-block area how they were feeling. Never bitched about it. Not to me.

He did the thing with his lips where he runs them like a motor. I could see he was figuring out how to tell me something. Gave me a little pause. Gaberson didn't shrink from the truth, or anything. Lean all around. He stood about six feet tall, wiry, tough; at the academy, he'd won the Kale Challenge half marathon the night after he drank Mark's Hard Limeade until dawn. He wore wire-rims and cut his hair himself, but you wouldn't have known it.

He was about to say something when his phone rang with U2's "Sunday Bloody Sunday"—his tone. He pulled the gadget out of his windbreaker, glanced, grimaced, set it on the table.

"How're you doing, Fitch?"

"Cut the crap." No edge to it, though.

He nodded; yeah, fair enough, he'd cut the crap. One more

motor churn with his lips. I took a sip of my Scorpion Bowl—coffee, Red Bull, echinacea.

"We're gonna have to chill for a while," he said, glancing up.

I let the words settle in. Nodded like I was thinking it over. But it was pretty clear what he was talking about. Gaberson and I had a mutually beneficial, if unofficial, relationship. He asked me to check into things now and again that might not meet the letter of approved police procedure and I asked him to run things through the databases, and no one was the wiser. It'd helped us each catch a few bad guys who might otherwise have slipped away or taken longer to net.

"The Argyle case?"

He nodded, pulled his lips tight. "Come home to roost," he said.

Had to figure it would at some point. Too much about it smelled too rotten below the placid surface. Before he could elaborate, his phone rang again. He reached to silence it.

"Take it," I said, starting to scoot out of the seat to give him some privacy.

"It's not a call."

"Text?"

He shook his head. He silenced the phone. "New app I can't figure out how to get off the phone." He rolled the gadget over in his hand like he was looking for some mystery button he'd not found. "Every few minutes or so it rings to let me know that it hasn't rung in a while."

"Sorry, I'm not—"

"Of course it doesn't make sense. It's an app to let me know that my ringer is still working in case I get panicked that I'm not getting anyone checking in. Truly insane, but like I say, I can't figure how to get rid of it."

I shook my head.

"Somehow, Bono got it on here," he continued. "Arranged it with Jobs, is how I hear it. People say they love the feature. Doesn't just let them know the ringer's still working but reminds them to check the phone in case they've put it on silent."

"But if you have it on silent, doesn't that mean you don't want . . ." I realized the folly of this conversation. Besides, something else struck me. "Isn't Steve Jobs dead?"

He shrugged. "When you're that big, you can put things in motion, keep them in motion, even after . . ." He laughed. "Jesus, the stuff I hear. Jobs is still pulling the strings. Anyhow, about Argyle."

I'd stopped midsip. "What do you mean Jobs is still pulling the strings?"

Another shrug. "Nothing. Nonsense, stuff you hear. He's still"—Gaberson looked around the room, eyes sweeping the ceiling—". . . out there."

"You're serious." Second time I'd heard something like this in the last hour.

"Not really. We're getting off topic. My bad. Argyle."

I let this odd moment pass. Turned my brain to the Argyle sextuplets, reaching their sweet sixteen when I first came across them. Great cover story, so to speak. Darlings of reality TV, traveled the country, backstage passes to every event, skipped through airplane security. Five boys and one girl, the mastermind. Then, after their six-month blitz run as America's darlings, they seemed to drop off the map and return to their San Mateo roots to run a summer tennis and piano camp in Mandarin. Gaberson, who was working the quasi-celebrity beat at the time, was instantly suspicious: Who doesn't try to parlay a reality show into a sequel? The Argyles, that's who. They were just lying low.

And kept rolling in dough.

So Gaberson asked me to do a little freelancing and it was clear within days that their hands were dirty with something. Late-night rendezvous, lingering in the back of the store after book signings, plane flights south of the border. Visits to South by Southwest when they weren't even presenting. You don't have to have worked in the ATF to recognize drug runners when you find them. I had it all zipped up by the time I gave it to Gaberson. It was smooth as silk right up until the bust.

Gaberson had me along for it, the vicarious thrill, and to point out any characters they might've missed. Took place at a grow house near Modesto that was licensed for medical marijuana but didn't have a damn thing growing inside. When the cops moved in, the family started shooting selfies, like they were poised for the police brutality lawsuit the whole time. I took the bait. Knocked a camera out of the hands of one of the toughs that always seemed to keep the family company, and may've knocked a couple of his teeth out at the same time.

"It wasn't what we thought," Gaberson said.

"They weren't bringing in unlicensed sativa?"

"Yeah, but that was . . . a loss leader." Gaberson took a sip of his drink without losing eye contact. "You've heard of the Tarantula Clan."

Who hadn't? One seriously ruthless and efficient cartel. Nodes and cells, loyal street guys, prison connections, hired killers, a team of Romanian hackers, the whole bit. You had to wonder how much was mythology, but if even 10 percent was real, it was some serious downside risk—for society, or for whoever messed with them.

"Doing business with reality TV stars. I don't buy it. Too public," I said.

"Front, like I said. They were market-testing, getting in with the kids, working the angles."

"For what?"

He looked around, lowered his voice. "These guys, the Tarantula Clan, they're in it deep. Moving huge quantities of the nasty stuff."

I waited for him to continue.

"Adderall." He paused, rephrased. "Synthetic Adderall."

"Isn't it all synthetic?"

"*Double* synthetic, with zinc extract for immune-boosting. Wicked powerful."

"Stimulant."

"Yeah, sure, with a twist—two, actually. It's causing a huge problem for the schools."

"Young addicts. What's the second twist?"

"Between us," he said, then waved it off. "Sorry, I know that goes without saying," he continued. "We're starting to see huge improvements in the CPAC."

"What?"

"State mandated tests in schools, and in the SATs. Across the board. The achievement numbers are through the roof. Perfect. These kids are hyperfocused."

"So the parents don't mind."

"You read me. Where it gets weird is I think there might be an angle with the testing companies. They're lobbying the governor for more dollars to put in more tests, create better strata, distinguish among perfect scores. It's spiraling. I have no idea how high this goes."

I looked down in the bottom of my Scorpion Bowl, thought about how tough it is out there for parents. Made me glad Terry and I decided not to have kids, for now at least.

"What's this got to do with me?"

"Very little, Fitch. Most of it. You remember Fievel Lavin, goes by Tiny."

"Little guy."

"Right. Well, he got in with the Tarantulas. Worked his way up. Got invited to their year-end gala, almost won a RAV4 in the raffle, the whole thing. He muled a message out to me last week. It was about you."

"Let's hear it."

"We'd kept you off the grid—on all of this stuff. Was always in my interest to do so. No one even knew who you were at the bust. Somehow, they put it together—you, the Argyles, the punch to the mouth."

"So."

"So that guy's teeth you busted? Number two Tarantula."

"Deuce?"

"Yep."

"I busted the guy's teeth. Practically a badge of honor."

"Not the night before his kid's ConfirMitzvah."

"The heck is that?"

"Half confirmation, half bar mitzvah. Part of the effort by the

Tarantula Clan to be inclusive; they think it builds loyalty. Whatever. So the number two is set for this big all-comers spiritual gathering and you make him look like a Canadian hockey fighter."

"I did get a good shot in."

"And they want to shoot back. Tiny heard it firsthand. They're going to make your life very miserable, way beyond a tooth-for-a-tooth, if you get me."

It was all I could do not to look over my shoulder. I took a second to digest.

"Thanks for the tip. So: see ya around?"

"Like I said, let's chill. That'll keep you out of the public eye, make it harder for them to find you."

"How hard can that be?"

"Not hard. Keep your eyes open, Fitch. These are not the kind of people to mess with, especially . . ."

"What?"

"The Adderall."

"What about it?"

"They are incredibly focused. Patient. They can stake you out for days, sitting there, Glocks loaded, doing sudoku, expert level. It's not fair anymore. We're totally outgunned."

I exhaled, patted the table.

I was getting up to go when I saw the hesitation in his eyes. "What are you leaving out?" I asked.

"It's for our protection too—mine," Gaberson said. "I was never supposed to have you involved. If this thing goes public, we get sued—again. We're already spending eighteen percent of our budget defending lawsuits and we'll get slaughtered if people think the Tarantula case was built by an outsider."

"Okay, Lieutenant. I'll consider myself chastened and fore-warned." I scooted out of the booth, and he took my lead. Then he paused and reached for the black box at his feet.

"Ask you something, Lieutenant?"

He cleared his throat. "Shoot."

"You know Captain Donogue."

"Scion took a dump on his bike?"

"That one."

"What's on your mind?"

"Anything going around about that?"

He thought about it, not for long. "I'll keep an ear open. Amazing what you can pick up if you just listen these days."

Said absently, a bit of a non sequitur, but I went with it. "Thanks, y'know . . . for letting me know."

"You'll be fine. If I hear anything about Captain Don, I'll get a message to you through some back channel. For now, let's lie low."

He patted my shoulder and walked off, mysterious black box dangling from his left hand.

FOUR

NOT EVEN FOUR blocks later, I picked up the tail. MINI Cooper with a Tarantula stuffed in it, no doubt about it. If memory served, I thought I must've seen him earlier, tracking me to the coffee meeting. The MINIs had become all the rage with the midlevel bad guys. Had to do with parking. It's how cities were raising most of their revenue—parking tickets—so bad guys figured they had an easier shot getting busted as a drug runner by double parking than by hawking meth out of a den. MINIs made it easy to get a spot, stay below the radar.

This was a nice one, the MINI. Gold on the bottom, white top. Crossed my mind to do a U-turn and run it over with my truck. But there was no sense in confronting without a plan. I took a sharp right onto Van Ness, then another right in front of the BMW dealership, figuring the Tarantula would start rubbernecking the new 7 Series. Sure enough, three blocks later I'd lost the tail.

I lucked into a spot with a broken meter out front of the Wells Fargo and stared at the main branch of the public library. It's where I web-surfed when I wanted to make sure someone wasn't monitoring my keystrokes. My basic working theory is I figure my phone is tapped, traced, hacked, laid bare by a nine-year-old working for whoever needed his services for free time on Xbox Live. I made sure my phone was off and hiked the majestic marble steps of the venerable institution. If I ever got money, I swore to myself, I'd put it into the last bastion of information altruism. It was just you and whatever your thing was, which, unfortunately sometimes meant pornography.

The only downside of this public utopia is they didn't restrict what you looked at; couldn't, the First Amendment and all, which I generally agree with. But the only terminal I could find was next to a guy watching his evident fetish: some deal, it appeared, where everybody got busy at an Abercrombie & Fitch. Not that I was trying to look, but the sounds of mall sex were unmistakable.

I lost myself in a search for Don Donogue. Captain Don. Wikimedia, the encyclopedia we get to write ourselves, to the point that some biographies explore the outer reaches of laudatory adjectives. Warranted, it seemed, in this case. Donogue had been engineering and picking winners as far back as Hewlett and Packard. His first big innovation helped reduce the size and range of a transistor to give troops an edge in Korea. It was a big patent that begat many more, and led to licensing partnerships with everyone from Mintel to Qualtech. Later, he personally hosted the House Brew guys, saw or partnered on all the big things. Time didn't slow his own innovation prowess, it seemed, as he co-owned a series of patents involving data compression to allow almost instant video capture and streaming. That was in the late nineties, pioneering, seeing ahead of curves. Courted by presidents, feted by nations, referred to by *Forbes* and *Fortune* simply as Captain Don.

The last section of his bio covered his growing interest in immortality, "solving" death. "Terminal illness—just another inefficiency," he was quoted as saying. Not that it should happen faster but that death, by its nature, "gets seriously in the way of productivity." The whole thing, Wikimedia conceded, was parodied as a hoax, mocked on late-night TV (Jimmy Fallon: "I'd just like a mobile phone battery that lasts forever—or at least until the end of the day"). Undeterred, as always, Captain Don and cohorts talked of marrying Big Data, biotech, and singularity—the idea of sentient computers—to somehow prolong life, create cognizant computers built around individualized DNA, so that a person continued to "think, communicate, and live" even when the body shell gave out.

I was pulled out of my trance by a sound coming from the terminal beside me and had the bad fortune to glance over and see someone at an Abercrombie & Fitch "asking if they have that in another size."

I looked over my shoulder to see if anyone else was dismayed and I noticed the Tarantula. Not the same one who was in the MINI Cooper. But suspicious nonetheless. He was eyeballing me and then quickly looked away to the shelves, pretending to explore them. Trouble was, he was at the braille shelf, which gave him away—that and the wifebeater and the tattoo of a spider with fangs.

Clearly, they were tracking me somehow. I'd turned off my phone, so that couldn't be it. Or maybe they just knew my habits, which was scarier yet. There was one way to find out—take this guy back into the stacks and let him chat with my knuckles.

First, two more quick searches. The first, for Tess Donogue, gave me more boilerplate. Dartmouth undergrad, where she'd snowboarded, Stanford MBA, sat on the boards of a bunch of nonprofits, including the InEf Tour Company. The bio described her opulent property in Woodside, west of the 280, 110 acres. There were two houses on it, which she had been alternately remodeling—living in one for two years while bringing the other up to speed, then switching and doing the same with the other. Repeat. One story I read reported that her latest trendsetting technique was sending American oak to London to be processed as flooring, then reimporting it. You could do the whole thing domestically but she called it a "domestic export-import," getting the benefit of both American-made and foreign-exotic—depending on your audience—and the whole idea had sent flooring prices soaring.

I peeked over my shoulder. The brain-dead Tarantula pretended to read a book in braille. I wondered when it would dawn on him that he looked like a horse's ass. Or maybe that was the point: the Tarantulas were being so transparent they didn't mind my grasping the extent of their stupidity. Capable of anything.

Last search was for Danny Donogue, the golden grandson. It was tough to find much on him except speculation. He'd created a lot of the mystery when he dropped out of school after eleventh grade, saying that high school was for people who couldn't "do." Now he'd set up a shop that seemed to have made his point. It was called Froom and was getting a lot of buzz, but I couldn't exactly tell what for. It was either in post-alpha or stealth beta, depending on which taxonomy scale you preferred. In any case, I'd have to at least have a Twipper account to even begin to guess what Froom did.

Maybe not even then. The younger Donogue had 2,825,209 followers on Twipper before he shut down the account a few months ago. Danny's partner at Froom, Rajeev Cohen, "Da Raj," got more of the face time. He was a proverbial old-timer: nineteen.

One more thing about Danny: he was a regular at the Video Game Olympic Training Center. That's where I'd heard about him before; he was a donor and sometimes coach, Wikimedia said. Nonsense. I shook my head, the Scorpion Bowl wearing off. I was going to need some more time, and besides, I knew what'd get my juices flowing: a confrontation with my tail.

I stood and turned around. The Tarantula had disappeared. Rather, was disappearing. I spied him heading out the door toward periodicals, closed my browser, and followed.

FIVE

I HUSTLED THROUGH PERIODICALS but then got waylaid at a climate-change exhibit, where you were not allowed to leave unless you passed a quiz about what you'd learned . . . or made a donation. I gave five dollars to a woman dressed as "the carcinoma cell you'll turn into if we all don't compost." But the way she said it sounded like she thought I was mostly to blame.

The Tarantula must've gotten caught in the same thicket because he was still in view when I hit the ground floor and saw him hightailing it through the revolving doors. Not many steps later, I revolved myself and . . . BOOM. I'd spun right into a full-body tackle. In broad daylight. Audacious, I thought as I sprawled across the marble steps. Took a lot of fella to do that to me, I realized as I felt my head slap against a stair, the lights momentarily clicking off and then on again as I shoved the dude off me.

I rolled over and stood, woozy.

"We know where you live," the Tarantula said.

"Then come by for coffee and a knuckle sandwich," I managed. It rang horribly cliché, like I was pulling dialogue from my first five years with a gun license. But my head swirled in a post-attack mess.

The guy was five feet away, stocky, poised to pounce, biceps set permanently on curl. He had that look in his eyes—focus—double-synthetic Adderall, I was guessing. But the tackle nicked him too; looked like a good scrape tore through his cargo pants at the knee. He panted, like me.

Around us, on the steps and the sidewalk below, a half-dozen people milled about and not a damn one of them even seemed to notice us—or what had just transpired. They stared at their phones.

"Can I get a witness?" I bellowed, just to see if this would awaken something from the iPhone zombies.

Nothing.

"Free Blue Bear Coffee!" Nothing.

"On DavesList, I just posted a studio for rent, South of Market, $3,850. Plus utilities. On the Gooble Bus Run."

This got their attention. Two of the zombies bum-rushed me. One, still typing as he ran, slammed into the Tarantula, who swatted the apartment seeker away with a backhand, causing the guy to careen down the steps and then, undeterred, start back up again.

"Oops, studio taken," I said. "Someone got it."

"Damn!" said the man. "Almost."

So now it was me and the Tarantula again, eyeing each other, sumo chess, when a muted sound came from the pocket of his cargo pants. He pulled out his phone. It was playing U2's "Sunday Bloody Sunday."

"Fuck's sake," he said to no one. "How did they get this on a burner?"

He dropped the phone to the ground and destroyed it with a vicious stomp of an indestructible work boot, then looked at me, message sent: *I can stomp you too.*

"Looks like you got the worst of it," I said. I was looking at the hole in his cargo pants, where a bit of shredded knee poked through from his landing on the steps after tackling me.

"That was nothing. Just giving you a taste, a little app," he said.

I shook my head. "App, or appetizer?"

"Appetizer. Sorry." He meant it. Then smiled ruefully. "The entrée's gonna suck. You messed with the wrong ConfirMitzvah."

"Yeah, yeah." This was turning out to be the worst day and I still had expense reports, and the work on the tenant in the Richmond whose landlord figured him for foul play.

"See you around," the Tarantula said. He whirled and started walking.

I pulled out my phone and texted Terry: *keep an eye out.* I should have gone home but I doubted the Tarantulas would act immediately. Clearly, they wanted to string this out. One part of life in which efficiency doesn't count: giving someone the slow bleed.

I climbed into my '72 Ford flatbed and took Geary to the avenues. I didn't see any Tarantula-toting MINI Coopers but they blended in at some point with the Fiats and Smart Cars and other MINI Coopers, and besides, I'd forced myself to turn my attention to the people actually paying the day's rates, Sally and Fred Pern.

The couple had come into my office a few weeks ago saying they suspected their tenant of shenanigans. In a nutshell, they said the guy had two residences, the one he rented from them and a second in the Bayview that he listed as his primary residence. Why bother? I'd asked. They practically laughed at my ignorance; turned out, if your primary residence was the Bayview, the low-income part of town with historically underprivileged families, you could get your kid into any public school without having to go through the public-school lottery system. Popular scam, the Bayview Double Switch.

"What's it to you?" I asked the Perns.

Two things. They'd just put their own kid in the public-school lottery and didn't want some snotty professional pulling the Double Switch to take their spot at Claire Lilienthal. Plus, the Perns said, they didn't want to face any liability themselves: complicity in the Double Switch could get you into big trouble with the city, harboring a Double Switch fugitive. On the other hand, you couldn't oust a tenant without cause. So the Perns needed proof.

And they said they couldn't afford to dick around. The couple owned a booming new restaurant called Urban Ketchup. Served only ketchup, 1,001 different flavors. Lines stretched out the door. The couple wanted to expand, buy the place next door, so they could also start selling fries, which they thought could send the thing into the stratosphere.

But that meant getting a permit from the building codes department, they informed me, and all the background checks and the rest. So they were paying me to make sure that their tenant wasn't involved in any funny business. And, if so, help them break the tenant's lease. Dirty business I do. Dirty city.

Took me nearly twenty minutes to get past Masonic, with fog inching over this part of the city. I took a left on Thirtieth, a right on Balboa, and a left on Thirty-Sixth, and parked halfway down the block. I could see Golden Gate Park and Fulton running alongside it, the thoroughfare not teeming at this time of day, midafternoon. Time had flown at the library. My stomach rumbled. I scrounged a bag of Baked Gruyère Cheesoes from under the seat and munched and stared at 811 Thirty-Sixth Avenue. The Perns' place.

Yellow trim on purple. The paint. This is what happened, I figure, when you painted in the fog. Can't actually see what colors you've chosen. Looked like some kid got ahold of the crayon box. Or maybe someone let the inner child pick the colors, knowing they wouldn't be easy to see in the low light.

From the corner, there was an explosion of noise. Fifteen dogs, at least, turned the corner, every shape and size. Right behind them, their walker. She had all their leashes connected by a single leash she was holding in a gloved hand, the kind you'd use to hold a hawk. And she'd lost control. The lead dog, a husky with one blue eye, caught sight of the park and broke into a sprint. The other dogs followed. They created a surge of movement and, suddenly, the dog walker took flight. Like a kite. Flying behind the dogs. She smashed into a light pole, bounced off.

I stepped from the car. She saw me, and began frantically waving. I momentarily wondered whether my pistol aim was still good enough to sever the leash with one shot. Time was, no one could touch my precision. But even if I nailed the wiggling leash, she'd go splat. I rushed across the street, which caused the dogs to pause, long enough, at least, for me to grab the woman's Velcro-strapped sandals. I pulled her down to earth and the dogs circled, smelling the Real Smoked Gruyère flakes from my Cheesoes.

"What are you doing?" she asked accusingly.

"Saving you from getting brained by the stop sign."

"I wanted you to take video. Are you an idiot? I'm training."

I could barely respond when she strapped her sandals into a snowboard she pulled from her backpack, muttered "asshole" and said "mush," and off they went.

I felt my attention yanked and turned and saw a van that I hadn't previously noticed. It was back across the street, the same side I was parked on. Dark-tinted windows. Silhouette of a guy in the front seat, looking my way. Logo on the side of the van of a dolphin jumping to the sun, and the word "Flippers." Not sure what about it snagged my attention. I turned and looked back to the house in question, the one the Perns own and lease out.

Really, there was nothing to see. A planter on a precipitation-worn balcony, paint-chipped, rusted railing. Cheap faux-marble steps. House attached on either side to like-modeled homes, one green on beige and the other orange on puke orange. One key difference between the neighbors' and the Perns' houses: the paint on the Perns' purple garage looked new. Fresh. Like if I touched it, my hand would come away sticky.

I looked over my shoulder at the van. Just sitting there, guy in the driver seat too shadowed to judge. Might have been sleeping, for all I knew. I doubted it. I'd done the job long enough to sense what was part of the landscape and what was not.

I turned my attention from the van to the surroundings. What was I looking for?

A trash bin.

Good luck. It was trash day—and recycling and compost. Neatly divided contents. Nice for a private eye. Once it was out on the street, you could pick through without violating anyone's Fourth Amendment rights. Sort of. I tried not to get too caught up in the nuances of law. I beelined for the tenant's black trash container. Opened it, without thinking, then recoiled from the smell. You needn't have a PI license to have realized this guy had a cat and this bin was filled with its litter. With a stick I found next to the curb, I poked around. There wasn't much to see unless the Perns wanted to hang this guy out to dry for putting glass into the trash can instead of into the recycling container. Might have been enough with this city—Failure to Segment.

Recycling was the next stop, the blue bin. As I opened the top, I heard the roar of an engine and looked up. Sure enough, it was the van. I could see the driver's head glance my way through the tinted glass as it sped off.

My phone buzzed. I put down the recycling top. A text, from Terry: *Everything OK?*

Yep, I tapped back. *Home shortly.*

I dug through the recycling. Looked typical but for a smashed picture frame, empty of a photo. Interesting but meaningless at face value. Also, oddly, most of the papers had been through a shredder. Maybe the tenant was hiding something, or maybe he was just smart. I couldn't discern what the scraps might be. Bills? Shopping list? On one edge of one scrap, I made out words and numbers: *Sheldon 415-225-196,* but the last digit was missing. I pocketed the scrap.

I made it back to the car just as the MINI Cooper rounded the corner. It was time to go home to warn Terry to oil up our Second Amendment rights. We'd been down this road before. There was no situation that rattled Terry. That's why I married him.

SIX

WE'D MET THE day of the Fillmore Street Fair, neither of us in attendance. Each of us had come to Grandview Park to take in the majesty in silence. If you've never been, there's no place on earth like it, a sand dune poking from the avenues into the sky, accessible by steep steps, enough room at the top for a bench and a few milling hikers with cameras.

With Terry and me, it was love at first nod.

I reached the top, heaving mildly with age, saw him feeding torn pieces of crusty baguettes to pigeons. There was one other person, a woman, who asked me to time her with a phone while she completed what she described as a "one-minute workout."

I caught Terry's eye. I gave him a nod, got one in return, and after two hours hanging out there, chatting now and again, watching the skyline mostly, we walked down the steps and never looked back.

On the outside, I concede, we're a matched set. Two large, burly men, Terry just two inches shorter, a distinction without importance at this size, neither of us much into talking, neither with a Faceburg page. Tweeping is more characters than either of us can manage most days. Strong and silent, we walk into a bar and some-times people give up their seats, a primitive instinct, I guess, that we might be part of a biker gang, which is only half true. Gang, no. Bikers, yes. Harleys. Rode 'em to the Russian River, where we were married by Terry's longtime Catholic priest, Fella O'Dell. Terry is deeply religious, one of the many differences between us when you got below the large, soft-spoken corpus aspect.

He dragged me each Sunday to St. Mark's, then afterward we'd go to a gathering at someone or another's house to snack and I'd stand around and look awkward. It was all part of Terry's Mid-west sensibilities, including, while he desperately insisted other-wise, some Tea Party leanings. It didn't pay to get him started on welfare moms or deadbeat dads, people who text and drive, art that doesn't look like anything, castration or forced birth control for bad parents, corporal punishment for kids who mouth off. But, underscoring where Terry truly did part ways with the Tea Party, he called for the beheading of Shawn Hammity for more reasons than I could ever remember.

But he was a real softie too, Terry. He was an accountant, worked at home, but when I met him, he was earning grad school money working for Lickety Sit, the babysitting service where you could hire a sitter in increments of five minutes so that the chil-dren didn't have to spend even a second entertaining themselves. Kids would climb on Terry like a hairy jungle gym until he flung them off in laughter (theirs, mostly).

"Good, you're home," he said. He stood in the hallway at the bottom of the stairs, wearing an apron, holding a spatula with some yellow goop on it in one hand, and a rifle in the other. "After your text, thought you might've been an intruder."

"The Winchester?"

"Messy but effective. If my soufflé falls, I'll use it on you. Come into the kitchen and explain your hysterical texts."

"I said to keep an eye out."

"My point." He turned and headed back to the kitchen, my cue to follow.

We lived in the upper Castro, halfway to Noe Valley, in an attached Victorian, sparsely decorated but for Terry's collection of international beer steins and domestic album covers. I conceded an appreciation for the latter as I walked past a framed limited edition of *The Doors,* and then an actual door, leading to the living room, and then a gold-framed *Born to Run.* Terry must have been procrastinating; the maroon runner covering the hallway floor looked vacuumed, and he was cooking.

We had neighbors . . . boy, did we have neighbors. To the left, we were attached to two women, the Perry-Pines, with two sets of twins, Piper and Polly, and the other two, Pippa and Dave. On the opposite side, a straight couple, Sandy and Sandee; I could never remember which was which and there was some tiny difference in pronunciation that was imperceptible to me, so I'd not used their names for years for fear of getting it wrong. They didn't have kids yet but had an adoption agency, egg donor, sperm clinic, a precious spot on the ten-year waiting list at the prestigious Bong Bong Nursery School, and had put $4,000 retainers on not one, but two, of the most-sought-after doulas in case Sandy or Sandee conceived and delivered.

The couple could afford it. One of them, I can't remember which, had started a booming company aimed at cutting down on driver distraction. It was called Real Fun Drive (trademarked). The technology projected onto an automobile's dash-board screen an image of what was actually going on all around the car. The driver then was not only allowed to look at the screen but was encouraged to do so, to use the steering wheel to navigate objects on the screen, and use the actual brake and accelerator to make the video car speed up and slow down, as if playing a video game. The idea was to try to "win" by getting home safely and not hurting anyone else. In fact, though, the person was actually piloting the car through the Real Driving Experience (trademarked), which was projected onto the screen. This, theoretically, solved two problems: keeping the driver attentive to the road while also allowing him to play a video game, which research evidently showed is much more fun than actual driving, even if the driver is aware that the game is a version of real life. They were working with their doulas to create a version of the software for childbirth and rearing. So one of them told me at a neighborhood mixer.

The soufflé smelled out of this world. I stood at the cooking island, sipping water, and explained to Terry about the Tarantulas and he raised an eyebrow but seemed generally unfazed. Law-and-order type that he was, a part of Terry had just been waiting to exercise his right to shoot a trespasser on our property. I had canceled the *Chronicle,* fearing for the paperboy.

I was about to launch into the rest of it when my phone rang. Private number.

"Fitch," I answered.

"I got another message." The voice sounded frantic. Terry gave me the who-is-it glance and I put up a finger, one sec. Tess Donogue sputtered on—something about someone named Gene and a monkey—but it was hard to hear with a clack-clack noise, then yelling, in the background. "Ms. Donogue . . ."

"Mrs. I'm not [garbled] divorced."

"I'm having trouble hearing you."

"I'm . . . construction . . . so they . . ."

"Can you go somewhere less loud?"

"Call . . . ack."

Click.

Terry raised an eyebrow and I shrugged my shoulders, which passed for conversation in our house. He got that I meant I'd tell him later. "Make it home for dinner?" he asked.

"Expect to. Don't shoot anyone who doesn't deserve it."

"Kneecap anyone who does," he encouraged.

I walked out of the kitchen, feeling like I'd told him what I needed to, about the Tarantulas, and made sure he was okay. I was at the front door when the phone rang again, this one showing up on my caller ID with the name Lester Wollop.

"Fitch."

"It's me again."

"Mrs. Donogue?"

I walked out the door and discovered that, uh-oh, Sandy or Sandee was standing beside my truck, glancing up at me, like he wanted to say something neighborly. I nodded. I clenched my teeth at the possible encounter, because I didn't know which name to say, but I had my headphones on, so maybe I could get out of it.

"Mrs. Donogue," I said.

"Sandee," said the man. "Aha, you don't know my name? I thought so—"

"No, I know. I'm on the phone." I pointed to the headset.

"I got another message," said Tess Donogue.

"Can you spare a second?" said the guy at the car . . . shit, I'd already forgotten the name—Sandee or Sandy. They sounded so similar.

"Who is Lester Wollop?" I asked.

"What?" said Tess Donogue and Sandy or Sandee at the same time.

"I'm on the phone," I said.

Again, a double: "What?"

"I'll call you right back," I said. I hung up on Tess.

The man standing next to my car, arms crossed, dark jeans, sneakers without laces, untucked flannel shirt, sleeves rolled up, lean face, light smile, looked deliberately casual, too casual. I asked myself: Does that seem more like a Sandy or a Sandee? In any case, he wanted something.

"Hey, Terry, can I have a word?"

"No, I'm . . ."

"I know, Fitch, Willie Fitzgerald. You don't think we know our neighbors' names?" He chortled. He was so onto me. "You have a sec?"

I exhaled and nodded.

"We got some terrific news," he said. "We got into Bong Bong, the nursery school. I'm sure you've heard of it."

Even those of us without kids had heard of it. It was the Stanford of nursery schools, an almost 100 percent matriculation rate into the kindergarten of choice, all the instructors have at least master's degrees in "free play." Given the waiting list, some people started signing up after a first date that seemed promising, hoping to time their procreation for when a spot opened up.

I looked for the right response. "Congratulations. I've really got to call . . ."

"Of course. I don't want to bug you. Maybe I could get some time later."

"Sure."

"In a nutshell," he started. Apparently this qualified as later. "We were way down on the list, at least five years off. But a spot opened up for a family with both parents' first names starting with *S*, one of whom has a quarter Republican heritage. Demographic they're looking for to round things out. But to hold the spot we need proof of embryo and we're not quite there."

"I . . ." My phone rang. Desperate to get out of this encounter, I looked at the caller ID: Lester Wollop.

"I realize," my neighbor said, putting his hands palm down and pushing, to add emphasis, "I *fully* realize this isn't your thing. You're doing really important work." Patronizing all the way. "At some point, I'd just like to ask if you might, well, frankly, help us find any loopholes."

I picked up the phone. "Hold on, Mrs. Donogue."

"This is Lester. Who is this?"

In the background: "Lester, get off the phone!"

"This is my house too!"

"Estate!"

"You cheated! You tramp! Who is this guy you're calling?"

I pulled out my earbuds.

"Loopholes?"

"Sometimes there are work-arounds," said Sandy or Sandee. "Ways of putting pressure on organizations, if you take my meaning."

No clue what he was talking about.

"Looks like you're swamped. Let's talk later. I'll just leave it at this: I wouldn't ask if it wasn't super important. The world is an insane place these days and it's just plain irresponsible to attempt to bring a baby into it without giving it a reasonable chance of getting an immersive multilingual education in a free-play environment with conflict resolution as a core value." I wasn't clear what *it* referred to: the world, the baby. He swallowed. Misty-eyed. "Not to insult you, but I can afford to pay you for your time. I know you're the best."

He smiled, then took two steps toward me, thrusting forward a fist. I managed to force a fist bump, unsure what I'd just committed to by so doing.

Off went Sandy or Sandee and I put in an earbud, unsure who I would be speaking to. "This is Fitch."

"I'm sorry about that, all of it." Mrs. Donogue's voice.

She continued: "That was Lester. My husband, sort of. We're separated but he continues to live on the property and his name still appears on the caller ID, which is a major sticking point and something, frankly, that we've been talking about for a while in counseling. Part of our marital discord to begin with—whose name is on the landline. Just typical stuff. But you don't want me to get into all that nonsense. And I need to tell you about the message."

"Slow down, Mrs. Donogue."

"And sorry about the noise earlier. I can explain . . ."

"It's okay. The message." I opened the door to the truck, climbed in, closed the door, and instinctively looked around—curious to see if there were any lingering Tarantulas. Nothing evident. Hard to see much from my vantage point, given the sharp inclines of the streets here, up and down in every direction, like an Escher painting. After about a block in each direction, the horizon disappeared.

"This one came on Snipchap, not Twipper," she said.

"Okay."

"It included a photo. It was a hand, beside a picture or several pictures."

"Was?"

"As you know, Snipchap messages disappear after nine seconds. I can't remember all of it, but I think there was a monkey and a bird and the name of someone, maybe Gene."

I didn't say anything.

"I have no idea what it means but I'm certain it was from Daddy."

"Why is that?"

"His hand—it was holding the thing, the image or whatever, the one with the monkey."

"But it disappeared."

"It's Snipchap," she said, sounding irritated. "That's the point. It's a superior business model, solves the very real issue that people don't want to have their information live forever. Even once they're . . ."

She had started crying.

"Gone," she whispered. "Gone-ish."

It sounded beyond suspicious. She had to be making it up.

"It just disappeared," I said.

"It's Snipchap! It protects people's privacy by automatically deleting information. What, you don't think people who are recently deceased-ish want their privacy? Have some compassion."

"Hang on." I could already see the next aggrieved group, the Recently Not Dead.

She cleared her throat. "Four thousand. I'm upping your signing fee. But you have to come down here, at least talk to Danny. I know he's at Froom tonight. They're hosting an invite-only event. I'm not invited, obviously, since we're currently estranged, but I can get you in. He knew Daddy as well as anybody. He was Daddy's little guy, the future of the family, Captain Don said." Then, "Please."

It sounded genuinely plaintive and covered with a film of sexual innuendo. What had Lester called her? Tramp? She was barking up the wrong large man.

But four thousand bucks. To go to a Silicon Valley invite-only party.

Close call.

I went back inside to tell Terry to have the soufflé without me. I didn't have to. He intuited the situation from the moment I walked back in the door, and met me halfway down the hall with a to-go container. Gave me a nod. I wanted to tell him to be careful, but he might use the shotgun on me for overdoing it.

I nodded back.

At least there's one serene place on earth. And I was leaving it. To go straight down the 101 and into the maw of the beast.

SEVEN

I DIDN'T GET FAR, not fast. Quarter mile before Van Ness, I was slowed to a veritable standstill by what looked, at a distance, to be a group of protesters. The march was headed my direction, signs and placards, chants I couldn't quite make out. They were still a long city block away.

I rolled down my window and caught the attention of a parking attendant at Lunza, a four-star restaurant off Gough, and asked what was up.

"Realtors," he said. "They've finally had enough."

"Of?"

"Hold on," he said. He reached into his uniform pocket and pulled out a phone. From the speaker: "Sunday Bloody Sunday."

"My ringer's working," he said happily. In the process of declaring this, he seemed to have forgotten all about me.

The crowd neared, swarming in and around the cars. I could hear the chants.

"What do we want?"

"Inventory!"

"When do we want it?"

"Before interest rates go up!"

First the Phippies, now the Realtors. Injustice everywhere.

I opened my truck door, trying to get the attention of a woman knocking along next to it to get her out of the way. She carried a placard that read *Make Down Payments, Not War.*

The woman, wearing a flowing black dress and pearls, broke into a smile. "Are you looking to sell your place? I will pay for staging."

"I want to move," I said.

"You're looking to buy!"

"Move my car."

"Willful ignorance," the guy next to her said. "No compassion."

"Edward," the woman says. "He's mine. I saw him first."

Edward, khakis and button-down, said: "No, I mean, no." Totally exasperated. He eyed me. "How can you be a citizen of this country, this once beautiful city, and not know that there is a huge shortage of real estate inventory?"

"For people to live in?" I played along.

"To sell. How are Realtors supposed to even eat—at Lunza? God, do you even read Instacharm?"

"I read the newspaper."

He looked at the woman, incredulous, as if I'd just said I didn't care about war babies.

"Look at me," he yelled. "It has been nine months, nine *months,* since I've had a decent listing."

"Not including the one on Magellan," the woman said.

"And the one in St. Francis Woods," he noted. "A flip. A fluke. I've got two mortgages just to feed myself."

The cars in front of me started to move. I hit the accelerator and then paused when I saw a police officer on the edge of the protest. He had one of those black boxes that Lieutenant Gaberson had carried around. Then he disappeared behind the crowd. "Hey, Realtors," I said. "Isn't this just, y'know, an ebb and flow in market conditions? What do you expect anyone to do about it?"

"You racist!" Edward screamed. This prompted people in the crowd to take an interest and surge forward. In the movement, I could see the policeman with the black box. He was on the sidewalk, holding up the box, pointing it in our general direction. I could see a little cone extending from it and then I totally lost him in the sea of furious Realtors.

"Move," I said to the horde, trying to keep an eye on the cop and his odd contraption.

A few protesters broke into song: "This Land Is Your Land, This Land Is Our Land. This Land Is Developable!"

Followed by: "We Shall Overcome Historically Low Inventory."

I slipped into an opening and zipped along, trying to look back over my shoulder at the cop with the black box. I couldn't find him, but lo and behold, I caught another one—cop—in the third story of a commercial building at the corner of Van Ness, holding another black box.

Odd for sure.

HONK!

I was holding up the line of furious commuters already detained by the line of the march.

I focused on the road, serpentining among a few more protesters, hit relatively open road, and soon I was zooming at ten miles an hour in commute traffic.

An hour later, I was still on the 101, still twenty minutes out from Froom, tapping the steering wheel to the rhythm of the thoughts in my head. First off, no way—*no way*—Donogue was carrying on from the afterlife. Defied all reason. But that didn't mean something else wasn't going on. Murder? Maybe. Financial foul play? Likely. Some family squabble? Most definitely. Involving money. My dad once told me that dough was the only thing people actually ever really fight about. I'd rarely had a case that didn't prove him right.

So that made our persons of possible interest in this otherworldly affair Tess Donogue; her estranged son, Danny; Lester Wollop; maybe dead Captain Don's business partner, Alan Klipper.

Separately, I thought, what to make of these odd black boxes the cops were holding, and seemingly pointing at protesters? Some new law enforcement device, I presumed. Easily enough solved. I'd ask Lieutenant Gaberson. He'd always been a straight shooter. But it was odd he hadn't mentioned anything earlier.

Still, I figured, why waste any time worrying about stuff I don't even know is a problem yet?

My eyes were drawn to a billboard, blinking neon: *Text #SAFETYFIRST If You're Focused on the Road. For a Chance to Win.*

Then another billboard with a picture of the Dalai Lama that read *Make Peace. Make* Anything. *With Macrasoft (making things since 1985).*

Then, from behind, a flash of light, something was coming fast. Shit. Twin Tarantulas. I picked 'em up in the rearview mirror, one in the gold-and-white MINI Cooper, closing hard on the right at fifteen miles an hour, and, on the left, also gaining on me, a red-and-blue MINI, gold trim, looked like a Beatles album cover. They were converging on me, trying the pincer move, catch my old beater between them. Rattle me at highway commute speeds. I gunned it, managing to get to twenty miles an hour before I slammed into the back of a late-model Chevy Continent, which had seating for twelve but required fuel at each exit. Nothing I wanted to rear-end.

I hit the brakes to try to avoid a double sideswipe. No luck. The MINIs converged on either side. Simultaneous BANGs. That was the sound, at least. All sound. No sensation. I realized with only a little surprise that I didn't feel a thing. Their cars must weigh one tenth of my truck and they went bouncing off and spinning away like Darth Vader's little insect-looking spaceship at the end of one of the Star Wars movies, setting up a sequel. Just like I knew one was coming with these Tarantulas. But I was safe for now. The Coopers spun off, winding about fifty yards behind me, hopelessly mired.

Dangerous, though, these guys. Stupid enough to try a double swipe in commute traffic, but focused enough due to double-synthetic Adderall to choreograph it. Made me want to call Terry and have him put one in the chamber and watch the front door.

To make sure the Tarantulas couldn't find me on the open road, I pulled off at the next exit. I parked on a frontage road and shut off my phone, figuring they might have been tracking the signal somehow. It was also possible they'd put a tracking device on the car, which would take hours to find, if I even could find it.

So, now, a new plan: I'd park six blocks from Froom and walk the rest of the way, making it harder for the Tarantulas to find me if they were tracking me through my car.

I reached between the front seats, the middle compartment, and unlocked it. I couldn't remember the last time I'd felt compelled to dig in here. I opened it up, got a jolt of adrenaline, opened a second compartment, also with a key, and eyed my Detective Special, the Colt, a wedding present from Terry. Black on black. Romantic as hell. Small enough for any occasion. Powerful enough with .38s for any six Tarantulas, one per chamber.

I left 'em empty, the chambers. Bullets were another level of escalation, though one I suspected would come across the transom before long. I put the shells into my left pocket and tucked the gun inside my worn sport coat, and off I went.

Ten minutes later, I parked six blocks from downtown Palo Alto, the center of the known universe, according to the people who lived there. It was 6 P.M.

Based on what Mrs. Donogue told me, the pre-pre-event at Froom started at seven, then a pre-event at seven thirty, and then an official lull until eight thirty when people who knew better would start showing up. Gave me time to walk over, take in the sights and smells, maybe ask the neighbors a few questions. For instance, it'd be nice to know what Froom was before I got there.

The main drag here was Onaniversity Avenue. It had been a while since I'd been, but I'd heard how it had changed. It was called a Retail Incubator, the shops of the future today, or something like that. Real beautiful stuff if you're into that kind of thing. Like the first shop I stopped at, called RescueToure. I glanced inside and saw racks of clothes with a twist. The clothes racks went only about knee-high and the clothes were tiny. Mingling about, a few people and their dogs.

There was a small sign in the window, some fancy font:

WHAT IS RESCUETOURE? THE LATEST IN FASHION, HAUTE COUTURE, SELECTED FOR ANIMALS BY ANIMALS. YOUR DOG OR CAT HOUSEMATE DESERVES THE BEST IN OUTER-WEAR. NOT CHOSEN BY PEOPLE BUT BY OTHER ANIMALS. OUR ANIMAL PARTNERS HELP SELECT THE GARMENTS WE STOCK AND HELP CUSTOMERS CHOOSE WHAT LOOKS BEST, FROM COLORS TO STYLES. WE FOCUS ON INDIVID-UAL NEEDS. BUT WE'RE DIFFERENT FROM EVERY OTHER ANIMAL-FOR-ANIMAL CLOTHING SHOP. HOW? EVERY SINGLE ANIMAL PARTNER IS A RESCUE ANIMAL. THESE ARE DOGS AND CATS (AND AT LEAST ONE FERRET! WE LOVE YOU, BLINKY!) THAT WERE STARING DOWN TOUGH STRAITS, NOT BECAUSE THEY ARE BAD ANIMALS BUT BE-CAUSE THEY CAME FROM TOUGH CIRCUMSTANCES. NOW THEY ARE UPWARDLY MOBILE, WITH A CHANCE TO MAKE THE KIND OF LIFE WE ALL DESERVE. AND 10 PERCENT OF EVERY SINGLE SALE GOES TO FAMILIES WITH ANIMAL HOUSEMATES WHO DON'T YET HAVE ELECTRIC CARS.*

*STORE OWNERS

A guy passed me walking an Irish wolfhound in Stanford sweatpants. Both the guy and the dog, actually. In the sweat-pants. They walked inside.

Wrong place to ask about Froom.

I took in the next few stores. One was called One Last Thing. Evidently, according to a woman window-shopping, it stocked only one item at a time and only one of that thing. When that was sold, they moved to a new item. Next store was called Sold

Out. Then a store called I Stand For, where you paid a membership fee to write on the wall what you stood for or you could choose from preselected stances, plus they sold frozen yogurt with toppings.

Three doors down from the address I had for Froom, I walked into a store called Ben's Bags, empty except for a guy behind the counter. Maybe a shot at a conversation. The store was narrow but deep, lots of pedestals, each with the same bag perched on top, looked like it was made of some fancy white canvas, if there even is such a thing, embroidered with the name Ben and looking a bit like old Chuck Taylor high-tops made into a handbag.

"Welcome," said the guy behind the counter. His heart wasn't in it. Out of place: ponytail, buckteeth, Vulcan ears. First-class nerd in the new Beverly Hills. "We're having a sale."

I pretended to glance at a bag. It cost $299. For a bag.

I looked up.

"Next few days, you buy a bag, you get a free shopping bag. Ordinarily ten cents."

He reached beneath the counter and pulled out a bag that looked identical to the one on the pedestal.

"So you get two bags for the price of one."

"Nah, this is just the shopping bag. That's the Ben's Bag. It costs two hundred and ninety-nine dollars, but if you want something to carry it out in, you can get this for free. We pick up the tab for the bag."

"I . . . but it's the same . . ." Didn't compute and I didn't bother trying to make it. "Lemme think about it. Hey, I'm supposed to be at a party and I'm looking for the address. Froom. You know where it is?"

This perked him up. Eyes opened, ponytail swished with activity. Then he looked down.

"A few doors down. Is it a plus-one?" He paused. "Joking."

"I might be able to work something out," I said.

"Really." More a statement than a question.

I walked over to the counter. I saw the guy had been scribbling on napkins. Numbers and signs. I realized I was looking at a coder. What was he doing working here? Could be making $250,000 at . . . anyplace.

"Maybe. Gonna be packed with movers and shakers. Danny Donogue. Heard of him?"

Ponytail nodded; hell yeah. "That guy is going to be the next Captain Don. Smart, poised, maybe a little behind. Really needs to stay focused, how I see it. Or wind up like the rest of us."

"He's eighteen."

"You take my point."

I decided to go for it. "How much you know about Froom? Seems to be a little on the down low."

He laughed. "Dude, of course I know about it. It's this place where they do . . . they, um . . . I . . ." He looked down. "It's bold and exciting stuff. The next frontier."

"You have no idea. What are you scribbling?" I looked at the napkins, Xs and Ys, a drawing of a bubble, a symbol that looks like infinity, the word "Eliza." Lines pointing to and from it, leading to a cloud. He covered up his work.

"Uh . . ." He took me in. "You an investor?"

"No."

"Oh, well, anyway. Without giving too much away, it's new and radically improved facial recognition software. Gonna be huge."

He pulled up his phone and shot my picture, without asking, before I could move. I managed a smirk. He hit a few buttons on his phone and showed me my picture.

"I don't like having my picture taken without my permission."

"Of course you don't," he said. "No one does. But that's because people aren't comfortable with how they look."

He pressed a few buttons. He held up the phone with my picture, but now it showed me without my scruffy facial hair and with a new haircut.

"Ta-da! New and improved," he said. "This way, when some entity uses facial recognition software—"

"Entity?" I interrupted.

"Law enforcement, a commercial business, new home security systems, whatever, it'll be your best face, the best you."

"You're kidding."

He shrugged. "I think part of the big resistance to facial recognition software is people would like to put their best foot forward."

"You don't think the resistance to facial recognition software is about privacy."

"Listen, you want to look foolish when you're ID'd, be my guest. Not my problem. Besides, I'm just trying to get the patent and then people can do with it what they want. That's where the money is, in the pat . . ." He paused, looked at me, seemed to hesitate, or realize he was wasting his breath. "You want a Ben's Bag or not?"

"I'm saving up to get something next door."

Bored, he asked: "At Already Broken or Exotic Yo-Yo?"

I shook my head. He was shining me on; this wasn't real conversation. Smelled wrong but I couldn't pinpoint why.

"You're holding out on me," I said. "You know more than you're saying."

He shrugged. "Nice bags we have here. Zuckerbaum got one for everyone in the wedding party. Enjoy Froom. Come back on the way out and let me know what the big secret is over there, or if you want to get in on the ground floor of my start-up. You'll be retired before you know it."

EIGHT

I WOUND UP TAKING stairs to a belowground doorway, which seemed like the right place, given the self-important sign on the doormat outside: *What Is* Froom?

"Exactly," I mumbled, letting myself in.

No sooner had I taken a step inside than I heard a voice: "Welcome Mr. Fitzgerald." The voice sounded computerized, and familiar. I couldn't place it.

I looked around. No one there. Just a sleek, slate-white reception counter with a computer monitor on it. All bathed in soft blue light. An empty chair sat behind the counter.

"Hello?" I ventured. How the hell did they know my identity? I patted my pistol, reminding myself it was there.

"Mr. Fitzgerald, please sign in at the terminal and get a badge. Would you like your usual?" Same digitized voice.

My usual?

Jesus, I placed the voice. Shirli.

Before I could respond, a woman stood from the other side of the counter, where she'd apparently been kneeling, holding a pen, maybe that she was picking up from the floor. Long black hair, soft features but plain, looks late twenties.

"Coffee, black?" she asked.

I stared at her hard. So this broad knew my name, drink of choice, and her voice was a dead ringer for Shirli, the digitized damelike voice loaded on everyone's smartphone. Before I could shake my surprise, I heard a sound from the right and a short man with dark skin walked through an open doorway.

"Thanks, Shirli, I've got this."

"The pleasure was mine," Shirli said. Freaky, just like my phone said it.

"Hello, Willie," said the guy in the plaid shirt, a stack of leather bracelets showing through on his left arm. "Rajeev Cohen. Raj. You prefer Fitch. You're early. The pre-pre-party doesn't even start for an hour."

I recognized the guy from my research. Rajeev Cohen, Da Raj, Danny Donogue's business partner.

"We feel so lucky to have stolen Shirli," he said. "The competition for talent here is brutal, but people get on board when they realize they have a chance to really change the world."

"Shirli," I said, still astounded.

All at once both of our phones said in response to me: "How can I help you?"

This prompted laughter from Rajeev and a tight smile from the real-world Shirli.

"I thought I turned it off," I said in the direction of my phone.

"Finding something for your cough," responded Shirli on my phone, totally mishearing me.

"Try enunciating," said the Shirli behind the desk, irritated.

"You're saying this is my fault?"

"Finding the nearest vault," responded the Shirli behind the desk.

"Take five, Shirli. It's gonna get nuts here later. We're expecting upward of two hundred," said Rajeev.

"Baking jive," Shirli answered.

"Oh, sorry." Rajeev smiled patiently. Then: "Baking jive."

"Taking five," Shirli said.

As she walked out from behind the counter, Rajeev turned to me. "Grab a badge, Fitch, sign the NDAs, and come back and see the future."

It didn't happen often but I found myself all but flummoxed.

"Don't look so surprised. Of course we know who you are," Rajeev explained as he neared the computer monitor on the counter and poked the touch screen. "We use facial recognition software and instant AI to immediately identify everyone who walks in the door, then layer it with taste analysis drawn from search habits so that . . ." He looked at me. "Do you even have an invitation?"

"I'm looking for Danny Donogue."

He smiled, wide. "Of course you have an invitation. You don't think I know that. And don't act surprised we know your search habits. Everyone does. It's in all those Gooble waivers you click when you surf the net. So wonderfully efficient. This system lets us get past all the small talk, inefficiencies, nonsense, and bureaucracy so we can instantly get you your badge and drink and move on to the important business of changing the world. Besides, it's the police surveillance you really have to fear. Fourth Amendment, baby!" He ripped a badge that had printed from the monitor. "Just sign these NDAs." He waved a pen.

"I don't think so. I'm here on business."

Rajeev laughed. I made a more in-depth study; his small stature was offset somehow by a slightly disproportionate large head, short dark hair parted and combed, a gleam to his teeth. Fancy jeans. On his feet, the latest fad: sandals with laces.

"Trust me, this nondisclosure agreement is worth it. Besides, you think you'd get taken advantage of by someone from your own tribe?"

"My own . . ."

"Irish Catholic, brother!"

Enough. "Rajeev Cohen isn't Indian? Or Jewish?"

Rajeev practically recoiled. "You racist!"

Not again.

"This is Silicon Valley," he said. "It's a meritocracy, the ultimate meritocracy. You are judged by what you do. You can be anything you want."

I sighed. Picturing my fee in my head. Could it possibly be enough?

"Listen, pal, you're twisting the meaning of 'meritocracy.' It doesn't mean you get to pick your own heritage."

He shook his head, like I was too simple to get it. "Suit yourself. Not everyone has a high EQ. Besides, I'm not in the mood to argue. It's too great of a night. We're moving from unofficial alpha to pre-official alpha with beta rising. We'll be doing one-on-one demos and our CEO will be here and the One Female Venture Capitalist and we have a taco truck."

"Danny. I'm looking for Danny. Let's cut the crap."

"You don't want to sign the NDA, fine." He shrugged. Before he turned away: "I wouldn't come to your office and ask you to share your secrets."

"Evidently, you know all my secrets."

"Touché. Feel free to see yourself out."

There it was, just one of those moments. I remembered the moment when Terry and I were about to say our vows. Ready or not? Leap into the unknown or hit the Harley and return to a life of solitude. That was a no-brainer. So was this one.

"I'll be on my way. Just one thing. You know about Captain Don?"

"What about him?"

"Took a dive on his bike."

Rajeev lowered his head, pursed his lips. "A great man. That was a guy who knew how to innovate. Right up until the end."

He started on some soliloquy. Captain Don helped build the Valley, deserved a spot next to Jobs, believed that what matters were ideas not who you are—unlike me, he was suggesting, giving me a look like I had Klan ties—and single-handedly made the world more efficient.

"I hear his death was no accident."

He looked up at me square with dark, piercing eyes. "I don't know anything about that."

It felt canned.

"You seem pretty sure of yourself. That's the first time you've shown the slightest indication you might not know something."

"You told me yourself. He took a . . . he fell off his Pinarello. Serious tragedy."

"So you said."

"The bike. Gorgeous."

"You're kidding me."

"Of course I'm kidding. It was okay. Old-school. Decent ride, nothing special, like an eighth of a pound heavier than it needs to be. But no reason to speak ill of the dead." He stood there with the pen in his hand, like he was holding his damn dick, waiting for me to sign or go.

I took one last, long slow sip of this guy, just a little too much of what you'd expect if you were scripting him. With a wrench and a pair of electrodes, I suspect I'd find he knew much more than he was letting on. Dare to dream.

"See ya." I turned to the door, feeling momentarily relieved to be free of this utter nonsense. That is, until I opened the door—and got an eyeful of danger. At the top of the stairs, back to me. A Tarantula. In a sleeveless leather vest with a spider on the back. Only a moment's extraordinary fortune seemed to have him looking the other direction when I nearly walked his direction. I quickly shut the door.

"Black," I said to Rajeev. "My coffee. But you know that. What is it I'm signing?"

"An NDA—says you won't share anything you learn tonight, blah, blah, blah."

I walked to the counter and looked at the paperwork and wished I could feel surprised. These things had been turning up all over the place. Everyone you work for requested you to sign an NDA. I figured that made sense for a private detective, but it wasn't just guys in my line of work or accountants like Terry dealing with confidential financials. The loaded guys were seeking NDAs from house contractors, flooring guys, painters; in one case, I heard from a barber who wasn't allowed to give away anything about the comb-and-part strategy of the venture capitalist he was cutting. And the fellow was bald.

"How come the Internet guys get to know everything about me but I'm not allowed to share anything about you guys?" I asked, inking my name.

"Well, you see the conundrum."

"What conundrum?"

"I can't answer your question or I'd be sharing information I'm not prepared to share." No self-awareness in his voice. "And sign this one." He moved aside the first piece of paper to reveal a second. "This NDA says you won't disclose that you signed the previous NDA."

I smirked. "Is there a third NDA to prevent me from saying I've signed the second?"

"Why would we do that?" Genuinely incredulous. "Come on back!" Big smile as he walked into the back, in his hand paperwork I had no intention of abiding by, lawsuit be damned. Something stank here.

Maybe it was the kiwi.

The second I'd stepped in the back, I inhaled the scent of kiwi and I could promptly see its origin—piles of the green fruit cut into perfect circular slices. They were stacked on a snack table along the far wall of the immense room. Next to the carved fruit, if I wasn't mistaken, large piles of sand with water spouting through the top, some sort of artisan fountain. On the wall to our right, a huge digital screen took up most of the wall. The screen showed a swirling image of outer space.

In the middle of the room stood a conference table, isolated, surrounded not by chairs but by odd-looking seating: backs to the "chairs" but no places to place your rear end. In the middle of the conference table, rising from the center, a hologram kept changing images: outer space; the African savannah; a dolphin jumping into the air in a vast ocean; two little girls holding hands and running across a green field.

"It's not *that* impressive." Rajeev laughed. Of course it was, he meant. "Froom."

"I can be out of your hair in ten minutes. I'd just like a word with Danny."

"Oh, c'mon, Fitch. You're not curious?"

I took a look at this half-pint and realized he was a veritable hologram himself. I was usually decent at reading people, but I couldn't tell if he was serious or not, or thought himself serious or not. Dangerous kind of creature, like a deadly spider that might crawl into your sleeping bag for a nap or an attack. *Deep breath, Fitch,* I told myself, *no need to dismiss this character before you've coaxed out of him what you might.* Besides, speaking of spiders, the Tarantulas were combing around outside.

"Yeah. The teensiest bit curious."

"You know what the greatest obstacle is to greater productivity? You know what really holds us back?"

"Slow boot-up times."

"Obviously. Those are excruciating milliseconds. I'm talking about something we can solve." He paused, milking this. Waiting for me to guess. I just stared at him. Part of me wondered if he would say *mortality.* Maybe he was in on the notes from the grave.

"Conference rooms," he said.

"Conference rooms."

"Behold the conference room of the future." He looked at the setting in the middle of this huge room. "Standard stuff. Reclaimed marble table, squatting desks. Stuff everyone can have, and should. The price of admission. But what turns this conference room into a Thinkference Room, into an Ideaference Room?"

"A what?"

"A place where we Change. The. World. Achieve Omniference."

"Kiwi?"

"Not bad, actually."

"What's not bad?"

"Kiwi. I realize you don't know what you're saying. You're talking about fruit. I'm talking about names, the names of conference rooms. Kiwi might be a great name. Rich with meaning."

Suddenly a full stop. He was waiting for me to get it. Which I decidedly did not. "Danny . . ."

"Patience. The conference room is the new garage, the start-up within the start-up, where ideas get generated and flourish, or they don't. And they will die, trust me, Fitch, they will never be born if the conference room doesn't have a what?"

"A what?"

"The right name! You think it's an accident that Gooble keeps generating new ideas, brilliant new ideas that actually have the potential to generate revenue? No way. Listen to their conference room names: Mandela's Sandals; Sans Permit; the Mad Hatcher."

"Let's move on."

"We're on the same page. That last part was OTR, off the record. I was number two in conference room naming at Gooble and I fully appreciate what they've done. Great people, pioneers in their own way. But they've lost their way. A lot of the brainstorming for the Gooble Mouthcam Platform was done in These Are Not the DDR2s You're Looking For."

"I'm not sure what you just said."

"Right?" He smirked. "No wonder Mouthcam flopped. Did anyone, *anyone,* think of the privacy issues of showing the larynx? Anyhow, the point is, we're notching conference room naming up by orders of magnitude."

"You name conference rooms."

"We christen conference rooms—but with you at the helm. For your individual enterprise, *your* vision. We tailor, design, evoke, stimulate. We Coopreate. Cooperate, create, and copulate."

"Copulate."

"Reproduce ideas at a frightening rate."

I almost jumped when I heard his phone ring. A U2 song. "Hold on." He put a finger up. "Sorry . . ."

I muttered: "It's just an app, telling you your ringer works. You can ignor—"

"Bono, what's the word?" he said into the phone. He listened: "Oh, sorry to hear it. Catch you on the flip side." He listened again. "See you, my Irish Catholic bro." He laughed and clicked off and looked at me: "Bono." Can't hide his pride. "Froom backer. Obviously I can't say the equity split but he's way down with it."

"I thought the Bono ringtone just warned you that your ringer was off."

"Maybe. Billy! Danny!"

Who? I turned to see where he was looking. At the opening from the front. In walked an odd couple: an older guy, tall, slender and sleek, gray goatee, white shroud-type thing hanging from his shoulders to the floor; and a stocky kid, more like heavyset bordering on fat, shaved skull, jeans and a T-shirt, round head, downward glance, looked like he'd have three-day growth were he fully pubescent.

"Fitch, the talent is in the house. I want you to meet Billy Winehouse, and Big D Donogue. Gentlemen, Willie Fitzgerald, he's with—"

"Myself."

I tried to make sense of everything. I'd thought Danny was the CEO. I said that: "I thought Danny was CEO."

"It's a nontraditional in-house position. Chief Existential Officer, our spiritual adviser," Da Raj explained. "We've decided to take the CEO position in-house, not use an outside service like some companies. That's how important it is to have our values front and center. It's a differentiator."

This older guy extended his hand to me. "Old-fashioned handshake," he said. "I don't think I could fist-bump if I tried." I grasped and we shook. I sensed instantly that the guy was down-to-earth, which he confirmed by saying: "Don't let Da Raj's youthful enthusiasm get to you. We're all going to work for him someday." He smiled beatifically at Da Raj, who now seemed a touch off balance.

I fist-bumped with Danny, who barely caught my eye and looked away.

Over the next few minutes, some details worked themselves out. Da Raj and Danny cofounded Froom along with someone they kept referring to as the Valley's One Female Venture Capitalist, and Bono. The explanations were a little hard to follow because Shirli had reentered and, in response to a request that she put on music, gave directions to Pasadena. Da Raj defended her: "One of the trade-offs you make when you hire truly creative people is that they color outside the lines. You need them to do that. That's why we let people work at the gym or a climbing-wall facility. We *encourage* that."

A few other early pre-pre-partiers streamed in. People stood at the kiwi table, sipping from the fountain of vitamin water that bubbled from the pile of sand. I was told this was a reminder to people that we're in the middle of a drought and as a way of encouraging people to drink judiciously and also to figure out new ways to monetize water. When I'd finally had enough, I approached Danny. The place was humming now, fifty people at least. Over the loudspeakers blared indie rock, the songs sometimes interspersed with driving directions.

"I'm sorry to hear about your grandfather."

"Yeah, well."

He fiddled with his phone, not looking up. I stared at the top of his pate.

"Did my mom send you? I know what this is about."

"Oh yeah?" I tried to keep it noncommittal.

"She wants me to go to college." He looked up. "Did Jobs finish college?"

I locked eyes with this kid, then he looked down again. Back to his phone. Fiddling with nothing. He said: "College isn't the only way to make it in this world. It's a joke. Four years that could be spent . . ." He trailed off.

I could barely hear the kid. "Is there someplace we can talk in private?"

He looked up. "How about my office?"

"I'd appreciate that."

"We're in it. What's on your mind?"

I looked around. I was in the left-hand corner of the Froom room, the farthest point from the door where we came in. The kiwi and sand table was a few paces to our right, the food line stretching behind us. A surge of new attendees streamed from the entrance. I glanced at the incoming crowd, my danger alarm sounding. Something wasn't right. I suppressed a sudden urge to call Terry, check in.

"We have open-air, standing offices," Danny said. "Promotes Coopreation. Feel free to squat."

"Oh, come on. Nobody talks like that. Listen, I'd like to promote privacy. Someplace we can have a bit more in-depth conversation?"

"Nothing worthwhile needs more than a hundred and forty characters."

"Look, kid, how many characters is murder?"

The kid stiffened. I saw the tension in his jaw. "Fitch, right? You're a private detective? You know my mom's a greedy weirdo, right?"

"You always talk that way about your mother?"

He shook his head. "I'm emancipated. Practically. This is a new world we live in. I'm making my own way and I don't need her looking over my shoulder, and if you have any self-respect, I wouldn't think you'd want to get involved in her dirty business either."

"What business is that?"

"You should go. At least out of my office."

What did that mean? Take two steps to my left?

"Call me anytime. Here's my card." Old-school but nice, heavy paper. Felt like a kind of peace offering. I couldn't get a handle on this guy. I slipped the card into my pocket.

"Listen, Danny, you're into something. Carrying weight. It's written all over your pimply face. What happened with your grandfather?"

He bit the inside of his cheek. A nonanswer that hinted at something else.

I picked up a ripple in the crowd. Da Raj, moving in our direction, along with the CEO. I look back to Danny, trying to place what was bugging me.

"Are you taking Adderall?" I asked Danny.

His reaction was a kind of half snort, like a forced laugh, as if to say: *give me a break*. Not very convincing.

Da Raj and the CEO continued in our direction, occasionally being backslapped and fist-bumped, slowing their approach.

"I hear he's been tweeping—your grandfather, Captain Don From . . ." I looked for the word. "Beyond."

Danny's eyes twitched, just as Da Raj and the CEO arrived.

"Whoa, aura," said the CEO. "Tension. Would it be okay if I broke in with a story?"

"Does anyone knock anymore?" Danny asked.

"Pardon the interruption. I think you'll like this. I was walking in Samoa. Talking to MELFIs," then, for my benefit, the CEO explained: "Mother Entrepreneurs Learning Financial Independence. Of course, this place had no mobile connections, none. How do they do it? How do they stay so serene with all the inefficiencies? What's their secre—"

There was commotion near the entrance. Two Tarantulas, unmistakable. Big guys, leather vests. They got a few glances, then people returned to their elevator pitches. Not me. I made eye contact with both of them, near as I could, trying to suss them out. They separated, going for the flanks.

". . . meditative breathing"—the CEO had continued his story—"from the diaphragm. It's ancient wisdom but applicable now as it was then, even without a walking stick. Think of your phone as a walking stick, handheld, a grounding tool . . ." I tuned him out, watching the Tarantulas nearby. I reached inside my jacket for my gun. I couldn't figure it; something too obvious about this approach, here, in this crowd. And then it hit me. Shit, it's a distraction. How did I miss it? To my right, other side of the kiwi table, a Tarantula. I'd picked him up earlier, a guy in an ill-fitting gingham shirt. What was in his hand?

"Get down!" I dove into Danny, Da Raj, and the CEO—trying to tackle them to the ground.

We hit the floor—I, the bowling ball; they, the pins. I heard screams and moans from the crowd. Business pitch interruptus. I pulled my gun, remembering, shit, I hadn't loaded it. What was the next move? Where was the nearest exit?

"Rajeev!"

It was the CEO screaming. His face was inches from Da Raj's. I managed a quick take and saw Da Raj turning blue. And something protruded right from his neck. A dart! Shit, that's what had been in the Tarantula's hand, some sort of toxic blowgun. Glassy-eyed, Da Raj stared at Danny. "You, Danny boy . . ." He trailed off. "I know. You . . ." He slumped, gasped his last breath—on my behalf.

Bastards. I stood and raised my gun. Bullets or not, I'd put the scare into them. That poor Irish Catholic kid had just taken a dart meant for me.

Over the loudspeakers, I heard Shirli dialing the phone. After a ring, someone picked up: "Emergency operator." Shirli responded: "Finding carpet cleaner."

The Tarantula with the blowgun gadget hit the exit, turned back, seared a look at me, and took off. I gave chase.

NINE

SHOUTS, MURMURS, A shrill scream. In my peripheral vision I picked up someone pointing at me: *stop him!* Halfway across the room, a hand snagged my arm and I yanked it away forcefully enough to send the person spinning, toppling into a few other people, prompting human dot-com dominoes to teeter and fall. Compostable plates and GMO-free, organic kiwi splashed into the air like confetti.

Somewhere in the recesses, it dawned on me that I'd become the face of this murder, the guy fleeing after standing next to Da Raj before he hit the floor.

At the wall that led to the little entry room, I paused. Could be Tarantulas hiding behind it. I'd have felt much better if the gun had been loaded. But even then, it would be three on one and I was coming around the blind corner. Another arm snagged at me and I swatted the person away and, the hell with it, turned the corner.

Nothing. Empty. Except for Shirli. She smiled. "Hello, Willie Fitzgerald . . . er, Fitch. Can I help you with something?"

Great, her first positive identification in months, and it was me. Just the kind of thing I needed her telling the police. As I loped to the door, I made a fleeting mental note to call Lieutenant Gaberson and set things straight. I burst out of Froom, bounded up the stairs, and discovered a world totally different from the one I'd left less than two hours earlier. For one thing, it was dark. And besides that, it was now wholesale bustle.

In fact, no sooner had I stepped off the top stair than I was practically assaulted by a guy trying to hand me a flyer. "Hey, I'm Tuck."

I ignored him and scanned the packed area. People paraded along both sidewalks, which were sufficiently crowded to cause some to stream into the street. Cars honked, pedestrians flowed among them. I craned to find a Tarantula. It was like Mardi Gras.

What had Da Raj meant when he looked at Danny with a deathbed accusation? Unmistakable, right?

The guy calling himself Tuck said: "Cornell, at a baseline, guaranteed, with all the usual caveats. Someone tells you they can guarantee Dartmouth or above, don't believe it. Is that a gun?"

"Water pistol." I scanned for Tarantulas.

"Oh, smart. Scare off the frauds. Nice. What year is your kid? Freshman or still in junior high? What percentile? I just mean ballpark, on the PSAT?"

I still saw no Tarantulas. But I did see the cops, a cherry-top half a block away down on the right, stopped in traffic. The passenger door on the police car opened.

"I get it," this pest said. "You're just checking it out, scoping the competition. Lot of fly-by-nights. Used to be just three of us here, two years ago. Now it's wall-to-wall test prep. We've got a track record. You cannot beat what we're offering."

No freaking clue what this huckster was hawking and no Tarantula in plain sight. A cop headed right for us, gun drawn. I looked at this joker. A head shorter than me, floppy hair, casual dress to a fault. He took my looking at him as encouragement.

"Just check us out, is all I'm saying. Your kid play an instrument? Obviously, he or she does. We can offer package deals with a local conservatory. We're just two doors down."

Cop closing in. I said: "Show me—"

"Tuck. Tuckster."

"Tuckster."

"Great. Great! You won't regret it. Full disclosure, I work on a commission basis, but I don't get paid if your young genius doesn't see a fifteen-percentile increase on the next official SAT, all the usual caveats. Boy or girl? My goodness, I didn't even ask. And I didn't catch your name."

"I didn't say." Absently, I followed him, scanning for bad guys, wary of the fuzz. I needed cover and to catch my breath. If I were a Tarantula, which way would I scurry? How had they disappeared so quickly?

The guy practically led me by the elbow and stopped in front of a shop I'd been in already. It was that damned bag store. Now the sign read: *Number Won Test Prep.*

"Look, college isn't for everybody. Jobs dropped out." Tuck paused. "Jesus, did you hear? He apparently Snipchapped this morning about user interface."

The cops were ten steps away. I feigned interest. "Who?"

"Jobs. Like: from his personal account. Everybody's saying it must've been hacked. He's dead and he's now got like twenty million followers."

"Steve Jobs."

He winced, like: *Who the fuck else could I mean? Was I from the moon?* He opened the door and I followed him in and saw a place transformed. What had been some retail outlet, with a few display shelves, now had six rows of kids sitting at computer terminals.

"Where's the bag joint?"

"That's the day scene. At night, we're like everyplace else in test prep central. Well, I misspoke. Not like everybody else. We've got a track record, world-class—*world-class* instructors," he repeated. "One board member sat on the SAT word-game subcommittee. He's got that section cold and it's where a lot of the difference gets made."

At the front, beside one of those digital chalkboards, a woman stood with a laser pointer, her red light pointing to an image: a teenager with one hand on a keyboard and another on a phone.

"What," she asked the class, "is the key to success?"

One teen shouted: "Having a great conference room name."

"Shorter boot-up times."

Another said, "Duh."

"Well, yes," the instructor said. She was so plain as to be nearly invisible; rail-thin, slumped shoulders, hair falling over her face and shoulders. "But I'm talking about something we can solve. The key to success is . . . being ambidextrous." Dramatic pause. "If you can use two hands on two keyboards simultaneously, then you can do what?" She paused again for effect, suddenly lighting up. "You can take two tests at the same time!"

I looked back to the street and things fell into place. Everyone who walked on the street did so in pairs: a parent and a kid, or, more precisely, young teen. Most pairs came with one instrument, a violin in a case, digital keyboard tucked under an arm; two oboes walked by. I'd heard about this, Résumé Row.

I turned back inside and saw my possible escape route, a doorway leading to the rear of the shop. Standing in it was a vaguely familiar face—the wonky engineer type with the ponytail who worked behind the counter at Ben's Bags. He looked perplexed, off balance, even shaken.

Tuck put his hand on my shoulder. "Oxygen shot? On the house."

I made a beeline for the Ben's Bag dude, eyeing a little stick dangling from his left hand. Tuck, holding tight to my shoulder like he was a car salesman in the death throes, nearly took flight rather than let go. As I neared the back, the guy in the doorway seemed to flinch. I made out the thing in his hand: a small flag, black and gray, with a tarantula in the middle of it.

"Where did you get that?"

"Fell out of the pocket of some weirdo who went flying through here. How was Froom? Was the CEO there?"

I pulled the flag from the dork's hand.

"Hey!"

"Glad you want to look around," Tuck said. "Our bathrooms promote ambidexterity."

I shook him off as I accelerated down a short hallway, bathrooms on both sides, a small kitchen area to the left, and then a back door that looked like it might well lead to an alley. So was this where the Tarantulas went? Awfully coincidental.

"Not again," Tuck said. "You with the guys dressed in leather? I can offer a package deal."

"What?" I turned to face Tuck and the ponytail guy. "Did a guy come in here with a leather . . . with tattoos, spider deal?"

"I got him in here," Tuck said. "Steered him right through. Big rush, that one. We understand. Time is ticking. If you're with them, we've got a two-for-one family deal, includes the SAT, music, voice lessons, and basic Generation-Z social skills, including how to let your parents feel like they're in charge."

I'd had enough. I lifted Tuck up by the veritable lapels and pinned him against the wall.

He protested: "You are in charge. Of course you are. It's just that we're letting them think that—"

"The guys who came in here with the spider vibe—where did they go?"

Ponytail piped up: "Shot through to the alley. One of them dropped the flag, fell out of his back pocket." He said he could show me where they went. I dropped Tuck to the floor, where he continued to pitch as I followed the Ben's Bag guy through a glass door into a dark alley. He nodded to the right. Ran to a small car at the end of the alley, he said, and lit off.

Must've been a MINI.

"Does this have to do with Da Raj?" Ponytail asked.

"How do you know about that?"

"It's trending. Was. His death was huge for more than two minutes."

"Whose bike is this?" I looked at the motorcycle kickstanding near the wall. One of those Zero motorcycles, no emissions, specialized rear jack, top box and rack kit, soft leather saddlebags.

"It's mine."

"I need it."

He laughed, like: *you're crazy.*

"I'm a cop." I paused. "Cop-ish. Those guys are bad guys. I need it."

"I'll make you a deal," he said.

"The other guy already tried. I'm not signing up for classes. I need your bike."

"I go with you, hear about Froom, you make an introduction to Danny, a good word, y'know, for relationship building, and I get twenty-five percent of the social media rights if this chase makes news."

It was all I could do not to shove this guy's head into the spokes. He picked that up instantly: "Okay, fine, yes. But I'm going with you."

"Get on the back," I said through my teeth.

Seconds later, I tore down the alley. Then skidded to a stop near the end of the alley as a teen walked crosswise into the opening playing an accordion while juggling a soccer ball on his knees. I looked left and right. No MINI in sight. But, realistically, it had to go right; to the left, middle of the road, a blockage, a big jam of people, bathed by streetlamps.

"SLS," said the ponytail. "Spontaneous Lecture Series event. So much bullshit. They're not even remotely spontaneous. Someone had to plan this or there wouldn't be a banner." It was hung over the street. It read: *Midlife at 15. What's Next?*

Yep, the MINI had to have gone right, lest it pile over the middle-of-the-street lectern and the teen at the helm. I gunned the bike to the right. I crossed Onaniversity Avenue. No way any of the Tarantulas took the main drag, too crowded, unless they were on foot, and the ponytail behind me had professed otherwise. I kept straight, hitting the flatlands of Palo Alto, one beautifully manicured ranch-style house after the next.

"Wait. Go back," said Ponytail. "I saw something."

"In the dark?" I muttered. But I hit the brakes. Middle of a residential block, the cacophony of Résumé Row behind us, a hum of sirens over the top. "What kind of something?"

"Look."

The ponytail pointed between two houses, and the fences that separated them. Even in the echoes of light from houses and garages, I could see something was on the ground back there. I shot the bike between the houses and, yep, something all right: lying right there in the alley between the houses.

A Tarantula. Flat on his back.

I flinched. Pulled out the pistol—I know, not loaded, but emotional support nonetheless—and whipped my head around. This was all wrong. I was moving too fast, getting yanked along, looking for the trap, trying to eye the guy on the ground who was decidedly not moving. Froth bubbled from his mouth.

It was dark but not pitch-black. A garage just to my right had those movement-sensor lights on it and they'd gone on when I pulled the cycle up. I looked both ways in the alley for movement, shadows, a trap to be sprung if I leaned down to examine this Tarantula bait. But there was nothing. Not a peep.

I dismounted with gun trained on the dude on the ground wearing the gingham shirt. Brown hair matted against his forehead, eyes rolled up. I didn't need to be a coroner . . .

I reached down to take his pulse and a sound exploded. I pulled back sharply.

Christ, it was coming from the Tarantula's mobile phone, which was in his dead hand. It was a U2 song.

"At least his ringer survived," Ponytail observed.

I reached down to snag the Tarantula's phone. Then another sound, this one in the distance but closing in: sirens. And, behind it, a little farther out, helicopter rotors. Circling cops, by air and ground. I turned to Ponytail: "I recommend you beat it."

"What?"

"Get on your bike and get lost. Otherwise you'll spend the next ten hours downtown answering questions."

"I didn't do anything."

I turned to go. "How does that software work? The thing you were telling me about—facial recognition?"

It took him a second to orient to my question. "You do investing? Weird time to talk about it, though. Can we meet later?"

It's not what I was thinking. Actually, I wasn't exactly sure what I was thinking. Maybe he could mask my identity, what with all these cops and the constant surveillance, the cameras on every corner. Jesus, what had gotten into me? This place, the nonstop optimism, like Hollywood but with engineers.

He pulled out his phone. "I'll infrared you my contact info." There was a beeping noise. Now I was connected to this freak too.

"When's a good time to meet?"

But I was already halfway down the alley, heading to my truck, the Tarantula's gadget in hand. Trouble in every single direction, including up.

TEN

HOOFED IT TO my truck and stood outside it, key in the lock, wondering: Surely, they were tracking me everywhere, but who were *they*? Tarantulas? Someone else?

My phone, presumably, easy enough to surveil. My truck, maybe, also presumably. Unless tracking technology somehow got thwarted by rusty paint and a radio that now only picked up AM. On the other hand, if they were tracking me, how come they weren't waiting for me here, six blocks from the sirens and oboes in downtown Palo Alto? Still, it seemed worthwhile to get a new ride. Hog time.

Thirty-five minutes later, keeping an eye over my shoulder, I was winding up the hills above Silicon Valley, unincorporated land. West of Woodside and Redwood City. God's country, even to atheists. Green and quiet, curving roads, at least where there were roads. You didn't need much of an imagination to picture the ghost of Sleepy Hollow. Too far out for the techies. Here, it was hippies, or wannabes, or freaks, what was left of them. Including Elron Lyme. Best chopper mechanic I'd ever met. On a

Baja ride we took years ago, he resurrected Terry's Harley from near death with a seashell, two pesos, and a tequila worm.

I parked a half mile from his pad to throw off any surveillance scent. With a deep breath, I loaded the gun and dumped some extra shells into my pocket. I checked again that my phone was off, discovered it so, and then remembered the phone I took from the dead Tarantula. As I suspected, it was a burner, a cheap text-'n'-talk-only device, the kind people got at the convenience store and bought the minutes in advance. I opened it up hoping just maybe there was some critical insight on this thing—a text with the name of cohorts, directions to my kill, that sort of thing.

Not to be had. Just a bunch of incoming calls from blocked numbers. Except for one—an outgoing call. An actual number. In the 408 area code. Didn't tell me much. The question was: Who would answer when I called?

Unfortunately, I wasn't able to find out, not at that moment; there was no phone service up here, zero bars of coverage.

I turned off the phone as I walked onto a road so narrow it barely would accommodate a motorcycle. Trees bent in over me on either side, moonlight blocked, darker now than Hades but for a dim light beaconing from the house where I was heading. My thoughts turned, for no reason in particular, to Terry. Not his style, this aesthetic. Honestly, if he had his way, we'd probably have gone the other direction—full suburban, a pool, picket fence, the muted California seasons erring on the warm side, furniture from this-or-that upper-middle-class name-brand place and lots of emotions stuffed into them.

I learned early on that Terry didn't much like talking about how he was feeling, or how the day went, or who said what to whom. There, we were birds of a feather. It's just that my behavior came from not liking the sound of my own voice and his came from a classic conservative upbringing wherein emotions, like children, were meant to be neither seen nor heard. His family's philosophy: *We will solicit your opinion after you reach voting age or kill a member of the Johnson clan* (latter part lost relevance after about 1850). Once, a famous client of Terry's was audited, giving both him and his client ulcers, and I didn't know a word about it until three weeks later when Terry wound up in urgent care. Even then, it was the hospital that called me; they handed the phone to Terry, who said: "Don't waste your time coming down here. Make sure to tape *Justified*."

I pulled open the gate of a five-foot-high fence surrounding a house that seemed more expansive than I remembered; woodland chic, not fancy exactly, more like perfectly blended in, two stories that melted into the trees, maybe because the structure was totally of this place. I took one step inside and heard: "Halt or I'll shoot."

I took the halt option.

"Your iPhone. I'll nail it right in the app!" Thus continued a voice I immediately recognized as that of Elron Lyme, followed by his deep, resonant laugh, like he'd said the funniest thing in the world. "Lemme guess, you got your private dick stuck in the spokes again."

"Howdy, Elron. It's possible you've gotten less funny."

The porch light went on. There stood Elron, tall and skinny and whiter than an albino who fell into yogurt in the British winter. "Honey," he shouted inside. "Fire up the moonshine."

The front-door screen opened and out walked Honey. That was Elron's husband, who had been christened something else long ago, took the name Honey, and looked just like it—golden-skinned, smooth and lumpy in spots. A mama-san of sorts but Caribbean style. Once I asked Honey where he was from and he said: "Tough to name a place I'm not from."

"I don't have time to stay," Elron said.

"What?"

"That's what you're going to say: 'I don't have time to stay.' I know you, Fitch. If it's late, you show up unannounced, carrying a piece, acting jumpy, you need a hideout or a bike."

"Or both. I don't have time to stay."

Elron laughed. "That's what Honey said after our first night together. And here we are like ten decades later."

"I don't have time to stay," Honey said.

"I've got a way of persevering," Elron said.

"I really *don't* have time to stay," I explained.

"It'll take me at least thirty minutes to get your ride together. So come in and catch us up. How's your better half?"

I sucked it up. No way around a little socializing. And so, forty-five minutes later, I'd caught them up and gotten their latest story, and had bathtub moonshine that tasted just like bathtub. But it did take the edge off. Elron sent me off, a bit miffed that I'd declined to tell them about the case I was working on; I'd denied them for their own protection. Honey handed me a chicken sandwich for the road.

The air felt great as I peeled out in a beauty, a Triumph Tiger from the mid-1960s, svelte bike, red on white, much too nice for the likes of me. Elron insisted and said it was the only thing he had handy and knew I was good for the $6,000 it would take to replace it.

I knew exactly where I was headed. No question about it at all. I was already in the neighborhood.

I just needed the address. That meant turning on my phone. Once I did that, how long would it take to triangulate my position if someone was tracking me? A few minutes. I needed to make this quick. I dial.

After two rings: "Hello, it's Lester, do you realize what time it is?" said Lester Wollop.

"Lester, get off the phone!" Now Tess Donogue had picked up.

"It's the landline, which is mine!"

"That's not what the mediator said."

"That was not legally binding."

"Hi, this is Captain Don," I said.

Sudden silence.

"Daddy?"

"No, sorry. It's Fitch. Your friendly neighborhood detective." I felt bad playing the dead-ish-guy card, but I needed to get their attention. "I've got news about your dad." Another lie. Lie-ish. "I'd rather deliver it in person. What's your address?"

Silence again.

"It's nearly ten P.M.," Lester said.

"Lester! Not everyone turns out the lights at nine thirty."

"You have no respect for sleep hygiene."

"It's in your head, Lester. You sleep just fine when we're on vacation."

"That's because you're not sitting up in bed with the laptop."

"Stop," I muttered.

"It's not a laptop. It's a tablet. Jesus. And besides, someone has to manage our affairs!" Tess barked at her husband (ex-husband?). "I mean, *my* affairs."

"Oh, that's rich. I've got as much right to that ill-gotten gain as you do. Anyhow, that laptop light is just like the TV. It delays melatonin release."

"Not if you're wearing eyeshades. You can't even see the light! Or tell that it's a *tablet*!"

"Stop!"

This did pause them.

"I need your address. I'm almost out of battery life and I have news."

Tess, Mrs. Donogue, spat out the address and said, "When you get to the gate, push the button and I'll let you in. You do realize it's late."

"Oooooh," Lester said sarcastically, "I didn't realize you could read a clock."

"Get off the phone!"

"It's my phone. And so is the wireless modem."

"We have joint custody of the Wi-Fi!"

"So you can troll the Internet for young-tech ass?"

"Lester!"

"Trollop!"

I hung up.

Ten minutes later, I was at their gate.

ELEVEN

BEFORE I HIT the buzzer on the massive wrought iron gate, I took a moment to reflect on the long day, trying to add things up. That morning, Tess Donogue had barged in and told me her dad was tweeping from the grave after he was murdered. The aggrieved daughter pointed me to her son, Captain Don's beloved grandson, who played coy. Mrs. Donogue also urged me to meet with Alan Klipper, Klipper the Shipper, who was working with Captain Don to build something called the Spirit Box. It somehow created a digital afterlife.

No sooner had I started poking around than the Tarantulas showed up and left Da Raj taking his last breath.

Too many pieces to make sense of. Especially with all the noise erupting. From somewhere on this expansive estate burped the sound of gears and pumps. It sounded like there was some massive industrial process at work. I couldn't determine the source of the sound but gathered that it was coming from the direction I was facing, over a hill behind the iron gate. The powerful sound must have made the neighbors murderous, unless they were acres away, which was possible; this estate stood isolated, down a narrow road in the Los Altos Hills, just fifteen miles south as the crow flew from Elron and Honey's place but a whole different planet. Money lived here. Money took long luxurious baths here, after it touched down on the helipad at the end of a long day counting more money.

I rang the bell.

"Donogue-Wollop residence," a female's voice said. "Visitor or life coach?"

"Visitor—for Mrs. Donogue."

"Mr. Fitch?"

"Fitch."

"You're expected. Come in."

The gate opened and I took a slow drive up a long, paved access road lined with tall, decorative streetlamps. The motion-sensor lights clicked on as I moved along. The terrain was tasteful nothingness; to my immediate left and right, open fields. Farther out on both sides, if my eyesight didn't deceive, groves of trees. Dead ahead, a slight rolling hill that hid what was on the other side. As I neared the undulation in the land, the industrial sound got louder, then softened, then increased again; its origin was still unclear. I rose over the crest and then had to stop at the magnitude of it all: what came into view was not one gargantuan home but two megawatt residences. One stood on the left flank, one on the right. They couldn't have been more different from one another.

The one to the left was a rustic, I guess you'd say, wooden structure, a log cabin of sorts, but, well, I had trouble putting any sense to it. It wasn't like anything I'd ever seen. The logs were stacked at various angles, as if designed by a kid with Lincoln

Logs and a sugar high. The house sloped upward to an apex in the middle, where a single room seemed like an observation tower. It was three stories in all, though if you'd have asked me to wager, I might've said the left side had four stories. It was that haphazard.

If this was what passed for modern architecture, I could've made a mint designing houses.

I looked over to the right at an entirely different façade. This one looked like a classic plantation—right from the pages of *Gone with the Wind,* while the log one was designed by the patients from *One Flew over the Cuckoo's Nest.*

"Grotesque," a voice said.

I looked and realized that Mrs. Donogue was standing next to me. I hadn't heard her, evidently, over the industrial sound.

"Where did you come from?"

"The tunnel system," she said. "We're tearing that down." She gestured to the southern-looking mansion. "Hardly fit for *Lester* to live in. You can leave your bike here. Come on in. Feel free to keep your shoes on. We're using the tunnel entrance."

"Because the front door is . . ."

"Lost. We're having trouble finding it." She took a step into a circular opening in the ground, a veritable manhole entrance. "C'mon, Fitch. There's something you really should see."

A few minutes later, we emerged into the Lincoln Log house, which my host described as the perfect mix of indoor and outdoor environments, open-air rooms conjoined with covered ones. "It's what makes the front door so elusive because you're not sure whether you're going inside or outside. That's what Daddy says. It's what he wanted."

"Mrs. Donogue, please—"

"He called it the troll house. Called it. He's mostly dead. It's ridiculous—this house, not Daddy," she said. Then, perhaps to herself: "Oh, Daddy, I'm so sorry. You loved this place." To me: "Would you like a tour?" She practically had to shout over the mechanical din.

"Pass. Let's get down to business."

"What do you have to tell me?" she asked.

"What?"

"On the phone, you said you had news—about the case."

I told her about Da Raj—in broad brushstrokes. I watched her face for reaction. Did she already know?

She said: "I'm sorry he's gone. He was a creepy kid." Then added: "I told you there was nasty business going on. What does this have to do with Daddy?"

"I'm working on that."

"I need to show you something," she said. "It's all teed up for you in the media complex."

She led me through a series of rooms, some open-air to the sky, others roofed, some with stairs leading up, others down. Finally, we reached a fully indoor entertainment room, practically twenty-foot-high wood ceiling beams and, back down here on earth, a comfortable-looking S-curved couch in the middle. On each of the four walls hung massive flat-panel television screens. On each of the screens, the frozen face of a man I recognized: Captain Don. He looked frumpy.

Tess Donogue picked up a remote control and clicked it, and in an instant, the industrial sound disappeared.

"Sorry about the noise!" she shouted, and realized she no longer needed to. She lowered her voice. "We're starting work on the other house."

I recalled what I'd read: the ample land had two houses, and Tess Donogue alternately lived in one while she tore down and updated the other, and then switched. In this case, she explained, she was adding a desalination plant. Piping water in from the Pacific, sending it through tight membranes that leached out the salt, then putting it into the toilets.

"Because of the drought," I said.

"Oh, that's an interesting way to think of it." It hadn't dawned on her. "A lot of people think it's a nice-to-have amenity, but I think it's a great-to-have. Design-wise, I think of it as future-proofing the place for the next three to five years, plus or minus." When she said "future proof" she did air quotes with her hands.

"What do you have to show me, Mrs. Donogue? It's late."

"You're the one who showed up here unannounced." She paused. "If the night wears on"—she lowered her voice—"I'm sure I can find you a place to bed down."

"Trollop!" A man's voice rang out.

In a doorway to the right, the man stood wearing a yellow rain slicker. Just when it couldn't get any weirder.

"He's a private dick, Lester," Mrs. Donogue said.

"Aha!"

"I mean an investigator. That's just a turn of phrase. A slip of the tongue."

"Aha!"

"Oh, give me a break. He's looking into Daddy's death. Speaking of absurd, what are you doing out here in your pajamas?"

"Somebody turned off the desalination plant. You know that sound is the only thing that puts me to sleep."

"It's in your head, Lester!"

"Oh, that's rich. It's an actual desalination plant. It's plain to see."

"I mean the insomnia. You sleep fine whenever we're on vacation."

I couldn't resist. "Maybe it's the damned rain slicker, making it hard to sleep."

Lester looked at me. He was round, but not super round, a muted version of Jackie Gleason in *The Hustler,* the original, from the early 1960s. Terry had made me watch it a dozen times if we'd watched it once. A round face topped Lester's round body. Nearly plump legs stuck out the bottom of the slicker, stumpy toes stuck into flip-flops. He had a mustache. Beneath his arm, a pliant, plump cat.

"What rain slicker?"

"Your pajamas—"

"State-of-the-art indoor-outdoor sleepwear. Jesus, Tess, you'd think you could sleep with someone who knows which direction is up."

"He's just a dick!"

Suddenly they were reduced to squabbling. I wanted to strangle both of them. I closed my eyes and pictured the check that Tess was going to write me.

"I'm leaving," I whispered.

This instantly shut everyone up.

"Lester! Go. To. Bed!"

"I'll stay, thank you."

"Fine."

And so, with Lester sitting on one end of the S-curve couch and Mrs. Donogue on the other, facing opposite directions, looking at screens on opposite walls, it was time for the show. Mrs. Donogue hit play on her remote control.

In the video, Captain Don started laughing. Laughing and laughing. It wasn't clear that he was aware that the videotaping had begun. He was lost in a private joke.

"Cap'n," a voice said. It was high-pitched, girlie almost. Hard to determine gender.

"We're on, then?" Captain Don looked straight ahead, mostly. Maybe owing to generational issues—he wasn't raised with a camera always on him—he was not looking exactly into the camera. But enough. His flop of white hair made him appear sage, not cartoonish, almost dazzling vivacity in his blue eyes, despite the ring of wrinkles and sagging skin. He was round too, like his son-in-law, Lester, a Freudian enough physical likeness.

"Much as I hate clichés," he started, "this is one."

He shook his head, closed his eyes, displeased with himself in some way. Then opened his eyes again, took on the camera directly. "This is the standard if-you're-watching-this-I-am-already-dead or dead-ish video."

Mrs. Donogue burst out a sob.

"I have a rare form of something-or-other. I can't even remember the name of it. It doesn't matter. It's gonna be something-or-other that gets us all in the end, one way or another. Tess, stop your bawling. It's going to be okay. And Lester!" Captain Don looked right into the camera. "Pet your goddamned cat yourself, will you?"

We all looked at Lester and saw that the cat he was holding was being stroked by a mechanical arm that extruded from the couch.

"It's like he's still here," said Mrs. Donogue.

"This was your innovation!" Lester yelled at the screen.

"I know, I know," Captain Don said, shaking his head, eyes nearly closed again. "I know it was mine. But it was no innovation. It was not, I repeat—NOT—an innovation. That word, that terrible, terrible word—"

"Stop the video," I heard myself say.

Mrs. Donogue pressed pause and looked at me. "What's the matter? Did you get rained on? I think we might have a leak. Do you want some pajamas?"

I ignored her. "Was this video made before he died? If so, how does he know what you're going to say?"

"Oh. That. He just kind of knew how everyone acted. We're fairly predictable—especially Whiner over there." She went on to say that Captain Don absolutely made the video weeks, maybe months, before his death. She found it on his bedside table.

"He lived here?" I asked.

"After Mama died, I took him in."

"Like every other man on the block," Lester said.

"Look who's stroking his cat," Mrs. Donogue said.

"So he lived here until the day he died." I brought things back on track. "Go ahead with the video."

Mrs. Donogue pressed play.

"Innovation. Innovation." Captain Don let the word roll around in his mouth like a marble. "Abomination!"

"Daddy!" Mrs. Donogue seemed to recoil as if seeing this for the first time. "He was out of his head, delirious with some sort of disease."

"When did merely naming something become the equivalent of having an innovation?" the Captain said on the video. "Marketing is not innovation. Saying the word 'innovation' is not an innovation. Making things more efficient Is. Not. An. Innovation!"

I realized what I'd understood when this video began: I liked this guy. He was speaking some earth-toned truth.

"Listen here," Captain Don said, jabbing a round finger. "I'm as guilty of it as anybody. I'm not pointing fingers."

"You are too pointing a finger," Lester said.

"I know that, Lester," said Captain Don. "I'm making a point. I'm as guilty as anyone, at least for the last quarter century of my blessed life. I stopped innovating and I started incrovating."

"Daddy! Good word."

"No, it's not. Incremental nonsense. It's not an innovation. It's language. And I'll tell you something else. I'll tell you the god-damned truth. I am afraid. I'm just as afraid as anyone, from any era, from any time and place. No matter how much stuff we come up with, no matter how much faster and more efficient we get. No matter how many e-things and i-things, it's still scary when the end gets closer. That's what I'm saying. That's what I'm trying to tell you. My greatest innovation. The thing I can best give you is a chance to pull away all these distractions, free yourself of the warp-speed ideas, sucking more time and money from everything." He paused, and he chewed on what he was going to say next. "Speed is not peace. Speed is speed."

"Dementia," his daughter muttered, and let out a sob. "You were right. I wasn't there for him."

The man on-screen went silent and he looked right at us, then dropped his eyes, shook his head. It seemed he was saying: *I'm not sure anyone understands what I'm saying, at least not this audience.*

"Turn it off," he said.

"Grandpa?" It was a voice from the person holding the camera.

"Turn it off!" Captain Don repeated.

The screen went black.

TWELVE

T EARS ROLLED DOWN Mrs. Donogue's cheeks. Real? Crocodile? And Lester snored. Deep zzzz's.

"Was that Danny who said 'Grandpa' while taping the video?" I asked.

"Yes. I assume."

"You assume."

"He's not in it, not visible. But I'm pretty sure it's him. I'd recognize our little baby's voice anywhere. Wouldn't you, Lester?"

Lester snored on.

"Lester, get up!" she screamed at him.

He sprang awake. "What's happening?!"

She chuckled haughtily. "See, you sleep just fine. It's all in your head."

He looked dazed.

"Did Danny take that video of Daddy? You can hear his voice."

"I guess so."

"You're not sure, Mr. Wollop?"

"It sounds like him."

Weird, I supposed, this moment of mild uncertainty. Maybe.

More generally, the video had me sideways. Not what I expected from Captain Don. Not the evidence I anticipated. I couldn't quite put my finger on why it was so unexpected. This anti-innovation tirade wasn't characteristic of the Captain Don that had so long been advertised. A deathbed conversion? How long ago was the video made? Had he expected to die?

"Can you e-mail me a copy of that?"

"Sure," said his daughter. "Of course you'll need to sign an NDA."

"You just showed it to me."

Lester guffawed. "Careful, or she'll get you signing a prenup too."

She took two steps in his direction and pointed the remote control at him as if it were a gun. "Are you saying I asked *you* to sign a prenup?"

"Nice try." He smirked. Then looked at me: "If—*if*, hypothetically—I had signed a prenup and if—*if*, hypothetically—I had signed an NDA about such a hypothetical prenup, then I'd be in violation of my hypothetical prenup and hypothetical NDA *if* I said anything about it. Then, POOF, she sues me and, poof, the divorce settlement goes poof." He looked back at her: "How stupid do you think I am? You think I'll fall for your petty tricks?"

"Very."

"What?"

"I think you're very stupid."

"Stupid enough to sign a prenup?"

"Yes, I think you're—" She paused. "Nice try, Lester!"

"Ha. You were almost in violation of the NDA. I mean hypothetical NDA, if there were one. Oh yeah. Woot! I've got Snozz-wanger, Veruca and Gloop on speed dial."

"His divorce-slash-patent attorneys," his wife explained to me, sounding bored.

"I'm not signing anything," I said. "You want me to get to the bottom of your father's death or not?"

Things got quiet.

"Death-ish," Lester said. "Have some respect in front of his daughter, will you?"

"Thank you, baby. You want some tea to help you sleep?"

"Yes, and turn on the desalination plant, snookums."

"You said he stayed here, your father. I need to see his room."

His daughter cleared her throat. "It's a mess."

"So?"

"You want to see it now?"

"Yes, now."

She chewed on this.

"What's the problem? You got something to hide?" I'd had enough.

"No."

"No, there's no problem, or no, you don't have something to hide?"

"You don't have crampons," she said.

"What?"

"The tunnels—they get steep."

"Take me to the room or find yourself another detective."

She swallowed.

"One more thing. I have to ask one more thing." I looked

hard at the pair of them. "Did Danny have something to do with Captain Don's death?"

Another moment of silence.

"No way," Lester said. "They loved each other. Birds of a feather."

Mrs. Donogue nodded in agreement.

"Mr. Wollop, I'm going to want a word with you—later," I said.

He looked at his wife and shrugged and nodded affirmation. And Mrs. Donogue and I left the room. A few minutes later, we found ourselves in a spacious, indoor-only master bedroom, the one at the peak of this log monstrosity. It overlooked the back of the estate through expansive windows. Presumably, it was once a great view but now opened on a large industrial project: the desalination plant—again barfing noises. At my request, Mrs. Donogue turned it off.

The tasteful, if modest, room had a drawing table, shelves, a worn recliner, and a bed, and every damn piece of furniture had one thing in common: they were covered with books. Books and books and books. Dozens, hundreds, strewn and stacked.

"I haven't had the heart to clean it up."

"He read all these?"

"Read, underlined, read again."

"But never put anything away."

"He did. Usually. I don't think he would've left things such a mess. He was very orderly."

We were standing next to the door. I gestured to a pile on the bed. "Do you mind?"

She nodded: go ahead.

I picked through the pile, glancing at titles. I wasn't much of a reader but enough of one to know this was a random—what's the word—amalgam. Nonfiction, fiction, technical, various genres, serious tomes, mysteries, science, lots of math and engineering. I'd heard of some of the authors and books: *Common Ground; Good to Great;* a bunch of books by Walter Mosley; *The Selfish Gene; Steve Jobs,* the biography; Martin Luther King's *Why We Can't Wait; Stalingrad; The New York Times Manual of Style and Usage;* Raymond Chandler's *The Little Sister; The Best and the Brightest; The Hot Zone* and *Into Thin Air;* and tons of technical books with names too boring to mention, some of them merely symbols.

Near the middle of the pile on the bed, my eye settled on *My Life* by Bill Clinton. I shooed aside the books and opened the autobiography, instinct and whim. Inside the title page, a note: *Captain Don, Thank you for innovating us into the black. My debt is to you. Sincerely,* and then the former president's signature.

"Impressive."

"He innovated that bed."

"How's that?"

"You've heard of the king and the California king? This is a new size, entirely, all new, the Silicon Valley king. It's in between the size of the California king and the Northern California jester and it has built-in Wi-Fi."

"You're kidding me."

"Patented."

"Why does your bed need Wi-Fi?"

"So it has wireless capabilities."

"Because . . ."

"What if you're in a place where there's no Wi-Fi?"

"What if?"

I eyeballed this woman, speaking of jesters. I couldn't help but think about Captain Don's video, his message.

I continued: "He didn't sound so proud of all these innovations. It seems like he wasn't entirely sure they were all so innovative after all."

She looked suddenly sad. Deep wells formed beneath her eyelids. She took a step forward, then another. A smile formed on her face, nothing real, but pained almost.

"It has a patented pillow lining, the Silicon Valley king. Very bouncy," she said. Another step forward.

Next thing I knew, she'd planted one on me. I push her away, tasting strawberry and grief.

"You're not my type."

She looked like she'd been stung. This one didn't get turned down very often.

"It's never too late for an experimental phase."

"What's your game, Mrs. Donogue? You're upset, you're tawdry, angry, sad. It's not all adding up to me in any way that makes sense except that it adds up to a lie. You don't have to be a math whiz like Captain Don to see that."

"You don't get it!"

"What don't I get?"

"Something was wrong with Daddy. What he said on that video, it was crazy talk. The talk of a madman. This is Silicon Valley. We innovate. *He* innovated, he was the Silicon Valley king. He was an OI."

"What the hell does that mean?"

"Original innovator."

"So you're upset that he spoke against conventional wisdom."
I watched her carefully.

"Something . . . someone got him talking like that. It goes against everything he stood for, everything he built. All of this . . ." She spread her arms out expansively. "It all came from innovation, F and B—fasterness and betterness, he was the Emperor of Efficiency. This is his empire."

"Your empire now."

"What's that supposed to mean, Mr. Fitch?"

"Fitch. And what it's supposed to mean is that you inherit all of this, right? Since he's gone."

"Gone-ish. But yes, sort of. It all has to be sorted out."

"How much?"

"How much what?"

"How much are we talking about? How much money is at stake? How many billions to be sorted out in his estate?"

"A few." Softly.

"There's a will."

She was quiet. "-Ish."

"There's not a will?"

"Well, he didn't leave one per se."

"So there's no will."

"No . . ." Then she looked up. "I think he was writing a will. But it doesn't matter. Next of kin, etcetera, etcetera."

"No will."

"Standard protocol. Maybe it'll be challenged by various parties who claim the man loved them more." She sniffled.

"Or maybe he was going to write a will and you didn't like what it would say."

"No!"

"You wanted to get control of the money, right? Is that it? You . . ." I was feeling it out aloud, letting my temper get the better of me. Usually, I didn't talk until I had things better figured out. "You . . . thought he was acting funny, talking strange. You were afraid he'd—what—give away the money? What did Lester call it—ill-gotten gain?"

"No!"

"Maybe Captain Don stopped believing he, or you, deserved all this wealth. Maybe he didn't think he was so innovative after all."

All of a sudden there was the sound of exploding machinery—the desalination plant, starting up with a belch.

Mrs. Donogue stared at me. She screamed: "I'd rather hear *that* than listen to your ridiculous theories!"

Now I had to scream: "Did you kill your father?!"

"What?"

"Did you kill your father?!"

"Can you speak up?"

"Did you—" I yanked the remote control from her hand. I pressed off. The sound died.

"Did you kill your father?!"

"Why are you screaming?"

"Mrs. Donogue, time to come clean: Did you kill him? Did you kill Captain Don to gain control of his empire?"

She looked at me, her lip quivered, and suddenly weak-kneed, she wilted to the ground.

"What was he so afraid of?"

She didn't answer. She was near sobbing, real or faked.

"He said, in the video, he said he was afraid. Was he afraid of . . ." I didn't say what nearly slipped out: *that someone would kill him.* I wasn't keeping that thought to myself because I was being polite, or whatever, but because I wasn't. That's what Captain Don was talking about. He seemed afraid of dying. Period. Like everyone, I guess. Who the hell wants to take that long walk off the plank?

So I just stood there mutely, like a donkey, lost in thought, stuck in a recognition that I had no freaking clue how to interpret. My accusations against Mrs. Donogue didn't feel exactly right. Not exactly wrong either, but not exactly right. After all, why would she hire a detective if she was the one who had done the murdering?

Hell, I was tired. That was it. I had no clue what time it was, maybe not even midnight, but it felt like two in the morning. Made me envy the Tarantulas and their steady stream of double-synthetic Adderall, and I'd never taken anything stronger than coffee.

"You want to lie down?" Mrs. Donogue asked me. "No wiles here. No games. You look like you've been hit by the high-speed rail."

"I'm a hundred percent. How far along was your father on his immortality program?"

"The Spirit Box? Far along, I think."

She repeated that he'd been, during the last few weeks of his life, in a frenzy of meetings with Alan Klipper, his friend and codeveloper. "Lives next door," she said. "Our neighbor. Next property over. Takes about ten minutes to get there."

"You seem anxious for me to talk to Klipper."

"I'm anxious to find out what happened to my father. You sure you don't want to lie down? We have ten bedrooms next door."

I let the idea sink in. I needed some sleep. I told her I'd take her up on it. So ten minutes later, after an underground tunnel walk, I was nearly asleep in a luxurious bed within the largest mansion I'd ever seen. Like something that got in the way of Sherman's March. At the last second, before slumber took hold, I shook myself awake, fired up my phone, and texted Terry. *On assignment. Back in the AM*. A second later, a response: *Don't get killed*.

Right back at you.

Next thing I knew, I was out, deep into REM, and having a dream with images and words and jumbles and spiders. Monkeys and bicycles and spiders. Spiders, tarantulas.

The sound of a shattering window. Not a dream, not that part, not the tarantulas. I opened my eyes just in time to see the big fellas moving toward me. Assassins in the night.

THIRTEEN

ONE SHADOWY FIGURE dove at me from the foot of the bed. Launching himself over the footboard. He was mid-air, nearly on touchdown atop my legs, when I spun left. Bad idea.

A second attacker stood right there, waiting for me, sumo stance, framed in the dim moonlight's gaze. He had something in his hand. He reached out with it, and I recoiled back to the headboard to avoid the object (a knife? gun?) or whatever it might propel (a bullet?). I shot my right foot forward to knock whatever it was out of his hand.

ZOOM!

From the bottom of my foot, electricity screamed through my body and I was instantly helpless. Well, nearly helpless.

Brain said: *Taser*. Brain also said: *indirect hit*. Because a direct hit would have left my brain saying nothing.

In the remote distance, like a dream again, I heard a woman's voice. "Recalibrating. Turn eight inches left."

What the fuck?

"Seven inches right."

That voice. *Shirli*. No way. Had I died and gone to hell?

It was coming from the device, the Taser.

"Hold him down," said the Tarantula with the Taser, his voice penetrating through my mucky brain fog.

I felt the weight on my feet, the spider who'd attacked from the bottom of the bed now getting a grip on my legs.

"Target interference. Recalibrating," said the Shirli voice.

"Get out of the way," said the guy next to the bed.

I had a feeling like my ears were popping and I realized I was coming out of my trance. I bucked my knees in an effort to destabilize the guy holding on, but he was hanging tight. New plan: I brought a right fist around to his temple. Not much leverage but lots of training. So a direct, if lightweight, hit. The stunned Tarantula froze, just for a millisecond, his bell rung. I used the instant to flail out my legs again with everything I had so that the Tarantula weighing down on me, the one I'd whacked, went flying toward his brother with the Taser.

ZAP.

The Taser went off, a misfire, or a misaim.

I saw the thin blue strands of electricity coursing through the Tarantula who had been attached to my legs. *Ugh-ugh;* he spasmed. I scampered backward to avoid the juice being conducted through him. Then I rolled to my left and onto the floor, nearly a full somersault, and I was on my feet.

"Recalibrating," said the Shirli voice. And my suspicions were confirmed: the digitized sound came from the Taser. She was everywhere.

I took a step backward.

"Recalibrating. Three steps forward."

The Tarantula with the Taser was standing still and I knew why, having been on both sides of these standoffs often enough to understand his hesitation.

"Math just got tougher," I warbled. "Was two on one and now it's just me and you."

He considered it. Lean guy, wiry, the kind that scares me the most; one doesn't get far in this business if he's built that skinny unless he can put out the lights with a single haymaker.

"Yeah, but still highly favorable," he said. "It's me and the Taser six-dot-zero. New OS packs way more punch than the Taser 5i."

"As your buddy discovered."

His fellow spider lay peacefully, a few hours away from a nasty hangover.

"The on-board nav gets finicky."

"They've thought of everything. But I have to wonder how many Tarantulas it takes to point a Taser."

I was buying time.

"Racist," he said.

"Finding nearest tapas," said Shirli.

He slapped the side of the Taser and I looked around in the moonlit room for a weapon—an umbrella, walking stick, fireplace poker. Something.

"Say good night, Fitch." The Tarantula stepped forward. I retrenched and moved left, running out of room.

"Six steps forward and three inches left," Shirli said.

I stepped left.

"Recalibrating."

I stepped right.

"Recalibrating."

The Tarantula crept a half step forward, wisely taking the cautious approach. The room was coming into low-light focus but nothing was presenting itself, no clear options, nothing to save me. I pawed at some waist-high, built-in shelves to my left, feeling a line of neatly placed books. Behind me, I sensed a nightstand and a bookshelf. Across the room, a curtain flapped. Must've been where the Tarantulas entered from one of the windows that stretched most of the way across the expansive suite.

"Recali—"

A step right. Inching along the shelf behind me.

"Recali—"

Here came the Tarantula.

"Fire!" Shirli bellowed.

I saw the flicker of blue electrical lines surging toward me. I curled my head sideways and to the back, milliseconds and centimeters from the blue arc. I tried to step back again, and hit wall and bookshelf.

The Tarantula took another step.

"Fire!" Shirli said.

I ducked beneath the oncoming curl of blue death. As I began to sink to the ground to avoid the electrical surge, I used a firm underhand fling to hurl, Frisbee-like, the book I'd pulled from the shelf. I watched it spin against blue light in the direction of the Tarantula's head and then nail him in the throat. "Whaa!" He groaned, and took a step back.

"Recalibrating! Recalibrating!" Shirli screamed in orgiastic frenzy and I took three desperate lunges toward the Tarantula, closing at Big Boy speed. Before he could get his bearings and raise the Taser again, I dove forward and slammed him to the ground while simultaneously grabbing the wrist of his weapon hand. He landed with an *oomph* and the Taser shook free.

We both reached for it, but I had the better vantage point and he was cowed by my weight. Seconds later, I was pointing the weapon at his stomach.

"Target at ninety-degree angle," Shirli said. She sounded tense.

"Device off!" the Tarantula said.

"I think you're looking for medicine for a cough," the Taser said.

"Oh shit," answered the Tarantula.

"I think you're looking for a surge of electricity," I said. I pressed the trigger, sending wild currents into the eyes-wide Tarantula. He went limp. Next to his head, in the blue light, I caught a glimpse of the hardcover book I'd plucked from the shelf and hurled at the asshole's neck: *Angle of Repose*. Wallace Stegner.

A classic. So I'd heard.

Score one for books.

Book. Shit. I realized what I'd been dreaming about. A monkey and a subconscious clue.

I heard voices, coming from somewhere. Outside? More Tarantulas? Taser in hand, I made my way to the bedroom door. I had to get back to the other house to see if my instincts were correct.

FOURTEEN

B EST ADVICE I ever got in ATF training had nothing to do with bad guys or guns or interrogation or surveillance tactics. Best advice was about bread crumbs. Came from this codger named Sammy who spent years undercover with gangs selling steroids to guys on the bowling circuit. Heavies who would do anything to strengthen their forearms and fingers and then do anything to cover up the evidence. Sammy was missing a pinkie on his bowling hand and never would talk about what had happened.

He was one of the few fellas I liked in the ATF. He didn't care what the rule book said if it didn't help you get the job done. They eventually weeded him out but not before I got a full dose of his wisdom in a seminar called Advanced Tactics 100. He told me over a beer one night that it should have been called "Cover Your Ass: Your Boss Is the Biggest Chump."

"Hansel and Gretel, Fitch," he said to me. "You know the story."

I nodded. Kind of guy you trusted to take this somewhere.

"Jackasses. Shoulda been eaten by that witch dame. Only one

thing they did right: bread crumbs. Marked their way home. Knew the surroundings." He'd been in Vietnam, so I figured that was the origin of his paranoid survival theories, but he didn't make the connection himself. "Don't trust this newfangled computer shit to tell you what's what and where you are. Know where you are. Best defense and best offense is knowing absolutely your attack and escape routes. Worst mistake PIs make these days is tuning out on their way to and from an assignment. That's where the best guys get their edge. You know the term they use these days: 'own the last mile.'"

"You said PI. I'm not a private investigator."

He laughed. "You will be. You're like me. You'll never last in this racket."

Goddamn if he wasn't right about all of it—the racket and those jackasses Hansel and Gretel. That's why I had been paying close attention the night before and knew how to follow my way back through this southern-style mansion to the tunnel on the ground floor that started in a mudroom behind the kitchen. Place was already growing cobwebs and I couldn't believe this family would throw it all away like so many shanties.

As I passed through the kitchen, I picked up the time on the microwave clock: 4:45 A.M. I couldn't quite see or hear movement outside, but I knew it was there, just sensed it. The spiders, they had to be out there. But unless they were working with an inside man (or woman), they didn't know about the tunnels. I dropped down, making my way on the wooden-rung ladder. The cool air stung—in a good way. I was still half asleep and Taser-worn. The gun in my jacket added a layer of comfort. I couldn't believe I hadn't thought enough to sleep with it under my pillow the way

Terry would've done. Sometimes he liked doing this when we were on vacation, just because. Even when there wasn't a care in the world. The Second Amendment, he said, never sleeps.

As I made my way down the tunnel, I asked myself a bunch of questions. Like: How come the Tarantulas went for the capture not the kill? How had they found me? That last question I wasn't too exercised about because, like I said, I'd gotten to the point where I always expected to be found. There was always some way or another to find anyone. Hiding wasn't the game anymore; it was being ready when they got to me. But they also knew just what bedroom I was in, so unless they'd been ransacking the estate, they might've gotten a tip. Or maybe the surveillance tools had become so precise that they could figure out what bed I was in and what I was dreaming about—a monkey and a gene.

I was at the end of the tunnel, facing a ladder going up. I did my Hansel and Gretel trick, visualizing the path home. If my memory was right, I'd pop out of this tunnel into the nut-free snack lounge. So the question was: What was on the other side of the tunnel door? More Tarantulas?

I put away the Taser and yanked out my firearm. Checked the chamber. Ordinarily, if I'd been going by the ATF style manual, this would have been at least a two-man job. One guy pulls out a smoke grenade, then pops open the top, then both guys, each wearing a gas mask, emerge back-to-back, guns leveled and firing at the first sign of life. Nothing worse than tunnel duty.

The tunnel opening wasn't made of much. A thin metal plate on the bottom supported the wood flooring on the other side. I strained to listen and felt sweat grease up my trigger finger.

I destroyed the covering in one explosion. The door flew upward. Then I shrank a foot down the ladder. My theory: the flying top would've elicited firing from all but the calmest dudes. But there was no firing, no sound. So either I was home free or dealing with a real pro.

I led with my pistol.

Nothing.

No light, no sound, no shooting.

I climbed into the room and I flinched again, waiting for a shoe to drop. I let my eyes adjust and tried to remember the layout of the house from the tour Mrs. Donogue had given me. I'd need to pass the kitchen, a library, something she called the TED Talk detox room. As I did my Hansel and Gretel visualization, I walked, a left and then a right, down a long hallway, passing pictures of Captain Don from his earliest years, then up some stairs. I soft-shoed it when I was past what I recalled were bedrooms. But with the desalination plant humming, I had some noise cover.

Up another set of stairs, past the swimming pool. Here I stopped, thinking of my conversation from the night before with Mrs. Donogue when she showed me the indoor pool as she was walking me to my bedroom. There was a tanning bed in there that left you with no tan, sparing dangerous UV waves.

"So just a bed. What's with this place?" I was finally irritated enough to ask. "The weird design, open-air rooms, total nonsense. It's an . . ." I'd looked for the word: "abomination."

"It's how Daddy wanted it."

"He wanted everything strange, backward?"

"There's nothing backward about innovation."

"I think he was mocking you."

"How dare you!"

She'd had her hand pulled back like she might slap me.

"Don't even think about it. That nonsense might work with your husband, but it's only going to make me mad. You're not paying me near enough to treat me like another of your servants."

"Don't you dare!"

"You need some truth, lady."

"They're not servants. They're low-wage helper-partners."

"You're a fruitcake."

"I do wonder, though, if Daddy was losing it."

"Yeah, how's that?"

She didn't answer. Not with words. She stared into her reflection in the pool, leaving me with the clear feeling that she was still holding out on me, but I also remembered feeling that she was being square with me in saying that she thought her father had been losing it. So what?

As I recalled the unsatisfying end of our previous night's conversation, I found myself standing outside Captain Don's master suite. It was time to refocus. If there was something going on inside, someone waiting for me, I couldn't hear it because of the water plant. Another blind entry. I held my breath again and put my hand on the knob. Gun drawn. Leading with the pistol, I flung open the door.

Crickets. Not even. Just the slightly louder industrial hum.

Everything just as we'd left it. A mess. Master Suite à la Book. I reached to my right and flicked on the light, then changed my mind. Too bright. I sidled to my right to a doorway that looked like it led to a closet. Eyes on the windows, scanning for Tarantulas. Without averting my gaze, I opened the door. Then a quick glance to confirm that yes, it was a closet, and then a stab inside at the wall, where I found the switch and clicked on the light. I cracked the door open six inches, enough to give me some light without shouting my whereabouts. Then I took a few swift steps to the bed because I was pretty sure that the pile of books on it was the one I'd come for.

It had been in my dream. The face of a monkey on a book. An image that Mrs. Donogue had described to me from an alleged Instacharm message from her dead father. She'd told me: picture of a monkey and the word "gene." At the time, I'd thought "gene" was a name. But my subconscious had put the pieces together, maybe. The thing I'd dreamed about—I'd seen it when we were noodling around in here. And seconds later, I'd found it. I could tell in an instant it was what I was looking for.

The book, with the monkey on the cover . . . it had a funny weight . . . too light. It wasn't right. I carried it over to the closet to get some better light.

I stepped inside the closet, keeping the door ajar. This was the part of being a PI that made the job worth the aggravation—not the X amount per day plus expenses but finding the lies. Sure as it was almost dawn, I could tell this wasn't a book at all. It looked like a book, sure. The cover had a monkey's face and the title *The Selfish Gene*.

But it was hollow. A crafty shell. A well-constructed hiding place.

I opened the cover, and sure enough, there weren't any pages, not in the usual sense. Just a few pieces of paper, folded into a square. I unfolded them. I knew in a second that this wouldn't be an easy read. It was some kind of gibberish with a few words I understood, like "herewith." Then symbols and numbers and other such nonsense.

I gritted my teeth. Did some dead guy really send an Insta-charm message to his daughter that then led me to this evidence? I shooed away this invasion of my brain. I'm not meant for the supernatural, if that's what this was.

Exiting the closet door, I tracked out of the suite, following my mental bread crumbs back to the tunnel that would get me the hell out of this place. I was halfway down a long hallway when I heard a voice, distant, muted. Damned if it didn't sound like a cry for help. I tried to discern the origin of the sound. Just around a few hallway turns. Not my problem, right? None of this was my problem.

Shit, I couldn't help myself. Someone was crying out. I took a few turns and homed in on the sound. It was coming from behind a thick wooden door. Even though it was muted by the closed portal, I could make out the plaintive wail. I opened the door.

Oh hell. There were husband and wife, Tess and Lester, each of them tied up on a bed, next to each other. First thing I thought was: professional job. Solid knots on the limbs, mouth tape that had fallen askew on Mrs. Donogue. Through the edge of the tape she called out, sort of. "Fit . . . Wat . . . gu . . ."

Blood trickled from Lester's forehead.

I turned around to shut the door so I could untie them and saw a whir of movement. Everything went black.

FIFTEEN

WATER SPLASHED ACROSS my face. I blinked and blinked. *Splash*. I made out a fuzzy image of a guy with a cup.

Splash.

From the distance, I heard a voice: "What do you think you're doing?" The voice belonged to another blurry figure, just entering the picture from my ten o'clock, somewhere behind the guy with the cup.

"Sorry, boss, I—" said the guy with the cup, but he got interrupted.

"Nope, don't apologize," this man said, someone else. This third man said: "Deuce, what did you do wrong?"

Deuce.

That name woke me up.

Deuce.

Shit, I thought; it's gotta be *that* Deuce. Otherwise known as the Tarantula number two. Deuce, he went by. The operations guy in the spider clan. Full name was Jorge Franz McStein, or rather, that was his full pseudonym. His given name was not known, not by the authorities, not by me, at least. It was him all right, I realized through fluttering eyes. He was walking toward me and the guy who was standing next to me, the one splashing water in my face. Then, trailing Deuce, came the third guy.

I had an instinct to reach for my gun or bring up my dukes. But when I tried to move my arms, I discovered that was a no-go. I was tied to a chair. I looked down, my neck being about the only thing that wasn't firmly secured by rope. The chair was secured to the ground. Even a cursory twist of my arms and a shake of my legs told me I was in deep. My head was killing me. Felt like I'd been blackjacked.

Pings of water dripped from the ceiling, hit the floor, and exploded into my brain, like a hangover mixed with a migraine topped with a Green Day concert. Looked to me like we were in a damp basement or the empty engine room of a boat. It was the kind of place where no one hears you scream.

"Deuce, what did you do wrong?" This was repeated by the third guy, the one trailing the Deuce. He was tall and thin, khakis and a button-down. Way out of place in this dungeon.

"But it's a drought, Dr. Simons," Deuce protested.

"Bob is fine," the man responded with feigned patience. "So how could you put it to . . ."

The tall thin man calling himself Bob looked at the guy splashing water in my face, and that guy said, "I'm Daryn—with a *Y*."

"Deuce, so there's a drought, and I think that upsets you. So what's a more effective way to put that to Daryn?"

I blinked. Was this real? I definitely recognized Deuce, stocky, shoulder-length hair, a surfer look that belied his cruel intensity; then there was a Tarantula named Daryn, someone I'd not seen before but whom I recognized thanks to his traditional biker vest that showed off biceps and spider tattoos. Then the mystery dweeb called Bob.

"Daryn," Deuce said, "if you waste water throwing it at this douchebag, we'll wind up totally fucked. On account of the drought." He looked at the dweeb for some sort of validation.

"Almost, Deuce. Close. Put it in terms of how it makes *you* feel. Don't blame. Own."

Deuce turned back to Daryn. "I feel like when we waste water that it will make things harder on our children and their children. And that makes me feel like I want to beat your face with a tire iron."

"I feel like that would hurt," Daryn said.

"We're making progress," Deuce said, slapping the Tarantula on the back. He looked at me. "Greetings, Mr. Fitch."

"Fitch." I could taste blood.

"Fitch, how does it make you feel to be tied up after having your skull nearly caved in?" He chuckled.

I eyeballed the SOB.

"Do you know why you're here, Fitch?"

"You wanted to take the afternoon off from selling dope to kids."

"Tough talk for the guy about to eat my fist."

"Deuce . . ." the doctor said.

Deuce nods. "That hurts my feelings, Fitch. And I think it will hurt my fist when I sink it into your face."

"Better."

I heard myself say: "Get on with it." Whatever it was, they should do their worst and I'd save my dignity.

"Dr. Simons here—"

"Bob, Deuce. Call me Bob."

"Bob here is one of the world's foremost experts in developing progressive corporate cultures, and in helping organizations attract and retain talent. That's critical in our business—any business, frankly, these days. You train people, teach them your culture, expectations, build trust, develop their ability to prison-rape and then, boom, next thing you know, they're on the market. You put 'Tarantula' on your résumé and you're golden. Isn't that right, Daryn?"

"I get calls from recruiters all the time."

"I bet a year ago you'd have taken those calls," Deuce said.

"Not without fearing you'd kill me and my wife and my children and their children."

"Do your children have children? That's not in your dossier. I digress. Bob's at Stanford, in the psychology department."

"I'd rather that stayed between us. Can he sign an NDA?" Bob said.

"Not without fingers," Deuce says. He chuckled again.

"I'm not doing anything unethical," Bob quickly inserted. "Academia is brutal these days, so we're all taking corporate consulting gigs. It's just that I like to keep my private business between me and the client. It's good for the client too, a competitive advantage, if competitors don't know you're putting best practices to work."

I must have smirked at how ridiculous this was because Deuce said, "You think this is a joke?

"I'll tell you what's *not* a fucking joke." He took two steps forward. "Ruining my son's ConfirMitzvah. His big day. That was not funny. He worked on his service material for two years with the best priest and rabbi money could buy and who also would agree to work together on a service with someone who was bapcized."

"Make some damned sense, Deuce," I heard myself say.

"Bapcized—half circumcised and half baptized. That was its own drama, trust me, seeing as how his mother's family is staunchly agnostic, but we are way ahead on this stuff. Anyhow, that's how many years we've been waiting for his ConfirMitzvah, since his bapcizm, and then, the very night before, you put my lights out."

He was talking about how I let him have it the night we busted him in the Adderall scam. Of course, his lawyer had him out practically before they could press his fingerprints. Nothing ever stuck. But he had a whopper of a fat lip the next day for the kid's event.

"So I need you to apologize."

"Deuce."

"Right, doc." Then to me: "I would feel a lot better if you'd apologize—not to me. I'm a big boy. To my son." Deuce turned his head away from me and to the other side of the room. I could see that there was a door at the far end of this dungeon. "Dutch Abraham, get your ass in here!"

In walked a mini version of his father. Stocky, surfer hair, just much younger, and within seconds I knew, much gayer. Just something you pick up on when you've spent years in the business—of being gay.

"Hey, Dad."

"Son, we have a guest."

He looked up at me, eyes lingering for a second. "Hi, I'm Dutch Abraham, nice to meet you."

"Ordinarily, he'd give you a firm handshake but that's not possible on account of the fact that you're tied up. But just know we're very serious about our manners. In fact, that's why we're here today, right, Scruffy?"

The kid looked down; evidently, he didn't like being called by his nickname in front of company.

"Dad, Mom says I have to finish my homework."

"Eh, listen to her. I thought it was a free-play week. Anyhow, this is important. Fitch, our guest here . . . he was the guy who blindsided Daddy the night before your ConfirMitzvah. He wants to say something to you, don't you, Fitch?"

I didn't say anything.

"Look, guys, it was unfortunate, what happened," Deuce said. "But doc here says that we can learn from everything, especially things that seem unfortunate. Daryn, do you remember when Lennox took his shipment of batteries and tried to go to Europe rather than delivering them to Walmart?"

"Batteries?"

"Yeah, batteries." Deuce leered at his henchman.

"Oh yeah, the batteries, boss. I remember."

"And that was unfortunate because his job was to get those to Walmart."

"Right, Walmart. I remember."

"And we gave him a polite but firm talking-to."

"A talking-to?"

"C'mon, Daryn, stop looking at your phone. Or you're also going to get a nice, polite firm talking-to. Where was I? This thing with the ConfirMitzvah. It's been lingering long enough, creating unnecessary tension that, frankly, is easy to move past if we just confront it."

"Very good, Deuce," said the dweeb.

"Fitch, we'll have you out of here in a jiffy if you'll just apologize to Dutch Abraham."

"Out of here." Daryn chuckled.

"Go back to your phone," Deuce said.

"Dad, I don't think it's a very sincere apology if you've got him tied up. That's coercion."

Deuce considered this. "What do you think, doc?"

"I think he has a point."

With the panache of a gunslinger, Deuce turned around, yanked a gun from a shoulder holster, and shot the doctor in the middle of the forehead. The guy fell straight backward to the floor. Blood gurgled from the tiny volcano beneath his hairline. Jesus, this coldhearted madman Deuce was everything I'd heard.

"Where were we?" he said.

"Looks like the doc got a talking-to," Daryn said.

"I feel better," Deuce said, sounding like he was talking to himself. "That's how I feel. I'd really like to get back to the matter at hand. Fitch, can you please apologize to Dutch Abraham? Without the doc here, I'm going to quickly run out of ways to moderate this. It's just not my core strength and I understand that."

Yep, I needed to get this over with—whatever this was.

I raised my head, sending acute spasms through my brain. Wincing, I managed: "Hey, kid, sorry about the thing."

"Fantastic! Absolutely fantastic. Dutch, what do you say?"

"I honestly have no idea, Dad." Earnest.

"Neither do I, son. Frankly, it would be great to have Doc Simons with us."

"I think he preferred to go by 'Bob,' Dad."

"Point taken. Well, I think you're supposed to say something, Dutch Abraham. Just go with it. How do you feel?"

The kid seemed to weigh this. He was pretty self-possessed.

"I feel better, Fitch. Thank you. That really bummed me out, what happened at the ConfirMitzvah, 'cause my dad was stressed and he put a lot of time and effort into it. The plus side is my school counselor says it could be great college essay material and all that, and I just need to figure out if I can write it in a way that's authentic and not . . ." He looked to his dad. "What's the word?"

"Manipulative."

"Right. Anyhow, can I go?"

"Yes. Well done, son. What do we say to a guest?"

"Nice seeing you alive one last time."

"C'mon, Scruffy." Deuce patted his son on the head.

"Nice meeting you."

"Nice meeting you *what*?" Deuce said.

"What?"

"Mr. Fitch," Deuce says. "C'mon, Scruffy."

"Mr. Fitch."

"Fitch," I said.

The kid turned around and left.

"Terrific EQ on that one. We've really worked on that. My son's got great empathy and I really value that. Okay, Daryn, get the electrodes."

"What?" Daryn said.

"Daryn, get your damn face out of the phone. What am I paying you for?"

"To torture people."

Deuce put his head down. "It's a rhetorical question. Get the electrodes."

The flunky walked to his left and started rummaging through a bin of various sickening implements. Clips and hammers, a rusty saw. Deuce walked dead center in front of me.

"Thanks for working with me there. That was a real teaching moment for Dutch Abraham. Conflict resolution, that's the thing these days. Doc Simon was a real badass in that area, a leader in his field. He'll be missed."

"Cut the bullshit." I spit it out, tasting blood. "You shot him in the head."

"Touchy."

"Get it over with, Deuce."

"What's the rush? You got somewhere to be? Maybe home with the mister?"

For the first time, my alarm bells went off. Big-time. I didn't mind taking a few body shots, but now he was talking about Terry. I swallowed my impulse to let my fury show. Tried to save my energy, keep my cards close, all that.

"Here ya go, boss." The flunky approached holding a gadget that looked like an iPod connected to the pincers of a battery charger for a car. A voice came from the gadget: "Deuce, who may I help you torture today?" It was—who else—Shirli.

"That broad is the only thing I hate about this new technology. Other than that, it packs incredible voltage and you can carry it in your pocket." He leaned down, eyeballed me, made sure I was focused. "Fitch, I assume you know how this thing works?"

I gritted my teeth, managed a fake courageous smile.

"Reduces a fellow to jelly, a blubbering pile of 'please-kill-me-now.'"

I was racking my brain: Any way out of this? I couldn't get my hands free. Could I stand somehow and flip the chair? Could I make a break for it through that distant door? I'd have been shot down before I got three feet.

"It's easier than ever, with the new UI, and the sensors. They not only send electricity through the clips but pick up heartbeat and other stress measures. Really helps one calibrate. Hell, I used this once during a workout when I couldn't find my Fitbit. But the main stuff is old-school. Put these on the nipples or the nuts, send electricity, watch the poor sucker wriggle and writhe to death's doorstep." He looked lost in space, a sadistic grin on this madman's face. Almost like I was no longer there.

"Quit the foreplay, Deuce. Get on with it. Get your pound of flesh."

He smirked.

"I wish. That would be nice. Just two days ago, if I'd had you here, I would actually have taken time out of my busy schedule to watch you electrocuted on our new live-chat torture platform." He pursed his lips, relishing the thought. "But things have changed. So I'll ask you again if you know how these electrodes work."

Now I was just lost. So he wasn't going to torture me? He could clearly see the confusion in my eyes.

"Listen closely when I explain how you use it. Because you're going to need to know how to use it."

"What are you babbling about?"

"I'm going to untie you, and hand this thing to you, let you walk out of here, and you're going to go out and put it to some decent use."

"Make some sense, you sadistic shithead."

"You're going to get me the Spirit Box."

"The what?"

"That immortality gadget. The one that tech pioneer was innovating."

"Captain Don," his flunky said.

"Captain Don. Word on the street is he was really close to nailing immortality," Deuce continued. "And word on the street is you were close to nailing access to the code."

"I don't know what you're hearing, Deuce, but you got it wrong."

"Yeah, set me straight, Fitch." He turned to his flunky. "Daryn, can you hand me a chair?"

The Tarantula scrub bounced over to the wall, where there was a wooden chair, and brought it back to Deuce, who, in turn, sat a few inches away and brought his face close to mine. My brain was doing somersaults of figuring: Can I head-butt Deuce, break his nose . . . and then what? No good options.

But then I realized I was overthinking it.

"Yeah, Deuce, you're right. What's the point in bullshitting you at this point. Hell, you got me tied up like a pig at a luau."

"Easy, bud, we run a half-kosher kitchen."

"I'm close, Deuce. Get me out of here and I'll get you the immortality gizmo, hand it over to you, and we'll call it all even."

"Now we're talking."

I made like I was thinking it over. "I've got two questions for you."

"You're not in much of a position to be asking questions." He laughed. "Daryn, get a load of this guy, thinking he's in a position to be asking questions." He looked over with a can-I-get-an-amen from his henchman, but the guy was buried in his phone. "Daryn, get your face out of your phone!"

"I . . . I'm sorry. I think I just got a text from Bono."

"What?"

"Never mind. He's just letting me know I'm still getting texts."

"Hey, Daryn, if you won't back me up on my maniacal laughs, I will. Find. Someone. Else."

Daryn swallowed hard. Deuce turned back to me. He flipped something into my lap—a book of some kind. I blinked hard and, through still-concussed faculties, made out the title: *e-Electrodz, V2.6, User Manual*.

"Two questions," I muttered.

"Free country."

"How do you know about the Spirit Box?"

Deuce smiled, then laughed, then his laugh turned haughty. He looked at Daryn, who laughed along haughtily.

"Lemme tell you something, Fitch, I know everything that happens in the Valley. It's my business to know. Nothing goes down from Fresno to the Oregon border without me knowing it."

Daryn laughed haughtily.

"You're overcompensating," Deuce said in his direction.

"Deuce, I didn't even know about the Spirit Box until yesterday and you've been gunning for me long before that. So something's changed. You're working with someone, or for someone, right?"

"Is that your second question or a follow-up?"

I exhaled; this guy was totally exhausting. Same as every person who got to the top of a corporate structure; he could outlast you, plain and simple. Same as the managers who got to the top of the police chain, no different there, or at Chevron, the White House, Starbacks, or the Tarantulas. The rest of us needed a nap now and then.

"My second question is: When did you start hiring guys who can't shoot straight?"

"What's that supposed to mean?"

"One of your douchebags had me in his sights with a blow dart at the Froom party and he missed by five feet. I might have to start telling the world the Tarantulas have lost their edge."

"That's bullshit, Fitch, and you know it."

"I'll get myself one of those Instacharm or Faceburg accounts and that kind of mistake will go viral. Can't wait to see how many re-tweeps that gets from the Black Widows."

I could talk the talk when I had to.

"Watch yourself, Fitch. We don't miss. Our guys are one hundred percent certified to hit what they aim . . ." He paused. It was dawning on him, crossing his face like the moon in a full solar eclipse. I'd been playing him with this question, eking something out. "Yeah, we sometimes get a few bad eggs. We use a hiring algorithm and sometimes it messes up." It was a paltry recovery.

"If you say so."

"Enough chitchat. Here's the net-net: we let you go, you take the electrodes or whatever other means you deem necessary and get us the Spirit Box. We want the code. Capiche?"

"Now you're the Godfather?"

"Racist."

"What do you want the Spirit Box for?"

"None of your goddamn business. We took your gun. It's too risky for you to be able to hurt one of us at a distance and there will be plenty of us around. Look closely, you'll see a Tarantula in the woodwork. Oh, and you have twenty-four hours."

This guy made me sick, the thick lips, fancy haircut with a touch of bangs combed to the side, just enough depth in his brown eyes to be mistaken for empathy; a banker you could trust in another life, CEO material, the puppet master who could motivate the workforce at any organization. Except for his maniacal killer streak.

"What aren't you telling me?"

"You're a smart one, Fitch. Daryn, bring me the phone."

Daryn, now at full attention, made his way to a table where I'd seen the bin of torture implements. He picked up a handsome navy-blue case, smaller than a shoe box. He stood in front of Deuce like a joker making a presentation to the king. Deuce opened the top of the box, revealing a phone nestled in a soft cradle of maroon fabric.

"The double iPhone 19s. Not even in production yet. Two of them in the world. This thing can tell you two days ahead of time that you're going to take a shit and predict the nearest bathroom stall." He eyeballed me. "I'm kidding. Turn of phrase. It's awesome, is my point. And look at the picture quality."

He turned the phone to me. There was a picture on it.

I felt my body come to a complete stop, every molecule freeze.

"Don't worry," Deuce said. "We're keeping him comfy. He's eating gluten-free."

Terry. Tied up, a lot like me.

"Here's the video." The Tarantula flipped to another image and pressed the play icon.

"Take these assholes out," Terry said. "I'm fine."

A fist came in from the right side of the screen and leveled Terry across the jaw.

Terry winced, then smiled wryly, like: *That's all you got?* Tough stud, my husband. I felt my eyes go wet, and held it back.

"Twenty-four hours, Fitch," said Deuce.

"That's some ugly business, Deuce."

"Is this the part where you tell me that I don't want to see you mad? Give me a break, Fitch. You're not in our league. You don't know from ugly. You break a few rules now and again. But in the end, you break the little ones, not the big ones, like the cops. Those are the guys who scare me. You're small-time with a heart of gold. And it belongs to this guy"—he held up the photo of Terry—"and the clock's ticking on his last day on earth if you don't get me the Spirit Box. Me, mine, alone. Got it?"

"Yeah, Deuce, capiche."

"Racist. Untie him, Daryn."

A minute later, I was free and blindfolded, but didn't need eyes to surmise I had two guns trained on me. Not a damn way around it. They took me on a drive. Next thing I knew, I was dropped in a wooded area. "One for the road," Deuce said, and he popped me in the jaw.

I shook it off and yanked away the blindfold and saw their MINI drive off through the overhanging trees. The motorcycle was there beside me, and so was my truck. At my feet, my phone

and the other phone—the one from the Tarantula—and the electrodes.

The bastards had Terry tied up somewhere. Where? Anywhere. Who the hell knew.

I don't break the rules, Deuce had said, or at least not the little
ones. These guys had no idea who they were dealing with.

SIXTEEN

FOR OUR HONEYMOON, we rolled north to Washington, parked our bikes at a friend's house, and then flew to Anchorage. Hop, skip, jump, and we were in a kayak, paddling and floating peacefully through the Kenai Fjords. The Serengeti on ice, wild and untamed, the zoo bars sprung open, orcas and humpbacks, black and brown bears, some bird Terry dug called a tufted puffin and one called a black oystercatcher, and then a porpoise leaped about three feet from the kayak and nearly overturned us, and damn if that wasn't one of the best moments I ever lived.

We camped on the banks. At one point, a bald eagle landed at our site, *at* it, not near it, and sat. And watched. Or, as I tended to think about it in my honeymoon-addled brain, joined us. I don't spend a lot of time thinking about how human beings got to this shitbag marble in space, but that made me wonder right there about a higher being and whether he or she or it might be blessing me and Terry and us tying the knot and calling it settled once and for all.

Peaceful as it gets.

Now I stood in another forest, electrodes at my feet, and I

vowed to smash some heads. I pictured myself taking their phones and GPS-equipped Tasers, their electrodes and Spirit Boxes, and saw myself unleashing on them one asshole at a time. I was tired to the bone, and even if they hadn't nabbed Terry, I was up to here with the nonsense of this place and all the greed and avarice couched as politically correct doublespeak. A few years earlier, when the weather started changing, Terry had said to me that we were just a few degrees away from being Hollywood, and not in a good way. Mellow exterior, progressive banter, free play for the kids and woot for the meritocracy, but it was all façade, like the cover on a chocolate candy that hides something foul at the center.

Our favorite diner in the Mission had turned into a trendy flower shop and we didn't realize it until we walked in one morning for a huge breakfast and the lady behind the counter asked us if we were looking for a bouquet to celebrate an acquisition or an IPO. When she saw our fallen faces, she said, "Oh, I see," then smiled. "In the back, I've got something for right-sizing."

"Right-sizing," Terry repeated, arms crossed, and I could see he was playing along. "We just fired half our staff. You call it right-sizing!"

"You're right, sir. Forgive me. Half the staff. I didn't realize. You must be *automating*! Wonderful, congratulations. I meant no offense. Let me call to see if our downtown store has something for the occasion."

They were just killers here, no different from stockbrokers and plaintiffs' lawyers, but in Teslas and black turtlenecks tucked into their jeans, separating their recycling from their compost as if that made them any less the robber barons.

I sat down on a rock, eyes glazed over, and, yeah, sure, I'll admit it, a fury so powerful it threatened to eat me. But not before it devoured whoever took Terry and turned a perfectly okay nine-to-five PI job into a nightmare.

Trouble was, I wasn't sure where to start. It was absolutely not helping that my capacities were dulled from taking various shots to the skull. I felt the puffy skin from attack in at least two spots, one above my right cheek where Deuce gave me a roadie and one on the top of my head over my left ear, where some coward nailed me when I'd walked in on Mrs. Donogue and Lester Wollop tied up. I wondered if they were still among the living.

And, quite to the contrary, I also wondered if they'd set me up. Not that hard to make it look like they'd been tied up by Tarantulas when they'd actually tipped them off to my whereabouts and then tied themselves up to make it look like they were just two more victims.

But why would they have done that? They'd already hired me and had me doing their dirty business.

There was one thing that seemed clearer than most. That Tarantula at Froom had shot Da Raj but not me. Tarantulas didn't miss, not like that. Deuce admitted as much when I got his feet tangled up with my question. Yeah, sure, maybe the shooter had gotten thrown off by the overpowering smell of organic kiwi and Shirli's annoying banter, but I doubted it. I was starting to think that I wasn't the target after all; besides, the Tarantulas wanted a capture, not a kill—at least when it came to me.

So why kill Da Raj?

In his parting breaths, Da Raj had seemed to point a finger at Danny. Tossed an accusation at him, or seemed to, nothing precise.

Something else Deuce said: up until a day ago, he hadn't planned to have me go after the Spirit Box. Suggesting what?

That he hadn't known about the Spirit Box before that, or hadn't known I was involved before that, or somebody tipped him off to both?

I glanced down at the two phones sitting in the dirt. Mine and the burner from the dead, frothy-mouthed Tarantula. Death by oxygen shot. How come they'd leave me with his phone unless they didn't realize it was an official company gadget or they were setting me up with it or tracking me with it?

So many unanswered questions. I'd leave them that way too if they didn't have my beloved.

I turned on the burner, and my phone too.

First thing I saw was the time: 4:50 P.M.—about twelve hours since I'd woken up in the southern-looking mansion, taken the tunnel over to the troll house, and found the book with the . . .

The paper I'd found in *The Selfish Gene*. I'd folded it into my back pocket. What were the odds?

I reached back. Yep, it was there. I pulled it out, unfolded it, and saw three pages of symbols and code or whatever you wanted to call it. I could at least make instant sense of the first part: *I, Donald C. Donogue, being of sound mind and body . . .*

And then the only other word I really understood was "herewith."

Was this a will?

If so, I couldn't understand it.

The next line read: *If index is not None (limit) > 89 . . .*

And on and on like that.

Computer code, if I had to guess. With a few words of English mixed in, like "herewith" and some symbols I recognized.

This was definitely a computer program.

For a second, I flushed. Could it be the Spirit Box? Was this the code that had everybody's panties in a bunch?

And if so, how the hell would I know it?

I hardly understood English, Terry sometimes joked, noting that it was hard to tell because I spoke so little. Terry, tied up . . . I winced; that was not something that could've gone down easily. Maybe the Tarantulas nabbed him in the middle of the night. But knowing Terry, he'd slept with the Winchester under his pillow and had the alarm working. I'd have bet even money that he took at least one of those suckers down with him. On the honeymoon, way back in from the fjords, we'd got to playing cards on the barge that carried us back to civilization. Stakes had grown to fifty dollars a pot, nothing really when you think of it, but Terry wasn't about to give in when a cantankerous fisherman with leather skin clearly pulled a jack from his boot. Terry said something not nice about the guy's mom and he threw a punch that Terry caught with his fist midair, like snagging a softball, and squeezed until the local yelled uncle, and that was the end of that. Happens when you grow up with brothers.

I glanced at the three pieces of paper hidden in *The Selfish Gene*. At least one line of English, sort of, that I could read. English alphabet at least. *Filed with: Snozzwanger, Veruca and Gloop.*

Now, where had I heard those names?

On my phone, I found enough bars to do a Gooble search. *Snozzwanger, Veruca and Gloop, LLC. Northern California's*

premier law firm specializing in patents, divorce investment strate-
gies, and disclaimers—and the first and only Silicon Valley firm to
write its briefs on 100 percent recycled hemp.

Now I remembered where I'd heard the name: muttered by Lester Wollop, his divorce firm.

Interesting.

I picked up the other phone, the Tarantula's burner. I saw the call log; a bunch of calls from blocked numbers and one call with a number listed. It was in the 408 area code. I hit send to dial the number, put the phone to my ear. *Ring, ring.*

Then: "Hello, you've reached Danny, at the beep, you know what to do."

Whoa. Da Raj's killer, the tarantula with the blowdart and gingham shirt, had been in contact with Danny Donogue. I let it sink in. That little bastard. Well, maybe the key to solving a murder, several murders, getting the Spirit Box, and bringing Terry home in one piece. Then pulling the Tarantulas apart leg by leg.

SEVENTEEN

GAMERS USA 2024. *Gold or Bust.*

That's what the sign read over an awning in the narrow retail outlet squeezed between a Ben and Jimmy's ice creamery and Splatz, which sold "indoor-outdoor footwear for a changing climate." Black tint hid whatever lurked inside Gamers USA, but I knew from basic Internet sleuthing that it was the Video Game Olympic Training Center. A regular hot spot for Danny Donogue.

On the door, a sign indicated hours of operation: 3 P.M. to 6 A.M. Place had just opened a few hours ago.

I was standing in a strip mall in Redwood City, just up the highway from Palo Alto. This was an area in transition, not yet fully gentrified, a collection of boxy apartments across the street, an old-fashioned diner in this strip mall, along with one of those shoe outlet places where you could get three pairs for the price of one. I heard voices behind me. I glanced over my shoulder to see a mother and a boy, her son, I gathered, looking to be around ten.

"Bobby, do you have your joystick?"

"You said *you* brought it!"

"No, absolutely not. Bobby, I've told you a thousand times: you have to keep track of your own gear. Do you think Ivan makes his mom carry his joystick?"

"It's pronounced 'Evan,' Mom."

"Evan."

"*E-e-e*-van."

"Isn't that what I said?"

"Sheesh, you don't know anything. He's only like the greatest first-person shooter who ever lived."

"I'm sorry, sweetie. I'm trying. Did you look for your joystick in your trademarked vid-back-snack-case?"

They'd stopped walking just outside the training center. On the boy's back, a pack covered with a complex series of zippers and straps, Velcro, and a water bottle holder. He started trying to take it off, to pull his arms from the labyrinth of straps, but he got tangled up, then more flummoxed, and, eventually, totally tied up in the various straps and lines and a buckle and he was flailing around starting to whine and his mother was trying to untangle him and then she was getting more frustrated.

"Help!"

"Relax, sweetie, breathe. We've gotten out of this before," his mother said to her son, a panicking but otherwise indistinguishable freckle-faced redhead who evidently had some video-game chops. His mother was an otherwise typical high-tech exec with drop-off duties.

I'd heard about these kinds of incidents before, people getting tied up in their specialized backpacks. In the paper there had been a story about a guy who got pretzeled by his VitaMan™ Day Pack on a hike up Mount Tam and started chewing off his own arm to escape. Another hiker came by and discovered that it was just a matter of unfastening the waist belt the guy had gotten wrapped around his arm, but by that time he'd bled out.

I saw my opening.

"Double sailor's knot, near the bottom left," I said.

Mother and child both looked at me. Then at the spot I was pointing to, and sure enough, it was just the tangle that needed untangling.

"Thanks," said the mom. "Hey, it's your joystick!"

"Didn't mean to overhear," I said. I gestured to the ice cream joint. "I was on my way into Ben and Jimmy's for a . . ."—I had to make this authentic—". . . granola-parfait-hold-the-ice-cream."

"No problem," the mom said. "I appreciate it. Mile-a-minute parenting, I'm sure you know . . ." She turned back to her son, handing him a joystick-type thing. She spun him around and lowered herself on her haunches and looked him in the eye. "I'll pick you up before school . . . and what's important here?"

"Results, not process."

He smiled and she smiled.

"Process, not results."

"I know, Mom. Love you."

I took a step toward the picture in the ice cream shop's window of a castle made of ice cream. *The Middle Earth Sundae. Battle your hunger to the death with six flavors, ten toppings, and a root beer moat.* My eyes glazed over. What I was trying to do was listen to what the video-game player and his mother said after she pressed the buzzer next to the black doorway.

"Yep," came a voice from inside—projecting through the intercom next to the door.

"Billy Bear," the boy said.

"Number."

"Hashtag seven-pound-nine-eight-four-two."

The door clicked open and the boy disappeared inside. Through the window of the ice cream shop, I saw the mom turn and put her face in her phone and walk away.

Shit. I was hoping for some generic code to get in. I squinted my eyes, thinking, when it hit me what I'd do next—what I had to do.

Coffee.

In Ben and Jimmy's, I ordered a regular coffee, black, and then talked the flummoxed teen behind the counter into not adding any flavors to it, then pounded the caffeine and waited another five minutes. Then I hit the buzzer on the door of the Olympic training center.

"Yep."

"I brought Billy's snack. He forgot it."

"Who?"

"Billy Bear. Forgot his . . . quinoa, um, protein gummies." Shit, what was I saying?

"Number?"

Number. I repeated what I'd heard: "Hashtag seven-pound-nine-eight-four-two."

The door clicked and I opened it. I was hit with a lilac fragrance that surprised me and dim lighting that didn't. It was a small entry room. Spartan. A teen sat behind the counter preoccupied with something on the monitor in front of him. There was an American flag behind his head. "Billy's in, uh, Milky Way, or Andromeda. You know the way?" He never looked up.

"Of course."

One of the few beauties of living in an era in which people have their faces buried in their gadgets is that they are not paying attention. Could be useful for a private detective but also, unfortunately, good for bad guys. I'd heard of a guy stealing a ride from a dude standing beside his car so lost looking at his e-mail that he hadn't seen the thief get in and drive off. Guy who lost his car didn't even realize what had happened for ten minutes and the thief would've made a clean getaway, but a few blocks later he'd been so distracted texting the chop shop that he ran into the side of a police car.

I walked through a doorway to the right of the counter and a new world opened up—one with the sound of shooting. I almost hit the floor out of instinct, when I realized it was video games. *Pop, pop,* copter rotors, *whiz, whiz, bang, tat-tat-tat* . . . this had to be what war sounded like. Maybe looked like too, at least the colors and lights. I stood in a long hallway extending the length of the building. Narrow though it was, it wasn't claustrophobic. That was because the hallway wall to my right was only waist-high. Above, it remained open and I could see a line of massive screens in the middle distance, almost the size of movie-theater screens, one beside the other, stretching the length of the building, six in a row. The screens were on the far wall, about fifty feet away from me, each one ablaze in a shooting game, each of them separated from the others by five feet of empty space. Now the setting began to make sense. I was on a sort of balcony—with the video-game players below me, controlling the action on the screens. And as my perceptions came into focus, I realized that there were small booths on this level, accessed through waist-high entrances in the waist-high wall; in a few of the booths, people sat and observed.

I walked two booths down, where I saw a woman holding something to her cheek. She couldn't possibly hear me approaching with the wall of sound. Then she turned and looked right at me. She had a blank expression and a walkie-talkie pressed to her cheek; she spoke into the device. "Tell her to try bending the wrist. Christ, for the last time: she's pronating like she couldn't make a club team in Boise." She eyeballed me. "You with Perrin?"

I was having trouble figuring out how the hell I could hear this woman so clearly. It was like her voice was being piped into my ears, overtaking this wall of sound.

"Billy. Forgot his protein. But . . ." I decided to go for it. "I have a note I'm supposed to give Danny."

She crinkled her nose. "I think he's in two. You know where it is?"

I pointed right.

She looked at me with a hint of dismay. I pointed left. "That's what I meant."

She shrugged and off I went. A few booths later, I recognized the back of the head of Danny Donogue. The distant screen displayed a tank emitting bursts of fire at a nest of enemies as it crawled over and crumpled a building labeled *Orphanage*.

Danny was not watching. He was looking down at something in his lap. I opened the waist-high door and slid next to the dead innovator's grandson. He turned to me, started to stand, and I put my hand on his shoulder. "No need to get up, Danny."

I settled in next to him in a cushy theaterlike seat and measured his stricken expression. He didn't look likely to run or call out for help. Just in case, I figured, I could always tell him I had a real old-fashioned gun, not the virtual kind. I decided to save that information.

"To what do I owe the pleasure, Detective?"

"Come on, Danny. No one talks like that."

He clenched his jaw.

"I come here to hear myself think."

I glanced at what was in his lap. It was a pad of paper. He was sketching in it, or making notes of some kind that I couldn't make out.

"You're joking. How can anyone hear anything?" Even as I asked the question, I was stunned to realize I could hear myself, and Danny, just fine. The sound of the video games became increasingly distant, dreamlike background noise.

"We pipe in AS."

"What?"

"Artificial Silence. Trademarked. Let it wash over you."

I did, I let it wash. Hell, it felt good. Silence. Like my brain getting a back rub. It was all I could do not to fall asleep in the sunken theater chair.

"Do you know where your food comes from?"

"Listen, kid—"

"Do you know?"

"I guess: Safeway. What? Not organic enough for you? Let's cut the small talk."

"Chateaubriand comes from the top of the cow, just below the filet. Meat and gristle. The key is that you've got to bleed the cow for a good period. You know why?"

"I'll play along. To let the muscle loosen up so the meat's not so tough."

"These cows, they're really just babies, the ones we eat. Probably less than a year old, but already eight hundred pounds. Hard to call them cute, though, or scared. Who knows what they're thinking. Not really our problem, is it?"

Now he seemed to be thinking aloud as much as talking to me. His eyes were focused straight ahead, looking at a cadre of animated soldiers shooting massive shoulder-carried artillery at a giant Godzilla-like creature wearing a T-shirt emblazoned with the Russian sickle. The creature started shooting lasers from its eyes and had just nailed one of the soldiers when words appeared on the screen: *Eat Gluten, Loser!*

"My husband grew up in the Midwest," I said. "Spent summers working farms. He used to say that the worst part was watching out that your foot didn't get stuck in a machine, a combine. I'd call him paranoid, but he did lose a toe."

"One of the important ones?"

"Eh, they're toes."

"This dairy farm Grandpa took me to had a get-to-know-your-cow attraction. For twenty dollars you could get in a stall with a cow and have a handler tell you about its personality."

I didn't say anything. This kid was heading somewhere, I hoped. And if not, he was getting comfortable with me, which could pay dividends. The best part about being a PI: sometimes you get furthest by blending in with the woodwork. Maybe I'd get a confession.

"So this woman is sitting on a stool next to this cow and the thing looks all droopy-eyed and she goes: 'You guys sure got lucky.' And Grandpa says: 'How's that?' And she says: 'Your cow is peppy.' Grandpa nearly fell over laughing."

Now the kid drooped his head, looking not much different from a cow about to get bled.

"Sounds like you loved the Captain."

"So next thing you know, he says: 'Let's go shoot one,'" Danny said without looking up.

"Who said that?"

"Just listen, dick. There's a Jeep outside of where they keep the calves and Grandpa let me drive and he pointed me in the direction of a field," the kid said, ignoring my question, or answering it in his own way. "I hit the gas and we bounced up and down along the ground between stalks of wheat and he didn't say anything and just pointed and we drove for like five minutes, maybe it was less. The watch function on Fitbit wasn't working because we were out of wireless range, like maybe Grandpa had planned that."

He was talking like I wasn't there and I wasn't planning to stop him 'cause I felt like, just maybe, he was working his way toward a revelation. On the huge theater screen in front of us, the game had switched to a triathlon: skiing, shooting, and taking selfies. In an apparent mix-up, the player skiing took a selfie near the bull's-eye target and shot himself in the face and Danny winced at the action but kept going.

"We get to this field and there's this cow, not much bigger than the calf we'd been petting, and I'm not an idiot, I know what's going to happen. Grandpa tells me to stop and he reaches behind him and he goes to the back of the Jeep and he gets out a gun." Now he looked at me. "I don't know what it was called, exactly. I mean I've shot a million guns on video screens but this one wasn't fancy like those. A basic shotgun, even more basic than the ones they have in Zombie Kill I, the original game with the horror-film graphics. Grandpa says . . ." Now Danny paused.

"Danny?"

"'You may not remember, Danny, but you used to love to go out with me for prime rib.' That's what he said to me when he handed me the gun." Another pause. "Anyhow, Detective, I'm making this story too long. Out of respect of time for both of us, I'll give you the Twipper version: he makes me shoot the cow in the forehead."

"Makes you?"

He looked at me again. "I asked you where your food comes from. That's where it comes from." It was tough for me to tell in the dark, but it looked like there was water in his eyes and tears running down his cheek.

"Pissed you off that he made you kill a cow, I bet."

"Oh, I liked it just fine."

I let the words settle in, measuring the tone.

"So is that the point of your little soliloquy? That you know how to kill stuff in real life? You're letting me know you're a tough guy?" I was asking in a mildly hostile tone, not liking his vibe, but I was genuinely curious too. I couldn't get a handle on this guy. He didn't sound like he liked killing that animal a lot.

"We're standing over this cow and . . . Captain Don tells me that, well, y'know . . ."

I wait for him to get where he's going.

"He's sick. He's got something or another. He doesn't go into details, but I got the point."

On the big screen, the virtual skier executed a somersault, jumped over a gigantic canyon, and shot a bull's-eye while using a selfie stick. Then, just before sticking the landing, the skier wobbled, and pulled a mobile phone from his pocket, and skidded and crashed. Danny brought a microphone to his lips and said: "What the hell was that?"

A voice responded: "I don't know, Danny. It was weird. The phone rang with a U2 song."

"That guy. Turn off your damn phone. We're training."

I took this moment to gather my thoughts. So Captain Don had taken the kid to a farm, a real-world field trip, back-to-the-earth stuff, and told him he was sick, dying. Maybe it was a cycle-of-life lesson; cows die, we all die. It didn't quite make sense, if I was even getting the straight skinny from this half-pint.

"Danny, I'm not sure what you're getting at with this whole cow story."

Silence again.

It was time to shake him up. "Was seeing the cow drop like seeing Da Raj go down? Same thing? Just another life-form hitting the ground with a thud?"

The kid clenched his jaw.

"Listen," I said, "I saw your phone number on the Tarantula's mobile—the guy who shot Da Raj. So we can quit playing games here."

He turned to me and now he looked stricken.

"Quit playing the aggrieved grandson. Acting the victim is your mom's game. You may have learned the behavior but you can't sell it."

"I'm nothing like her!"

"Yeah, yeah. Danny, let me level with you. Can you handle that?"

He rolled his eyes, tried to.

"Da Raj fingered you right before he died. I heard it, and that spiritual-nut CEO of yours heard it. *You* heard it. That testimony is locked up tight. Then I've got your phone number on the phone of the Tarantula that spit the blow dart. This is starting not even to feel like circumstantial evidence anymore. Even if I haven't got you pinned on your grandfather's death, you can go down for Da Raj."

"I don't know what you're talking about. *He* was threatening *me!*"

"That right." I was egging him on. "And you let him know who was boss, by putting a slug into a cow's brain."

"You don't know what you're talking about! He was going to expose . . ." Danny slowed down and then hit a full stop. "I'm done. You can talk to my lawyer."

"Danny, listen. You're a decent kid. That's my take."

"Don't patronize me, Detective."

"Fair enough. But you are—a decent kid, somewhere under there. But you've no idea who you're dealing with when it comes to the Tarantulas. I think you hired them to kill Da Raj because he was going to expose you and something involving your grandfather. Let's stop pussyfooting around—"

"You're so far off base."

"Straighten me out. What was Da Raj threatening to expose?"

He smirked. Then he said: "I didn't get where I am by fighting worthless flame wars."

"That what you think this is? Just me throwing taunts your way? If I find out you were involved with your grandfather's death, you're going down. You, your mom, every damn greedy one of you. I don't know how yet, I'll admit that, but all of this ties together with a neat little bow made of money. Billions at stake in inheritance, that's what I think, that's what people fight over. Or, just maybe, there's no inheritance at all."

Danny stared at the screen. The game had changed. Now it was bowling with virtual balls shooting flames at pins that were jihadists.

"Your jaw just clenched again, kid. That idea strike a chord? No inheritance, no money. Captain Don isn't dead at all, maybe. He's alive, the Spirit Box carrying him into eternity. Cheating every damn one of you out of the billions you think you're entitled to."

At that point, I was just riffing, testing out ideas, trying to shake the tree to see if coconuts fell out or maybe a confession would hit the ground with a thud. But nothing, not a peep; he'd clammed up, I could see that. He was done. I stood.

"I'm older than you, Danny. A lot older. I went to college. I've shot some people and been shot at. And the sum of that experience is this: the Tarantulas will eat you alive. If you're in with them, and even if you're not, they're a bad, bad group. I can see that you're proud, maybe like your grandfather, and you're alone. I'm your best hope."

"Wow, college sounds really helpful. Did you major in making speeches?"

I sighed. I reached into my wallet and pulled out one of those old-fashioned cards I carry around.

"It's got my mobile number and e-mail."

I dropped it in his lap; I started to walk out, then paused.

"How come you stopped using social media?"

"What?"

"You had a huge Twipper following, millions of followers, right? And then you went dark. Why was that?"

He shrugged. "Got old. I needed to focus."

"On what?"

"Other stuff. Social media is awesome, don't get me wrong. But sometimes it gets in the way."

Meaningless verbiage this kid was tossing out, sounding canned. "Give me a call when you're ready to get clean," I said. I turned and left behind a troubled kid and artificial silence before stepping back into the sound of machine-gun fire and screaming, inflamed jihadists. Then I was outside, and back into the dusk.

EIGHTEEN

I DIALED LIEUTENANT GABERSON.

"I thought we agreed you weren't calling me," was the first thing that the lieutenant said.

"All bets are off when my husband gets kidnapped."

This gave him pause and I explained the outlines. I gave him Terry's cell-phone number and other key details and asked if the police might start a search; maybe they could track his phone. Presumably, Terry didn't have it with him when he was kidnapped, but maybe he hid it somewhere. He was resourceful.

"We don't track people's phones," said Lieutenant Gaberson. "That's laughable. Absolutely ridiculous. Not without a proper warrant."

"Jesus, Lieutenant, it's me. Not the ACLU."

"Sorry, we have a department policy requiring us to read that disclaimer. I'm all over tracking him. How else can I help?"

"I need to know about Danny Donogue."

Silence.

"Lieutenant?"

"What're you into, Fitch?"

"Background check. That's all I need. Can you help me out?"

"Related to Terry?"

"I don't know."

A heavy sigh.

"We're not supposed to know each other right now, Fitch."

"I wouldn't ask if I wasn't drowning."

"Meet me tomorrow, usual place?"

"Not soon enough."

"I'll call you back."

He hung up.

TWO STOPS I needed to make, one to Alan Klipper, the Shipper, and the other to a law firm that seemed to have its hand in everything, Snozzwanger, Veruca and Gloop, described to me as a firm alternately doing intellectual property work and divorce funding, whatever the hell that was. I checked the time: 5:40. Would the firm even be open? Of course, those guys go round the clock, but I was already halfway to the Shipper's place, winding up the same hills I'd ridden to get to Tess and Lester's place. I kept looking over my shoulder, but no sign of the Tarantulas. I guess they figured they already had me by the lapels.

After a jag down an unpaved side road, trees overhanging, I found Alan Klipper's estate, looking stately and surprisingly unguarded, at least at first glance. There was no fence between me and the expansive home, which was brown-shingled with white trim and lit with footlights. Then I saw the sign: *This Property Is Protected by a Zero-Deforestation 12-Foot-High Electric Fence.* On close inspection, I could make out the occasional line of jagged blue electricity. An invisible fence. On the ground, to my right, I saw something crumpled on the ground and leaned in, and made out a UPS driver's discarded uniform that looked crispy around the edges. No trees harmed, but humans seemed to be getting a raw deal.

I also found a doorway standing in the center of it all. No fence, just a door, steel-framed, with a doorbell. I was standing fifty yards from the house, staring at a doorway in the middle of nowhere. What a perfect damned metaphor. I hit the buzzer. No answer.

My phone rang. I pulled it from my pocket and glanced at the screen. Private number. I answered. "Fitch."

"Fitch, it's Fred Pern."

"How ya doin', Mr. Pern."

"Call me Fred. I'm fine, but I want . . . I want to know what's up with my tenant. Any progress?"

The tenant, right. It took a second to pull the case to the surface. The Perns ran Urban Ketchup and owned a house in the Richmond that they rented out. They suspected their tenant of foul play, thought he might be working the old School District Double Switch to get his kid into a better public elementary.

"I spent some time there yesterday. I have a lead I'm working on."

"Great, tell me about it."

Truth was, I didn't have much of a lead, but I didn't need this guy knowing I wasn't taking care of business. I remembered that I'd found some scraps in his tenant's trash. "He's gotten himself an attorney."

"An attorney?" Pern sounded alarmed. "Sheesh, figures."

"How so?"

"He's up to no good. Of course he's lawyering up."

"Why don't I try tomorrow and give you an update?"

"Okay, sounds good. We're up to our ears, Fitch. We're trying to build up our french fry operation—to go with the ketchup—and the city has us crazy with permitting. We have to promise that our subcontractors will be locally sourced and have all the paperwork permits but we also have to promise we won't ask them for their immigration status or for their work permits. I told the city that I didn't understand how I could accomplish both things at once and they told me it sounded like I might enjoy opening a restaurant in Marin. It's costing me an arm and leg to get through this process. What the hell, Fitch?"

The question sounded rhetorical.

"Christ, and this tenant. It's like you don't even own your own property anymore."

"How do you mean?"

"Nothing, I'm rambling. Let me know when you make progress, will you?"

"That's what you're paying me for."

"See ya."

We hung up.

I looked back at the Shipper's place. What did I know about this guy? He'd first made his mark selling automation software for fast-food restaurants. You know how the clerks at those places only have to click on a picture when you order, rather than having to key in a cost? That was this guy's thing. As lore had it, he was so keen on making it fail-safe that he tested it on cats, to see if they could hit the right picture—and they actually did most of the time. Not coincidentally, he also was the first guy to make money with cat videos. Genius, they said. Later, once he was swimming in the dough, he invested in everything from Gooble to Snipchap and raked in his winnings while becoming the yacht king of Silicon Valley. His boats had a freaking zip code.

And then there were the dolphins. They'd become his pet symbol, part of the empire, a brilliant bit of branding, I had to admit. Made him seem smart, I guess, if you fall for that stuff.

I laid on the buzzer, really hit it.

"Hello, Mr. Fitzgerald," the voice came over the intercom.

"Mr. Klipper?"

"I've been expecting you." The door swung open. I cautiously entered, walking a stone path between manicured succulents. Far less ostentatious or weird than the last place I'd visited in this hood. I walked up the porch steps of the three-story house, wide enough to have wings. The door opened and there stood a guy I recognized from the papers, tall and thin, bald but for gray stubble on the sides where he'd shaved, weathered face, Stanford basketball T-shirt, jeans, leather moccasins.

"Pretty nasty defense system. Fried a delivery driver," I said.

"I seriously doubt that. More like an uninvited guest in a driver's disguise. Our regulars know to use the service entrance. Come on in and we'll talk about it."

He looked around the property, like maybe keeping an eye out for something. Odd.

Clueless as to where this was heading and why he so readily let me in, I followed him, let the estate wash over me: an ornate staircase bisecting the house and leading up, an open doorway to the right exposing a massive dining room, more like dining *hall*, and an opening to the left that my host entered. I followed as we made our way through a traditional living room, then down a hallway and an underground ramp and into a brightly lit court-yard. I emerged to view a gargantuan fish tank. Understatement. Like an indoor ocean.

It took up the entire side of the wall we were facing, with the tank extending both well below us and also upward, maybe to the top of the house. It teemed with fish, mostly small, but a few big ones.

"Is that a dolphin?"

"A rescue, more like a hand-me-down," he said. "Lillybud. She was part of a Gooble X project aimed at figuring out how dolphins reacted to various digital stimuli, pop-up ads, incoming texts, and data bursts sent in dolphin language, their sonar. They tried to figure out if Lillybud could use sonar to organize songs in a playlist, a way of testing dolphins' intelligence and our technology. The big question was whether sonar would be the next Wi-Fi. Could we interact with our devices using our minds?"

"You've got to be kidding me."

"Right, ridiculous. I mean, we've invested so much in Wi-Fi. Anyhow, Lillybud got so juiced up on fast-twitch data streams that she developed a terribly short attention span. She started craving stimulation. Can't stay focused. She'd be midflip and she'd switch directions."

"Mid what?"

"What?"

"What did you say she'd be in the middle of?"

"I forgot. Where were we? I've lost my train of thought," he said.

"I've got a problem, Mr. Klipper. I need the Spirit Box."

"You . . ." He started to laugh. Not disingenuous, not maniacal, a genuine laugh. "Don't we all."

He was standing to my right, staring at the fish, shaking his head, finding this all so laughable. The largely empty courtyard echoed with the tail end of his laughter. Behind him, against a wall, an elegant wooden table held several models of yachts. He crossed his arms and I noticed how frail they looked, the thin arms of an old man. Had to be late seventies, this one.

"I need the Spirit Box."

"You're serious."

"And then some. It's at the center of some bad business."

He clenched his teeth and looked pained as he watched Lillybud the dolphin swim back and forth in a jerky motion.

"You see that fish," he said, and walked toward the tank.

"There are millions of fish. I'm talking about the Spirit Box."

"I'm telling you about it. Be patient. You see that fish, over by the sunken ship? The rainbow-colored thing, small. You see it?"

"Mr. Klipper—"

"Do you see it? I'm trying to tell you about the Spirit Box."

I joined him. Yeah, I guessed I saw it. There were a lot of damned fish.

"It's a hundred and sixty years old," he said.

"Give me a break."

"In human years. In fish years, it's four. But it should have been dead six times over."

"Okay."

He turned to me. "This is nothing, Fitch. This isn't even close to science fiction. Using stem cells, we can regrow organs, give people 'Fresh Flesh,' which is a term I've trademarked but, respectfully, I'd ask you not to use it in public until I get the paperwork through. My point is, we can use stem cells and genetic engineering to make entirely new body parts. It's happening, today. Look, you see my shoulder? This thing is the shoulder of a twenty-five-year-old. I had to go in for rotator-cuff surgery and they slapped some stem cells in there and my ligament is now ten years younger. I can hit a hell of a spin serve, but then I'm so tired I need a nap, so what's the point?"

"You took the words out of my mouth. What's the point?"

"We're not so far from being able to rebuild the physical parts of a human being. We're on the cusp. In a few years, we'll be manufacturing tissue like tissues."

"Like what?"

"You know, Kleenex, but that's trademarked, so tissues, unless I win that one in court. The point is, that's not enough. Tissue is not what makes a creature. That's not soul, spirit. That's not our essence."

"The Spirit Box."

He turned to me, and answered in the affirmative with a serious look. His arms were crossed, eyes watery, bloodshot, tired, old—emotional, moved.

"It's not immortality if you keep a body alive. Hell, we can put people on an IV drip and leave them in a chair for years, long after their brains have left the building."

I held the silence. He was getting somewhere.

"You bet your ass it's personal to me, Fitch. I can see that's what you're thinking. My wife got Alzheimer's and she's sitting in the other room like a vegetable, sucking pureed soy protein from a feeding tube. She doesn't even recognize me. Little better than Eliza."

"Who?"

"Early artificial-intelligence program."

Heavy, real, I thought. No BS here.

"So you and Captain Don came up with the Spirit Box. Somehow it keeps the brain alive, or immortal, is that it?"

"It's not that hard, see." I didn't see but it was almost like he wasn't talking to me anymore. His eyes had glazed over. "The brain is circuitry, it's a motherboard, electricity lighting up connections. It's the Internet, basically. It's an algorithm. It's just math!"

"Who are you trying to convince? Me, or yourself?"

"Think about this: we can already rebuild the body, parts of it anyway, and now, with the Spirit Box, we aimed to copy and replicate a person's essence—like giving them a new hard drive. You follow?"

"I guess I don't." I found my thoughts drifting to Terry, the only person who made me feel there wasn't a single sacrifice too big. I could understand the terror this guy must feel at the loss of his wife.

"People aren't that complicated. We are predictable. Unique, maybe, but predictable, that too. It's why artificial intelligence works. It was what Eliza showed."

"That program you were talking about."

He nodded. "Human beings can be replicated. We tend to say the same things over and over again. If we can map that program, we can copy it, completely." Now he looked me dead in the eye. "We were *this* close. And then . . ."

I waited for him to finish.

"Don got sick. He had something or other, wouldn't say what, exactly. It's something or other that's gonna get you eventually, was all he'd say. I guess I didn't realize the extent of it. He started acting weird, weirder than usual."

"How's that?"

"He was spending time tinkering with the Spirit Box, said he was onto something."

"Tinkering? Like perfecting?"

No answer.

"You guys were spending a lot of time together, that's what his daughter said, Mrs. Donogue."

"Yes," he said absently. He was looking at the fish again. I watched him watch the dolphin swim one direction, then turn and swim the other. Then it swam high to the surface and I could see it jump out of the water and flip.

Flip.

Shit, that gave me an idea. *Flippers.* Where had I seen the name: Flippers?

Suddenly there was a sound of "Sunday Bloody Sunday," the U2 song. Klipper reached to his belt and looked at his phone.

"Ha," he said, bemused but distant. "Long after I'm gone, my ringer will still be working."

"So do you believe that Captain Don got the Spirit Box working and he's . . . out there? What does that even mean?"

From his belt, his phone barked: *new voice mail.* He pushed a button to ignore the message and he walked over to the table on the wall with the models of the yachts. He seemed to want me to follow him. A second later, we stood by the ships, intricate, extraordinary models.

"I assume you know how I made my money?"

"The fast-food thing."

"Right, decent idea, but nothing extraordinary. Pictures on cash registers. Anyone could've thought of it and maybe some others did before me. I just happened to get the patent. So I get a hundredth of a cent every time someone pushes the french fry picture. Double that on burgers but that's because the picture turns out to be more complex, depending on the cheese factor, lettuce, tomato, etcetera. And I tossed in shakes for free in the settlement. Anyhow, then I took my winnings and parlayed them into various investments."

"Anything else you want to confess?"

"Yeah. I'm not the brains. Rather, I wasn't the brains, not of the Spirit Box. Don. He was the one. He could've made it so. And now he's gone. Er, gone-ish."

"Meaning?"

"That's what I can't figure. He's been sending messages, so says his daughter."

"Meaning you think he's . . ." I looked for the word.

"Maybe he figured it out after all. Maybe he's . . ." He looked at me. "You know he was smiling when they found him—on the road."

"I wasn't aware."

"It was like he'd figured something out and he was taking his last ride."

As I chewed on his thought, the Shipper directed his gaze downward, seeming to look hard at a four-foot-long yacht model with tiny words etched on the stern: *Infinite Quest*. "Guess what this cost?"

"The model? Fifty grand?"

"Model? Hell, no. This is no model. This is a genuine yacht.

The smallest on the planet. I'm the first guy to go tiny with yachts. Most of those guys, like Epperson and Jango, the new money guys, they tried to best me for the biggest yacht. Let them have it. They can't touch this for innovation." He fingered his tiny boat. "It has twenty-seven bedrooms, fifteen plumbed bathrooms, two chef's kitchens, and does fifty knots."

"But no one can use it."

"That's what they said about Snipchap, and it went huge. The bigger problem is keeping it from getting eaten. But we'll solve that."

"When I came in, you said you were expecting me, Mr. Klipper? Why was that? And why did you look around like bad guys might be out there?"

"Cost me twelve million. I'm more proud of this than I am of *Speak Freely* or the *Lone Shark*."

"The what?"

"The world's most medium-size yacht." Something came over his face, a return to the moment. "Fitch, I don't know what to tell you."

"About what?"

"Tess Donogue told me you'd come by, told me you'd want to know about the Spirit Box and Don. But I don't know what to tell you. I was as anxious as the next guy to get it finished and I was pushing Don to do it. But he was, as they say, the captain, and I was, at best, first mate. Yeah, I'm the guy who put the pictures on the fast-food registers, but Don came up with the proverbial Big Mac."

"Speak English."

"I can't help you," he said. He looked so tired, desperately weary. "I'll see you out."

NINETEEN

HEARD THE DOOR close behind me and I turned and pushed it back open—gently—before it could click locked.

"You forgot something?" the Shipper asked.

"The Spirit Box—do you actually have it? Is it a thing?"

He smiled, almost kindly. "You're catching on. No, it's not a physical thing. It's software, as you might imagine."

"But it has to exist on a computer or gadget, right?"

He smiled again, now a tad on the patronizing side. "I guess I didn't think about it the way you're thinking about it. You can see the last version I had. Come on." He gestured with a neck crane for me to follow him back in, then, again, he looked over my shoulder, casing the surroundings.

This time we walked to the right, through the dining hall, and past a room where, through an open doorway, I got a glimpse of something jarring: a woman in a recliner watching a giant screen with videos of cats pawing at cash registers. Well, sort of "watching." Even at a distance and even with a passing glance, I could see that she was glazed over. But she seemed to be amused. This must've been Klipper's demented wife.

Next stop, two doors down, a spacious office. Big oak desk, and gorgeous built-in bookshelves filled not with books but with what looked to me like computer tablets, one after another. "Library of Congress," he said, "a complete copy," but all on e-readers. "The whole of human literary accomplishment, alphabetized." He walked to an oil painting of a yacht called the *Last Dolphin* hung behind his desk. He pulled on the right side of the frame and I could see that it was mounted on a hinge . . . and he revealed a safe. He keyed in some numbers, opened it, and pulled out a rectangular object I recognized as a hard drive.

"The Spirit Box," he said.

He held it in his palm, black and shiny, smudged with a few fingerprints.

"That's it?"

"I know, right? Don used off-the-shelf parts."

"Why didn't you tell me earlier?"

"Because it's worthless."

"So it doesn't hold the key to immortality?"

"I doubt it. It's most of the way there—the code. But when I hooked it up to a processor and monitor, it just kept sending out an e-mail: *this thing is revolutionary!*"

"Sending out an e-mail?"

"From my own account, to everyone on my contact list." He looked solemn, sad. "That's not revolutionary. It's just an e-mail blast. Revolutionary was the fast-food pictures." He just looked sad. "Revolutionary was my idea for self-brushing hair. Revolutionary was—"

He looked up at me and I cut him off. "Do you hear yourself?"

He took the hard drive and sat down at his desk and used a cord to plug the box into his computer. On the monitor, words materialized: *this thing is revolutionary!*

"That's all it does." He unplugged it.

He sighed. "Here." He handed me the box. "Take it."

"The Spirit Box."

"I'm done with this. Take it and go. Maybe you can piece it together. I've got to sing to Barbara and put her to bed."

OUTSIDE, BACK BEYOND the electric fence, I held the hard drive in my hand and I nearly prayed: *let this be the thing that sets Terry free.*

But I didn't believe it would be, not for a second. Would the Shipper give it up this easily? I stuffed it into a saddlebag on the bike and headed down the dirt path.

A COUPLE OF minutes later, lost in the night air and letting my mind go, I reached the estate of Tess Donogue and Lester Wollop and kept going. Then I saw the MINI. It was behind me, heading the same way I was. I sped up the bike, took two quick turns to give myself some distance from the diminutive car, and made up my mind to act.

While still riding, I reached back and pulled out the hard drive and put it in my pocket, then, after the next turn, I slammed the brakes, killed the ignition, dropped the bike in the middle of the road, and sprinted for the cover of the trees on the right.

Fifteen seconds later, the MINI appeared, and as I'd hoped, it stopped. I probed with my hand for a stick or heavy rock as I waited for the Tarantula to appear. The door to the MINI opened and a guy stepped from the driver's side, cautious, looking around, and then took a few steps from the car to the downed bike.

And I almost said: *What the hell?*

It wasn't a Tarantula.

"Freeze!" I shouted. "Or I'll shoot."

I didn't have a gun but this guy didn't know that. He froze.

"Put your hands on your head."

"My head? Fitch, is that you?"

"Walk away from the car."

"Absolutely. Fitch, I thought that was you. Can we chat?"

I walked out of the trees and eyeballed the hapless engineer from Ben's Bags. The guy who'd helped me find the dead Tarantula. What was he doing here?

"You don't answer my calls or texts, Fitch?"

"What are you doing here?"

"I . . . I'm really trying to get a meeting."

"Drop the car keys."

"They're still in the car. What happened to your bike? You want to go grab coffee? I realize it's late, but I know a place that has short-acting caffeine, it's not GMO-free, obviously, you've got to mess with the coffee bean to take the edge off, but sometimes you have to make sacrifices to have late-night, short-term focus."

"I'll ask you again: What are you doing here?"

"I've been trying to find you. You said you'd help get me in with the guys at Froom. I've got a killer idea on this facial recognition thing. I need backing. You know what I mean."

I didn't know. I didn't trust this guy. What was he doing in a MINI? I was struck by an idea and I went with it.

"I saw you leave the Donogue estate," I said.

There was just a momentary pause and then he said: "What are you talking about?"

I hadn't actually seen him leave the Donogues, but now he'd given himself away. I took three quick strides forward, and without thinking much about it, I gave the guy a quick jab to the right cheek. Not too hard and I tried to avoid direct impact to his nose. I was sending a message, not putting out the lights. He stumbled backward.

"What the . . ."

"That's your last warning, kid."

Without looking to see his reaction, I walked to the driver's side of the MINI and said to him: "Get in." He walked around the front of the car, rubbing his cheek, and got inside. I flicked on the inside light and glanced at him, and then around. Nothing noteworthy, the car clean.

"What were you doing at the Donogues?"

"Looking for you. I'm this close, Fitch. I need a break, man."

"Bullshit."

"You know the story of eHaggle?"

"I'm only going to ask you one more time."

"Just listen, Fitch. EHaggle, the biggest auction site in the world, made billions for its innovators. That's the official story. And it's a bunch of bull crud. They weren't the first with the idea. They weren't second. They were *third*. Third! You don't read about that in *Forbes*. You sure as heck don't read about Andrea Pinsky."

"Who?"

"She had the idea first, she wrote incredible code, pure garage start-up genius, and then . . ." He trailed off. Then: "She couldn't get out of her garage."

"What?"

"The door, it got stuck. She was racing to beat the eHaggle guys to Sand Village, where all the VCs hang their shingles, and her garage door, it got stuck and she couldn't get out. It's a problem you don't hear about very often, but it's a real problem with these garage start-ups. The door fails, or, worse."

"Worse."

"The entrepreneurs get stuck in the door, rushing to get out. The guy who came up with the first online dry-cleaning site was in such a hurry that he didn't see the garage door coming down and his spine was crushed. He still crawled his way to Sand Village, the venture capitalists, but by then ePress was already funded."

"Cut the crap. I told you that I wasn't going to warn you again."

"Someone's going to beat me to this facial recognition thing. I don't want to get stuck in the proverbial garage door."

"Where did you get the MINI?"

"I knew you'd be attracted to a car like this; you'd think it was a Tarantula. See, it worked. Can you get me in with Danny?"

I punched him again. This time, a little rabbit smack, right in the rib cage, enough to keep one lung from doing its business. He sucked for air.

"I thought you weren't warning me again."

"Consider yourself lucky, smartass." I paused. "Here's my theory. You're . . ." I paused again.

He looked at me, waiting. And maybe he realized what I realized: I didn't have a theory.

"You're in the middle of this," I said, noncommittal.

"Of what?"

"You just figured I'd be at the Donogues'; that's what you're selling me?"

"You said you were looking for the kid."

"The kid." This nerd was a kid himself.

"Besides, this gave me a chance . . . an excuse to knock on the Donogues' door. I . . . I don't know, I thought I'd pitch them on the facial recognition software."

"And?"

"And they wouldn't let me in. What did I expect?" His head was hung.

"Where'd you get the money for the MINI?"

"Money?"

"For the car." I flexed my fist so he'd get the idea another warning was on its way.

He recoiled. "I got a zero-down lease and tossed the sales guy some equity if things pan out. He offered to do biz dev during his off-hours, but no way I'm gonna take on a partner when I'm this close."

"Let's get something straight . . . what did you say your name was?"

"Floyd. Floyd Chiansky. It's half Chinese, half Thai, half Polish."

"Three halves, huh."

"Anyone ever tell you you're a racist?"

"About a hundred times in the last twenty-four hours. You're an engineer, right?"

"I do engineering. I don't like labels. I think they're confining."

"You do engineering?"

"Like I said."

"Well then, it's time to prove your loyalties."

"What's that supposed to mean?"

"Don't move," I said by way of a nonanswer. I snagged his car keys from the cup holder in the middle. I got out of the car and uprighted my bike and rolled it off the road and parked it behind a tree. Then I returned to the MINI, started it, and drove about twenty yards until I came to the first turnoff—to the right— just another dirt road leading to just another gargantuan estate. I drove ten yards in, cut the engine, then I turned on the car's inside light. I reached into my back pocket and I removed the papers that I'd pulled from the book *The Selfish Gene*—the papers left by Captain Don.

I unfolded them and looked at what appeared to me to be gibberish.

"Read this to me," I said.

He took a long sip of the pages. He pursed his lips; I could see his brain moving on his face, tics and teeth grits, modest undulation betraying deep thought, or that's what he wanted me to think. He sighed and looked at the second page. Finally, he looked up at me.

"Don't hit me," he said.

"What's that supposed to mean?"

"When I tell you what I'm reading here. Don't hit me."

"That is officially not a deal."

"Then I'd rather not say."

"Not saying won't spare you." I wasn't usually this big of an asshole but I was starting to see this big clock in my head and it was counting down to the Tarantulas putting a bullet into Terry.

He nodded. "Point taken. Look, the short answer is: I can't read this to you."

"Why not?"

"It's computer code."

"Right, and you're a geek."

"How have you even survived in the Bay Area with all the labels you give people?" He must've seen the ire in my eyes and his tone changed. "Anyhow, yes, I read code. But you don't just read code. You have to program this into a computer and then you have to see what happens."

"You mean make it run."

"Exactly. Don't think of this as code, but, rather, think of these as machine instructions."

I nodded. It met the smell test. "So how do we do that?" But I obviously knew the answer. We needed a computer. "Floyd, let me put this bluntly: Is this the Spirit Box?"

He shrugged. "I guess I'd doubt it. Maybe. But it's not very long."

It was just three pages. "How long is the facial recognition software?"

"The what?"

"The program you're working on."

"Oh, right."

"Oh, right?" I raised my eyebrows. "You've told me that it's all you can think about, that you've been chasing me around to discuss, your damn life's work, and you just suddenly forgot about it?"

"Are you saying you want in? You want to invest?"

"I'm saying I don't trust you or your story. So I'm changing tactics. I'm going to offer you a deal."

"So now *you're* starting a company?"

"Not like that, Floyd. Stop horsing around. It's much simpler than that. I'm going to drop you off somewhere with a computer—your house, an Internet café, whatever. You're going to find out what this does and you're going to tell me and you're not going to tell anyone else. If you fail to follow these instructions, I'm going to give your name to the police in connection with the murders of Da Raj and Captain Don."

"That's ridiculous. You're bluffing."

"Maybe. That's the nature of a bluff."

"I had nothing to do with those murders."

"That will not be my problem. That will be a matter for the police."

"This is insane!"

"I'll tell you what's insane: Insane is the likelihood that you're following me around so that I can introduce you to Danny or some other prospective investor. Insane is that you happened to see a Tarantula wander through the back door of Bob's Bags. Insane is that you happened to see the felled Tarantula by the side of the road while we were driving around and I didn't see him. All these things, every one of them, falls under a heading of something I don't believe in: coincidence."

"It's called Ben's Bags."

"What?"

"You said: Bob's Bags. It's Ben's Bags."

"Whatever."

"There was a Bob's Bags but it was a pretty classic tale. It was actually first to market, before Ben's Bags, and the founder—Bob—he was brilliant, an idea guy, of course. But he had no business sense. He had this idea that you could—"

"I don't care."

"Just listen to me. He had a phenomenal idea about how to build market share. He started giving away the bags."

"For free. I know, I've heard about this—"

"Just listen, okay. His idea was better than that. He was giving away bags for free and the bags were filled with money. People couldn't get enough of these bags. They were an instant sensation."

"That's the stupidest idea I've ever heard."

"What? No, we must not be communicating. He had huge market share. And then, one day, he just went out of business."

"That's because he was giving away money."

"What? No! It's not that simple. He needed professional management. The Founder's Dilemma. He didn't know how to manage growth, and then along came Ben's Bags and just picked up the pieces."

"I don't give a rat's ass—"

"I'm telling you that great ideas come along once in a while, founders who also have business sense. I'm your guy, Fitch. Take a chance on me."

This time my uppercut got his full attention. It struck his chin at just the right moment to cause him to bite into his lip. Blood trickled out and he blinked back tears.

"You are bullshitting me on about five levels, Floyd. Pretending to sound stupid with rambling stories, pretending to be running some start-up. I don't know why or what your game is, and I don't care. Now shut your mouth and sit there until I drop you off someplace of my choosing. I'll pick you up in a few hours and you'll give me my answer. Or I go to the cops. Got it?"

I took his whimper for affirmation.

TWENTY

AT A COPYMART, we made a copy of the computer code. Then I dropped Floyd on a residential corner in Menlo Park, just one swanky town over from Palo Alto. He said I couldn't take him all the way to his house because, he said, he still lived with his parents and it would be embarrassing for everyone.

"You're in your thirties," I said, guessing. "And living at home."

"I'm supposed to buy a place? It costs two million for a shack? The worst part is my parents keep jacking up the rent, trying to; they're not supposed to make more than a ten-percent rent hike until you move out and then they can go to market rates. They were hippies in the sixties and now they say that capitalist forces are the only true thing, along with fiber. Real misers."

"You know the terms: you have a few hours to get me the results or the cops start knocking."

He opened the door.

"Hey, Floyd."

"What?"

"I noticed that you haven't asked me about your car."

"My . . ."

"The MINI, your new car."

"I got it with zero down."

"I think you're into something up to your ears." I grabbed his arm before he could get out and I gave him a good hard look to let him know I meant business. Then, right before I was going to let him go, I was hit with a question that I didn't realize had been nagging me until that moment.

"Tell me about Eliza."

"Huh?"

I'd had this moment of clarity and connection. The Shipper had talked about Eliza and I remembered where I'd seen the name before.

I said: "When I came into the bag store, you'd written the word on a piece of paper."

He took it in, shrugged. He explained what I already knew: that it was an artificial-intelligence program. He claimed that he'd written the word down because AI underlies so much computer code these days, including facial recognition. AI, as he described it, was just an overused phrase, a catchall for much code.

"I have a stupid question," I said.

"There are stupid questions."

"What?"

"Usually people say there aren't any stupid questions but there are definitely stupid questions. I'll allow it."

I ignored him. "Does Eliza die?"

He pulled his neck back, almost like he was surprised.

"That's actually a fantastic question." He explained to me why. Artificial intelligence, he said, grows from existing patterns.

A computer program makes decisions based on the kinds of decisions that have been made previously. By way of example, he said that there are a million programs that make assumptions about human behavior based on the amassing of tons of patterns, so-called Big Data.

"You seem to know a lot about it."

"Just sounds like that because you don't know anything."

"Fair enough. So does Eliza die?"

"First of all, Eliza is long since dead. It's a generic term, really, a placeholder. AI has come so far since that. So forget about Eliza. But, again generically, AI doesn't exactly die. It can, though, peter out."

He explained that over time, an AI program that isn't refreshed with more data stops being able to accurately mimic future behavior or ideas. I was having trouble following and I wasn't afraid to admit it to him. The AI programs, he explained, get stale.

"Humans get random," he said. "It's hard to predict random by its very nature. There is an internal spark, creative chaos, you might call it."

"Spirit."

This seemed to jar him and he eyed me hard.

"Maybe."

I noodled it.

"You have three hours to figure out what's on that paper," I told him.

"Three hours, c'mon!"

"Go."

He got out. I followed him two blocks at a distance until he disappeared into a modest ranch-style home that probably did cost $2 million. Only thing I was sure he was telling the truth about: real estate prices here were out of control.

I GUESS I didn't think I'd given Floyd the keys to the Spirit Box. My gut told me that wasn't what was on those pieces of paper. And, even so, I had a copy. And I had the worthless black box in my pocket. Maybe the two things went together—the black box and the paper.

Regardless, I was at the point in this madness where I had to start taking big chances.

OUTSIDE A STARBACKS, I called Gaberson but he didn't answer and I left him a message.

Inside, I ordered the Moon Roast, which the barista said had enough caffeine to fuel a rocket jet. "No kidding," she said. I had to sign a waiver saying that Starbacks was not liable if I started looting. I took a few sips and felt the energy coursing through me, the synapses firing, and pulled out my phone. An idea had been percolating, I guess, and it surfaced, the coming together of a bunch of random thoughts: a dolphin; flipping; the high cost of housing; market rents; ketchup.

I did a search for "Flippers." No sooner had Gooble returned my answer than I realized I'd probably solved the Pern case. It had come together—the tenant, the lawyer, the Perns desperate for money.

I let out a fat exhale. Who cared? It might have felt nice twelve hours ago to dispense with that minor mystery and then go home and eat soufflé with Terry.

There was no joy in this modest revelation, and in fact, I just felt beaten. There was no Terry to go home to. I clenched my teeth and closed my eyes and remembered a story my husband told me about his dad. They'd gotten back from the last Little League practice of the year. Terry would've been around ten and his dad was the coach. His dad asked him if he liked playing and Terry said, basically, eh, it was all right. His dad pressed a bit and asked if there was anything he'd miss about the team and Terry said: Johnny Fairbanks was cute.

They rode the rest of the way home in silence, and when they got home, they opened the front door and Terry's mom said hello from upstairs and his dad said: "Lenore, I think we've got a situation."

I laughed every time Terry told the story because the way his dad said the thing was so damned kindly and, if I understand the word correctly, unfazed, like maybe telling his wife that their son had lost a tooth and was growing up. That's why Terry was such a great guy; he came from great people, straight talkers. He and his dad were best friends and damned if it wasn't one of the worst days of my own life when Terry's dad stroked out and I had to see Terry hit the dumps.

"You want a refill?" asked the barista, who had walked over.

"No thanks."

"It's locally sourced—from Guatemala."

"That's not locally sourced."

"Sure it is. If you buy it there."

I growled and she got the hint and took off. I willed from my head visions of Terry being tortured by Tarantulas and I pulled out a pen and did some back-of-the-napkin calculations. On the napkin, I wrote:

Captain Don
Mrs. Donogue
Danny Donogue
Lester Wollop
Alan Klipper (the Shipper)
Da Raj
Deuce, Tarantula #2
Floyd
Law Firm
Spirit Box
Eliza
Froom

I tapped the pen on the napkin, thinking, processing. I drew some lines connecting various people who were connected and quickly discovered that most of these people were connected in one way or another. Through family or business or both.

I circled the words "Spirit Box." That was the thing that connected everybody.

Everybody wanted a piece of it, it seemed, with a notable exception: Captain Don himself, the guy who created it. I mean, I couldn't say that for sure—he was dead; dead-ish—but from everything I could tell, he wasn't that into innovation. From his video, he seemed also to be getting peaceful with the idea of dying. He had something or other and he knew it and he was saying good-bye and urging others to let him go.

That just nagged at me. So why the Spirit Box and even more confounding: Was it actually working?

Was the Captain out there?

What did that even mean?

My phone rang. The caller ID said: *Lester Wollop.*

"Fitch here," I answered.

"I got another message," Mrs. Donogue said.

"You're alive."

"Why wouldn't I be?"

She'd been tied up last time I saw her.

"Mrs. Donogue . . ."

"Tess, please. I'm trying to reestablish my independence."

"I thought that—"

"Something happened with me and Lester. He tried to draw me back in. We had . . . relations, and it was great and all that, but I need to get back to me. I'm taking back my first name."

"Tess, did you get attacked?"

"That's kind of personal."

"Tess!"

"What? No need to shout. The desal plant is off."

"Did you get tied up by attackers, in your house?"

She didn't answer.

"Tess, please. I need to know what happened. When I left your house, I saw you and Lester tied up. Who did that?"

"I don't see what this has to do with—"

"Why didn't you call the police?"

"We tied each other up, Fitch. Okay! Leave it alone. Then I guess we fell asleep. I did, anyhow."

I wasn't buying it for a second.

"What's the message, Tess?"

"Message?"

"From Captain Don. What's the new message?"

"'Yer headed in the right direction.'"

"That's the message?"

Yep, she confirmed. That was the message. *Yer headed in the right direction.*

"When did it arrive?"

"Just a few seconds ago."

"Can you send a note back?"

She didn't answer right away and then said: "I guess, I never thought about it. What should I say?"

"'Say something useful or stay dead, asshole.'"

And I hung up.

FIFTEEN MINUTES LATER, I looked out from the driver's-side window of the MINI at what even I would have to admit was an architectural marvel. Terry would call it sublime. Snozzwanger, Veruca and Gloop. The law firm at the center of Silicon Valley. It stood at the corner of Onaniversity and El Camino No Real, the thoroughfare that courses through the region. The three-story building, taking up nearly a full block, glowed with low, ambient light that looked like it seeped from the building.

A storied place. Word was that the salaries of new hires from premier law schools started at $175,000 or more, which actually was the equivalent of double that since the new lawyers worked ninety hours a week and had no time to spend the money. Very lucrative, it was said, if you weren't one of the ones hospitalized for dehydration. The law firm had living quarters and a scrip store for purchase of office supplies and counseling services. But the thing that had me most intrigued was something I'd not previously heard about, and was frankly shocked to see: a drive-through window.

It was my only option this late at night. I'd tried the front door and had neither the proper key lock nor any excuse that the desk clerk would buy when I tried to get in to see someone, especially since I didn't even know who to ask for.

The drive-through was to the right of the building, and three cars were lined up in front of me. A sign overhead read: *Open 24 Hours*. The sedan in front of me moved forward and I followed in lockstep and came across a menu. It showed some items for purchase and then prices in two categories: "regular" and "after-hours." The prices struck me first, most of them ranging from several hundred to several thousand. The categories included: notary public; make-a-deal; late-night equity round; disclaimers; insta-file-a-patent; insta-patent challenge; instant coffee; protein shake; grab bag.

In front of me, I could hear a voice come through a speaker. The speaker was located at the mouth in the face of a stately English barrister painted on the wall of the building. "Welcome to Snozzwanger, Veruca and Gloop. My name is Chuck, I'll be your barristerista today. How may I help you?" the voice asked.

From the sedan in front of me, a woman stuck out her head. "First Mover Advantage Special, please. I have a GropeOn."

"Victoria, is that you?" said the voice.

"No!"

"It is too. Victoria. Move along."

"This one is great. I know it. Please! I'll pay in equity."

"Victoria. I have to cut you off. Believe me, we'd like your money, if you had any, but you're not taking care of yourself."

"I have one word for you: meditation."

"Victoria—"

"It's totally inefficient. What if we could speed it up, use technology to make it really zoom? Squeeze out the fat."

"Victoria!"

"What?"

"This is your third company idea this week."

"I'm rolling. I've been meditating."

"Get out of line or I'll call your bankruptcy officer."

Victoria practically stood in her seat, bringing her face up close to the painted barrister. She had long brown hair and wore a headset. "Hey, asshole, you know what?"

"What, Victoria?"

"Someday I'll have so much cash that I'll build a robot to dance on your grave until the end of time."

"Victoria, we really do appreciate your entrepreneurial spirit."

"You do?"

"We do. But this level of support is not intended to be perceived as a commitment of any kind."

"What?"

"The usual disclaimer, Victoria, you know that. Also, legal services we provide may backfire and lead to bankruptcy, bad decision making, carpal tunnel syndrome, paper cuts, and gout."

"Gout?"

"From carrying reams of paper."

"Fuck off."

"Can I take that as confirmation that you have heard and acknowledged the disclaimer?"

She drove off. I found myself in the position of having to figure out what the hell to say. I needed a way into this place. I had this feeling, just this aching feeling, that this building and the people inside of it held important secrets. Donogue used this firm, and so did Lester Wollop.

"Hello, Mr. Fitzgerald," the voice said. "My name is Chuck. I'll be your barristerista. Welcome to Snozzwanger, Veruca and Gloop. How can I help you?"

Deep breath. "Good evening."

"Right back at you. Seems like you're a first timer, so I should tell you that billing starts at this point, unless you plan to do an equity cash-out, but that would need to be negotiated. Are you familiar with our services?"

"I have some important documentation involving the estate of Don Donogue."

"So, an estate issue? Is this pertaining to loopholes, er, technical issues?"

"Yes and no. Don Donogue was a client here, or is. He died, more or less."

"I'm sorry, say again."

Holy shit, I was starting to speak the nonsense talk of this place. It was getting to me, like a virus.

"Yes, an estate issue. Involving a will."

"Great. Do you have a GropeOn?"

"What?"

"Coupon. We have a Life Closeout Special. I'll honor it anyway.

When you get to the first window, you'll need to provide death certificate and proof of overseas tax shelter. Our data entry specialist will fill out the paperwork, and at the second window you'll pay and get your form. Anything else?"

"I'd like to make an appointment."

There was a pause. Then: "To meet with someone in person?"

"Right."

"But . . ." He seemed taken aback. "That's fairly inefficient. We stopped even pricing for that because most people don't want it."

"I have documents that involve the estate of Captain Don Donogue. Do you know the name?"

"Of course."

"I have documents that involve . . ."—I decided to go for it—"millions of dollars."

"I can recommend a firm down the block."

"Billions, multiple billions of dollars."

"Why didn't you say so? I think Veruca Sap handles the Donogue account. I can see if she's in. Why don't you pull up to the next window? We're getting backed up. We're hitting peak hours." In the rearview mirror, I could see three cars behind me. I pulled around the corner to a drive-through window. In a chair, wearing a headset, sat a young man—early twenties, I'd say— eyes wide as full moons. So animated that it looked like his freckles were dancing. "Ms.-Sap'sin-anapping pod!" he said.

I had no idea what he was talking about, but I instantly recognized an unrelated truth: this guy was on a stimulant, much more powerful than coffee. This Adderall was everywhere.

"Can you say what you said but more slowly?"

"Ms. Sap is in a napping pod."

"Slower, pal."

He took a deep breath. "Veruca Sap is in a napping pod, please leave a message at the next window."

"Got it. Listen, can I give you some advice?"

"Skip college? I know. It's for people who can't doooooo!" So wired he seemed unable to stop his roller-coaster sentence.

"Get off the speed."

He laughed.

"I'm serious."

"It's got IMMUNOBOOST!"

"So do vitamins. You can take vitamins and get some sleep and you'll be better off."

"You-just-blew-my-mind. Next!"

I drove off.

Next window. Another guy in a seat, this one wearing white barrister hair. "Mr. Fitzgerald, Ms. Sap can see you tomorrow morning."

"Really?"

"Does eight A.M. work?"

This caught me totally off guard—the ease of access. "Sure. Any chance she can see me tonight?"

"I'm sorry, after her nap she'll be deep in a disclaimer."

I recognized the voice of the guy who came through the speaker. Same guy. A brown ponytail showed through the back of his white barrister wig.

"Are you bobbing up and down?" I asked.

"Bike desk. Ms. Sap will meet you in the lobby tomorrow at eight. Anything else?"

I looked in my rearview mirror and saw that the next car

hadn't pulled up yet. "Listen . . ." I lowered my voice. "Let's say that a fella was interested in getting a divorce. Hypothetically. What kind of services can you provide?"

"I can't give legal advice."

"I'm not asking for legal advice. I just want to know how the divorce thing works."

He stopped pedaling. He looked sad.

"What's going on, Chuck?"

"I was a child of divorce. It'd be great if you could try to work it—"

"Chuck!" He was interrupted by a voice coming from inside the building. Chuck, the barristerista, turned his head toward the person yelling. She continued: "Last warning!"

Chuck swallowed hard and started pedaling again. In a very mechanical voice, he said: "Net worth?"

"What?"

"Snozzwanger, Veruca and Gloop provides the nation's premier divorce investment services. We provide marriage dissolution investment counseling and representation funding. Our strategy firmly aligns the interest of the firm and client in securing the fairest and largest divorce settlement."

"Speak fucking English, Chuck."

"If you want a divorce but you don't have cash to afford a topnotch lawyer and investigative costs, we carry you up front. Then we take a cut of the divorce. It's a simple business transaction, if that's how you want to view a precious relationship that should transcend the ridiculous capitalist forces that have overcome all emotion in this godforsaken place."

"Chuck!" yelled a voice from the side.

Chuck looked in the direction of the voice and then back to me. "I quit!" he said, and yanked off his headset and started to stand, like he would stomp off, but he appeared to trip. "Frickin' stirrup! What's wrong with this place! Why can't I just sit!"

"Chuck, you're fired."

"I quit already!"

"There goes your severance."

"You don't offer severance!"

"Well, you wouldn't have gotten any anyway!"

"This place is ridiculous!"

"If you want to sue us, we can fashion you with an attorney."

I left the bickering in the background and pulled away. I'd gotten what I came for: a little more information, a few insights into this nuthouse law firm at the center of Silicon Valley, and an appointment to get in deeper still with someone named Veruca Sap. Captain Don's attorney. I wasn't sure why, but I had a sense she could shed some light.

That said, my sense of accomplishment was modest and fleeting at best. What was I really going to get out of this place? I was pulling at vapor, looking for anything to help me unravel the mystery of Captain Don's death and the role of the Spirit Box. Not that I particularly cared. In fact, I'd have long since left this madness behind. The answers held the key to Terry, finding him, saving him. As I drove down El Camino No Real I gritted my teeth so hard I thought they might crack. I had nothing. Nothing. I lowered all the windows of the MINI, let the night air flow through, let the whistle of wind suffocate my thoughts. I kept going north until I decided to go west to a place where I might get a moment of respite. And some very serious artillery.

TWENTY-ONE

SIX MONTHS INTO the ATF gig, we got a tip about guys sending counterfeit stamps across the Canadian border. This wasn't usually our kind of gig. But they were armed to the teeth. "Video-game-armed," Sammy, my mentor, said to me. Meaning: jury-rigged weapons so powerful and multifaceted they would seem to exist only in the world of fantasy. They'd caught one guy with a semiautomatic that sent flames and shot grenades and also hurled insults.

"Just to smuggle in counterfeit stamps?"

"Stamps be cash," Sammy said.

So before we stormed the bad guys' castle—really just a shack north of Albany across the border but with a 3-D printer—we did some heavy-weapons training. At the range, we practiced shooting dummies using a MAC-11 with a silencer. Nasty weapon. Generally illegal without a very specialized license. The M11 .380 fired 1,380 rounds a minute. Twenty-three rounds *per second*. Technology at work. At night, I got nightmares, seeing the land covered with shredded flesh. Got to the point where I hated pulling the damn trigger.

"The man's conscience shows itself again." Sammy laughed at the range the next day while I stood there sipping coffee, stalling, unable to shoot.

He handed me a sawed-off, short-barrel pump-action shotgun. I took it, ran my hand along the 8.5-inch barrel, and blew a dummy into the next county. And then another. I looked at Sammy and his smarmy smile.

"You're cured."

"Nothing to cure."

"Sure there is. You got a case of the dinosaurs."

As I drove north toward Floyd's parents' house, I thought about Terry's ticking clock and about how I might spring him and what firepower that might require. I pulled over to the curb a block from Floyd and texted. He immediately texted back: *need more time.*

Time's up.

My phone rang.

"Floyd, get your ass out here."

"I'm close."

"You're close to going down in a murder conspiracy."

"You're bluffing, right?"

"Get out here, Floyd."

"Listen! Please. I think I know what this is. It has to do with encrypting messages."

"English."

"It's a new program, an innovation, obviously—he was Captain Don. Some way to send messages that is secure and that eliminates the problem of hacking and identity theft. This could be big."

I noodled it. "So not the Spirit Box."

"I don't think so, no. I need a bit more time. I haven't even gotten it to run yet. I'm just seeing the outlines. I think there's more."

I looked at the clock.

"Are you bullshitting me, Floyd?"

"I swear."

"Okay, here's the deal. I'm going to wait around the corner from you. I'm in the MINI. I'll touch base in a bit."

No silence but it sounded like maybe he gulped.

He hung up.

I couldn't get a full read on him. He seemed excited about what he was uncovering, but I still didn't trust him for a second. And what to make of the idea that Captain Don had yet another new innovation—this one involving a new way to send secure messages?

Still, I had no intention of sitting here for the next few hours. I needed two things—rest enough to think, and guns—and I headed northwest to get them. Forty minutes later, I arrived at the porch of Elron and Honey.

"He's baaaaack!" Elron said. "Honey, fire up the moonshine."

He turned altogether less playful when I explained I needed a place to stay for a few hours and his best work on some munitions.

"Does Terry know what's going on?" Honey asked. We stood on the porch in near darkness but I could see his head cocked to the side with suspicion.

"Let's go inside," I implored.

I felt their eyes on me.

"Where's Terry?" Elron pushed.

When I didn't answer for a second, Elron said: "You want me to get Tucker?"

Tucker Fields ran the Barkers, a biker group that Elron did the maintenance for and sometimes rode with. A tougher SOB than Tucker there never has been. One of the few fellows who actually made my knees knock.

"Not necessary. Just a couple of guns. One intimidating, the other discreet but angry."

"Just like us," Honey said without much humor. This was a dark moment, clearly. "Come inside and get a few hours of sleep while Elron does his business."

I hit the pillow in a wood-framed room no bigger than the king bed stuffed into it. I heard light wind rattle a bird feeder on a nearby tree and fell into a dead sleep. I woke up to a tap-tap on the door and Honey greeted me in a colorful kimono with a cup of coffee, steam swirling over the top. "Crows are up and I got the sense you might be on a deadline," he said. I squinted at a digital clock perched on the headboard and saw 6:05, and for a second I felt like a million bucks after the dead sleep, and then remembered Terry and the rest of it and dusted myself off and creaked from the bed.

Just off the rustic kitchen a round table needed its sturdy wooden legs to support the huge pile of pancakes that was on it and two very serious guns. They looked for a second like utensils, one on each side of a plate that Honey had set out for me. But you'd not confuse either for a spork.

"Abbott and Costello," I heard a voice say, and turned and realized Elron was standing in a doorway to the left. His arms were crossed and he looked grave. "It's what I call this pairing.

Costello, the big one, she looks tough and is tough, but I sawed it off before the choke so it's likely to spray. I got the feeling that might not be such a bad idea." He seemed to eye me for my reaction. "Abbott . . . well, watch the fuck out." I looked at the smaller and thinner of the guns—not too long, and lean. "Made to settle all disputes," Elron continued. "It's almost all chamber. Houses ten .270—"

"I doubt that."

"Don't test me, Fitch. They come out fast. Spare telling me how impressed you are and have some of Honey's double-gluten frozen berry pancakes and tell me what the hell is going on."

I sat and I ate and didn't say much at first, despite their prodding eyes. Then I finally relented and spelled out most of it.

"Where do you think they've got him?" Elron asked.

"No idea," I said, staring at a pancake bite hanging from my fork.

"But you do have an idea," Honey said.

I didn't respond.

"How can we help?"

"You've helped. I should be on my way."

Elron sighed, and for the first time that morning I realized how tired he looked. He'd been up all night sawing and retrofitting. At the doorway, Honey met me with a tan leather jacket. "Perfect for the season and concealing weapons." He fitted it over my shoulders and it hung down below my waist. It felt heavy. "I sewed in a flak jacket," Honey said. I felt the weight of ammo in the pockets.

Outside, Elron stood beside the MINI and a motorcycle.

"Figured I'd give you an option," he said. "The car is nice but it's not the single most powerful engine I've ever built—the cycle hums six hundred horses and zero to infinity in four seconds. Your call."

I took him up on his gleaming silver chopper, but it did little to erase the pained look on his face, or Honey's. As I warmed the engine with a rev, I could've sworn I heard Elron say: "I hope to hell you know what you're doing."

I GOT A block away from Floyd's place by half past seven and parked in front of a small house. From inside, a woman in a handsome navy business suit appeared, walking purposefully in my direction. Before I could escape, she said: "Are you here for the garage sale?"

I had no clue what she was talking about and couldn't get the bike started again before she was practically at my back tire. "Nice bike. You must be on at least your third company. You'll love this. Nearly two hundred square feet of great workspace, a mini-fridge, and a pedigree. The last owners ran eWhale, which got swallowed by GuppE in that reverse consolidation."

"I'm—"

"Wait, don't make an offer yet. Not until you hear about the mini-fridge."

"You're selling your garage."

"Of course." She looked stung. "The people who lease are taking advantage of you and your terrific ideas. Wait." She paused. "You're in your thirties already. Forties? I'm sorry to ask but we won't take an equity stake if you have kids and may not be willing to work around the clock. You have to understand the reali—"

I didn't hear the rest as I gunned the engine and thought *screw it* and drove right up to Floyd's parents' place. It was single-story, bungalow style, unkempt front yard, weed-infested. I pulled into the driveway and parked over the unattended-to pavement cracks. I texted Floyd that I was outside and got no answer. I called and he didn't pick up.

It was irritating, at the least. I considered my options and then I called Lieutenant Gaberson.

"Hey, Fitch."

"I'm running out of time."

"I'm coming up empty."

"Bullshit."

"Fitch—"

"Sorry, Lieutenant."

"I understand."

"We live in a police state. You can track anybody."

"I don't know anything about that."

"It's me, remember."

"I know, sorry. But I'm telling you, I can't locate him."

I chewed on it. "What about going at it another way?"

"We're really pushing it."

"Lieutenant, can I ask you something?"

"Shoot," he said.

"You know that big box you were carrying around when we had coffee?" I was thinking about that contraption that I'd seen him with and that I'd seen other cops using at the real estate protest.

"What about it?"

"You tell me," I said. "What are you up to?"

"Fitch, did I detect a threatening tone?"

"I'm just curious."

He didn't speak for a second. Then he half chuckled. "A curious Fitch is a dangerous thing. Leave well enough alone on our new hardware. Mind your business. Everything has been lawyered. I'm told that whatever we're doing with these boxes is close enough to being constitutional. But I'd just as soon not have you poking around. So what's your other idea for finding your spouse?"

I told him: Do surveillance on the Deuce and his family. Check the whereabouts of Danny and Lester Wollop and the Shipper.

"You're asking a lot." He paused. "Speaking of which, I did some checking about the Donogue kid, like you asked."

"Yeah?"

"Squeaky-clean. Bit of a hole in his record for six months or so when it looks like he was off the grid. No credit requests, that sort of thing—about a year ago. But he's young. May not mean much."

"Okay, thanks. Lieutenant, you help me find Terry and it'll be only one-way favors from now on. You'll have me by the balls."

"I'll get back to you ASAP."

I turned my attention back to Floyd's parents' house and then looked down at my phone. I couldn't pinpoint what nagged at me. A ghost idea, a whiff of clue that was too indistinct, too amorphous to name. I glanced at my call list. What was it?

I looked back at Floyd's parents' house, dismounted the bike, and walked around to the back.

I hopped a waist-high, chain-link fence without pausing to think whether I'd get dog-bit. Usually, that's rule number one in the PI business: watch for dog. Luckily, it wasn't relevant here. The only things taking up space in the small backyard were old electronics. It looked like a computer graveyard, which struck me as odd given that this was supposedly his parents' house. I was starting to wonder. I stepped over and around the crap and made my way to the ratty back door. I peered through the top half into a kitchen that looked about as well kept as the backyard. I knocked. Nothing. I peeked at the neighboring houses, and seeing nothing, I put my elbow through the glass above the handle. The leather absorbed most of the sound and any risk to my person.

I walked inside and nearly puked. I hadn't inhaled something this noxious since breaking up the Garlic Boys' hideout in the old sock factory. It screamed: bachelor engineer. Discarded cereal boxes, a piece of curled yellow cheese stuck to the fridge, something on the counter that might have once been sushi. I covered my nose with the inside of my elbow and knew at that point that Floyd definitely was not there. He'd have since appeared. After all, he should've been up. It was nearly . . . Hell! It was nearly eight. I was supposed to be meeting the Donogue lawyer in just a few minutes.

With all the finesse of an elephant, I cruised through the cottage, skimming for anything useful. In a bedroom, at a desk, I rummaged through scribbled notes. Most of them had no meaning. They looked like code, unreadable by me. At the bottom of the pile, a manila folder caught my eye. On the front, a name: *David Skellow*.

I'm not sure why but I opened it up, and there were more scribbled notes and an official document. It was a transcript from Colester College in Maine. It showed that this guy, David Skellow, had gotten four A's and a B-plus in his first semester. Along the side of the transcript a handwritten note said *Da Raj,* and *pay dirt.*

I stuffed the curious but meaningless transcript into my pocket. I glanced around for anything else obvious in the way of evidence and, finding none, decamped to the bike, hit El Camino No Real, and practically flew to Snozzwanger, Veruca and Gloop.

In the lobby, I signed in and sat down and glanced at my phone. That number of Floyd's that nagged at me. Then I pulled out the other phone, the one from the Tarantula, and started flipping around in it.

Bingo. A hit.

No sooner had I realized what was nagging me—a huge revelation at that—than there was an orchestral noise, beautiful, like something to accompany the descent of angels. Then the music turned to a thumping version of the already thumping rock song "Eye of the Lion." It had been used in that boxing movie. Sure enough, the elevator door opened and a maroon carpet unfurled and there stood a tall woman in workout gear shadowboxing to the beat. She looked up. "Mr. Fitzgerald?"

"Fitch."

"Come on in. I won't bite."

Which clearly was not true. I put the phones away and followed.

TWENTY-TWO

SIXTEEN HUNDRED, ONE-EIGHTY, Harvard, Yale, JD, PhD in engineering, partner in name, and head of the new driverless division," she said.

"What's that?"

"SAT, LSAT, CV, honorifics, blah, blah. Just getting it out of the way. Most people want to know and we waste time as they dance around asking. Is that Naugahyde?" She glanced at my coat with pity she could not hide. She was lean in every facet, speedy metabolism incarnate. For just a second, I could imagine that she ate food and it burned instantly into muscle and then disappeared into the ether. We reached our floor and the elevator doors opened to an orchestral sound.

On the third floor, a receptionist behind a desk stood. "At ease, Alfred. Please bring Fitch the drink selection on his profile. This way," she said, and whisked to the left and I followed. Down the long corridor we walked until we reached the last door, the corner office, and she took four gulping strides and sat in a high-backed office chair behind the stately desk. Behind her, through corner-office windows, shone the Palo Alto Hills, and I ached for a second for Terry's suffering and possible fate and stuffed the feeling away.

"Your time is your time. I want to be respectful of that. What can I do for you?"

I caught my breath and realized from her tone that I might like this no-nonsense woman. Intense, sure, but pretense, no. She wore her sentiments on her sleeve, which was made of some multicolored, stretch athletic-wear fabric. I glanced at her shelves, which were filled not with books but models of cars—in unusual shapes and sizes.

"Driverless cars?" I asked.

She nodded. "I'm happy to mention that, but each half minute here counts."

"Is that what those are—the cars of the future?" I didn't really give a damn, but I also wasn't planning on paying this woman a cent and I wanted to set the tone that we could hash things out, not rush them along.

She nodded again, acknowledging that I'd permitted her to explain. "In a nutshell, it's a patent frenzy. Everything, every single part of the twenty-first century car, is in play—from the sensors that read the road, obviously, to the engine and electronics that control every aspect of steering, braking, nuanced response to road and weather conditions, and all the ancillary aspects of the experience that computers will take over from the primates." She smiled and shook her head. "You can only imagine the things people are coming up with."

"Such as?"

"We just filed ten patents for a guy from MIT for something he calls EnRage. It's a driverless road rage system, soup to nuts.

If a car cuts off another car, the system can determine if the appropriate response is honking or flipping a middle finger or racing up ahead to cut off the other car. You don't even need to use your own middle finger. The technology employs a projection system to simulate a bird-flipping so that the driver doesn't have to do anything."

I shook my head, like: *absurd*.

"Yeah, maybe. But this is the patent economy. Captain Don knew that, obviously."

"How so?"

She studied me. "Listen, tell me why you're here."

I nodded. "Indulge me for just one more second—on this patent thing. How do you mean that they are the economy?"

For the first time, and just for an instant, a look of curiosity mixed with concern crossed her face. She wiped it off so quickly that most people wouldn't have noticed, but that's what they pay me for—noticing the small stuff.

"You obviously know that a patent holder effectively controls a new innovation."

"Check."

"Which gives the patent holder the right to license technology, share in royalties, or extract revenue in any number of ways. That doesn't mean all patents have value or, at least, immediate value. Sometimes, a patent gets filed and approved and sits fallow for a few years and then suddenly becomes relevant. Who knows, someone might actually want a driverless middle finger and then the patent becomes an ATM."

"Spitting out cash."

"So what can I do for you? I do want to respect anything to do with the estate, but I've got an eight forty-two with a guy injured by a garage with a faulty disclaimer. Allegedly."

I reached into my back pocket and pulled out the three sheets of paper I'd found in *The Selfish Gene*. I laid them on the desk next to a photo of her with three kids and a husband and a large fish they'd nabbed on a boat called the *Institution*.

"These are?"

"A last offering from Captain Don."

"Offering?"

"An idea. A new piece of . . . software code."

"Respectfully, what does that have to do with you?"

"Let me turn the tables on that one. Why are you seeing me today?"

"You made an appointment." She leaned back in her chair, settling in for some low-grade verbal sparring she had no intention of losing. She was in her element.

"Sure I did. I'm sure the great Veruca Sap makes time for every dick on the planet."

"You've got a checkbook just like everyone else."

"I doubt that. I assume you checked with Tess Donogue."

She twirled in her chair ever so slightly, a tiny tell, then said: "I'm not at liberty to disclose but, yes, off the record, we checked with her after you made the appointment. And, in case you're wondering, she's agreed to pay the tab should you malinger."

So Captain Don's daughter knew I was here and approved of it.

"Back to the matter at hand," I said, gesturing to the three sheets of paper.

Veruca picked them up and smoothed them out in front of her on the desk and sat looking, muttering "mm-hmm" and "aha" and "yes." She looked up. "Interesting," she said. "This appears to be—"

She was interrupted by a loud buzzing. It came from her phone. She looked so exasperated I thought she might smash the thing, and then paved over the look. She pressed a button. "I thought I asked not to be disturbed."

"I know, I'm sorry, Ms. Sap. It's important, um, an important call."

"Who is it?" She looked at me and mouthed, *Sorry*.

"Bono," said her receptionist.

She shook her head. "Put him through." She picked up her handset and held it to her ear. "Darling," she said, and smiled. Then she seemed to look perplexed. She pulled the headset from her ear and looked at it. She pushed the button on the phone on her desk. "There's no one on the line," she said to her receptionist.

"Oh, I'm so sorry, Ms. Sap. I think it was one of those automated programs that makes sure our phone is ringing and that you can be reached."

"Are you serious?!"

"It's quite useful, Ms. Sap. What if our phones weren't ringing and we didn't know it?"

Sap shook her head and then slammed the phone down so hard that pens flew from the desk. Then she regained her composure.

"You won't be billed for that. Where were we?"

"You were telling me what that is."

"At first blush, there are a few things here," she said. She explained that the first part of the document—the part that was in

English and I could read—mentioned this law firm as trustee of the Donogue estate.

"That has already been established," she said. "Nothing new there."

"Can you read it?"

"More or less."

"You can?" I was surprised because Floyd had told me that he needed hours to figure it out. Then again, I had just realized about ten minutes ago in the lobby that Floyd was a whopping fat liar and maybe much more dangerous than I realized.

"Of course I can read it. I'm an engineer and part borg"—she smiled as if telling a joke but I wasn't sure—"and this isn't that complex, I mean, in general terms. It's from the mind of Captain Don, so I'm sure it's more nuanced than I'm giving it credit for."

"So . . ."

"So it's code, obviously. It's a messaging system of some kind, a way to send secure messages, is what it looks like. If you're wondering how I know that it's because, as an intellectual property specialist, I look at a million pieces of code and start to see patterns. Not because I'm a borg"—she smiled—"or is it?" Another smile, then she got serious again and continued to explain that she'd need to run the code to get the details.

"How long would that take?"

She shrugged. "Couple of hours, tops. We do this stuff all the time so that we can tell if something is original enough to patent."

"Do it."

She blinked, put off momentarily by my command. "Of course."

At this moment of standstill, a natural pause, I found myself wondering what was so important about this innovation—this not particularly fancy piece of code—that it would be hidden away.

"At that point, you can decide what you, or the family, want to do with the code. If it's patentable, then, of course, we can file for you."

"Uh-huh." I just had this feeling I wasn't getting anywhere.

"I'm not sure to what extent you're working on behalf of the family, but we may want to consider putting it in a trust."

"Yeah, okay." Whatever.

"That's really the only way for the family to benefit—at this point."

"At what point?"

"Well, you know, presuming that the Captain is . . . y'know, well, that Mr. Donogue, our wonderful innovator, passed."

I perked up. "What are you saying?"

"Nothing. He was a great man, that's all. I'm looking for the right honorific."

"Not that part—the part about him dying, and the family benefiting. What was that part?"

"Just the obvious. If he's dead, clearly, he no longer holds the patents. To put it in crass fashion: he expires and his patent rights expire with him. Unless they get put in a trust. There are ways."

"So . . ." I paused, realizing what she'd said. "You hang on to your patents as long as you're alive."

"Yep." She nodded as if to say this went without saying.

"May I ask just two more questions?"

She looked at the clock. Our time was up. "Sure. You can have the seconds Bono took up. That guy . . ." She smiled as if talking about an old friend who could nag.

"Captain Don's estate, all his patents, are they held in a trust—the kind you're describing?"

"That's the family's business, Fitch. Your other question?"

"You represent Lester Wollop—in his divorce proceedings?"

"Same answer, family business. In general, I can say that we often represent both sides in a transaction, but when we do that, the lawyers are segregated into different cages . . . Not cages, did I say cages? I meant: parts of the building. On such matters, we have a Chinese wall. In this case, I do mean Chinese wall, built in China, yes, I'm sure you saw those stories in the *Post*. It's ridiculous, the accusations."

"What are you talking about?"

"Nothing. We took heat for being early to have our Chinese wall made in China. Of course it was made in China. It was a *Chinese* wall. But some of the workers spent too many hours in the factory and there was a fire. We knew nothing about it. Nothing. And as soon as we learned about it, we took very firm steps and now our entire supply chain and all manufacturers have been vetted as humanitarian by Amnesty International."

"You're doing it," I said.

"Doing what?"

"Talking like these people. Sounding nuts."

"When in Rome. And I'm Caesar," she said, and smiled, in on the joke. "See your own way out. We'll be in touch about the program."

TWENTY-THREE

OUTSIDE, IN FRONT of the building, a guy wearing a suit and tie stood with a sign hanging around his neck that said: *Smoker*. I took out my phone. "No pictures," he said. "No Instacharm. Please. I've humiliated my family enough."

I wasn't intending to take a photo, never crossed my mind.

He pleaded: "It was *pot*. I swear it. But they didn't believe me. It only *looked* like a cigarette."

"What are you talking about?"

"I'm doing public penance, for smoking. The Scarlet Letter *C*."

Cigarette. I walked past him and used the phone for what I'd intended to do in the first place: look up the two things that were bugging me about Floyd. One was his phone number. I glanced at it, and then looked at the burner phone I'd picked up from the dead Tarantula—the guy we'd found in the alley frothing at the mouth.

It was what I thought: the Tarantula had used his phone to call Floyd. It was a number in the 408 area code, the very same number that I'd called and texted when I'd called Floyd myself.

But there was more. A day earlier, I'd used the Tarantula's

phone to check the very same 408 number. When I'd called it, I'd gotten a voice mail saying it was Danny Donogue's phone. So who did the phone belong to—Floyd or Danny?

I hit the number from the Tarantula's phone and it rang once and a voice-mail message came on: "Hello, you've reached Danny, at the beep, you know what to do."

I hung up.

Then I called the same number, but this time I called from my phone (not the Tarantula's). After one ring, voice mail picked up. "It's Floyd, you know what to do."

What the hell?

"Hey, pal," a voice said behind me.

I turned and there on the sidewalk stood the guy with the smoking sign around his neck. He leaned in close.

"Can I bum a cigarette?"

"Get lost."

"Wait, listen, being out here is so stressful. I've never smoked before. I was framed. I just want one, y'know, to take the edge off."

"Lemme ask you a question," I said.

"Yeah, sure." I could see he thought this might get him some tobacco.

"Is it possible to program your phone so that different people calling get different voice mails?"

"So your wife gets one response and your mistress gets another?"

"I'm gay."

"Are you accusing me of being racist? God, I smoked one damn cigarette! I mean, one *doobie*. For, um, glaucoma. I'm not a racist!"

"You're not a racist, fine, good. Is it possible—the voice-mail thing?"

"Of course. Are you, like, disabled? I'm sorry, I didn't realize."

"Thanks, pal."

"So you'll help me out."

But I was already walking again.

"C'mon, pal!" he yelled.

I pushed him out of my head and put the pieces together or made my best guesses. Floyd had been in contact with the Tarantula but then had programmed his voice mail so that if the Tarantula called it would seem like the voice mail belonged to Danny. Why?

Of course!

He had done that for my benefit. He realized that I'd taken the dead Tarantula's phone and didn't want me to figure out that he (Floyd) and the Tarantula assassin had been in contact. That, at least, was my theory. Only way to prove it would be to get Floyd to fess up, and I'd have to find him first.

I arrived at the motorcycle and straddled it and thought some more. If I was right, why was Floyd in contact with the Tarantulas? How did they all connect together?

I remembered that I had another piece of evidence to explore and I pulled it from my pocket: the transcript from a college called Colester, located in Maine. It was for a freshman named David Skellow. He'd attended Colester two years earlier. I called up the Colester web page and found a link to "student and alum fotobook." It was password-protected.

In the Gooble browser, I typed in "David Skellow" and I clicked for "images." They started to materialize, and the first few belonged to people who, from their advanced years, I doubted were freshmen. Then I got a direct hit—a picture for David Skellow that I recognized.

"No way," I heard myself mumble.

My phone rang.

"Watch out," the person said by way of a greeting.

"Tess?"

"I just got another message from my dad. It says: 'Watch out!'"

"What does that mean?"

"Beats me. But Daddy hated exclamation points, so I thought it might be important."

"Gimme a break."

It was all I could do not to hang up. I laid my head back on my neck, thinking. "Tess, I've got a question."

"Sure. Sorry, it's hard to hear you. I'm underneath the table."

"Why?"

"Daddy was warning me about something. I'm sure of it."

"Okay, listen. Did Danny attend college?"

"What? No! What?"

"Did Danny attend Colester College?"

"Why would you ask me that?"

"Tess! I'm looking at a picture of a kid who attended Colester College and he's a dead ringer for Danny."

"My son has been very clear that he, y'know, did not attend college and that college is something that people go to if they, um, can't do. He can handle things on his own. School of hard knocks and all that."

"Cut the bullshit."

"Please don't make things any worse. I love him and he thinks I'm a terrible, greedy person."

"Hold on."

Down El Camino No Real, I saw them coming. Two MINIs, fire red. Half a block away. Tarantulas for sure.

I turned the key in the ignition and revved the engine.

"It's the Apocalypse!" Tess yelled. "That's what he was warning me about!"

"That's my motorcycle," I said. "Not the Apocalypse." I didn't add: *Holy shit, could Captain Don have been warning me? From beyond? But how?*

As the MINIs neared, I gunned it west on Page Avenue, the phone still to my ear. "AHHHHHHH!" I could hear Tess shrieking, and I could imagine that she was mistaking my six hundred horses for something terrible. "Lester. Hold me!"

I let the phone slip into my pocket and watched the MINIs fade with my speed.

Then I saw the same MINIs in front of me. I thought for a second I was going nuts when I realized, with a glance in the rearview, that the pair was still behind me and this was another set, matching, fire-red MINIs.

I skidded a sharp right onto a side street and hit the accelerator. Bad move, I realized instantly. This was an industrial park, which I promptly surmised was likely a closed loop. A glance behind me showed four MINIs. I could feel the cool comfort of weaponry beneath my heavy jacket as I kept straight ahead on the park's main drag. Arteries to the left and right offered little possibility; both ended in a cul-de-sac. When I neared a dead end, I took the last artery right. It ended abruptly in a parking lot where a curved two-story building wrapped around the cul-de-sac and a bit of a crowd; there was some shouting in the parking lot near the front—about twenty-five yards from me. Calm suddenly washed over me. This wasn't as challenging a situation as I'd initially thought. MINIs, no matter how many, couldn't chase me over the grass between these buildings and back out to the main drag. I could see my exit—a paved alleyway between the building directly in front of me and one next to it marked *The Cloud*.

I turned the bike to go and looked back to discover the four MINIs were following. But three of them had stopped at the right turn to this artery while one glided forward slowly, its driver waving a white flag out the window. I put my feet down on the ground and steadied the mechanical beast I was riding. I put my hand inside my jacket and pulled out the smaller of the guns. I left it hanging by my side. The MINI stopped fifteen yards from me. The passenger door opened. I recognized Dutch Abraham, the son of Deuce. Holding a white flag in his left hand, he raised his arms, surrender. The driver remained seated.

I wasn't buying it.

I did a quick look around. Behind me, the crowd seemed to be engrossed in some action taking place in their midst but I couldn't figure what. In front of me, the MINIs remained stopped while Dutch Abraham made his way slowly in my direction. No weapons, near as I could tell. A smattering of parked cars nearby might've provided cover for a Tarantula, but it didn't stand to reason that one of them had anticipated my arrival here and had hidden.

"May I approach?"

I gestured with the gun. *Come on ahead.* Dutch didn't much look like he wanted to do that. He looked stricken.

"Come on, kid. I won't shoot you unless you give me a reason."

He looked over his shoulder at the MINI driver, who nodded, as if to say: *go ahead*. Dutch took two steps forward. Then another two. Ten feet away. "Close enough," I said.

He looked at his watch.

"Seven hours. You have seven more hours."

"You like the family business?"

He tried to square his jaw, I could see it. The adolescent had no chest to puff out but made an effort nonetheless. "What matters in this world is what you do, not how old you are, Detective."

That nonsense mantra again. "Killers," I said. "Your dad can dress it up any way he wants to but that's what they are and what you'll be."

"He said you'd do that."

"Do what?"

"Try to test my loyalties. That's what the smart ones do, he told me. So forget about it. You've got seven hours." He took another step forward.

"Did he tell you I'd shoot you if you got too close?"

"He said you'd threaten to. Then he told me that we do things the right way. I am duty bound to tell you that you have seven hours to get us the thing you promised you'd get us or the other thing will happen that we promised would happen."

"Yeah? Did he tell you what thing that is?"

"No." He kicked the ground.

"He's going to kill my husband."

Dutch was looking down.

"After torturing him," I continued. "That's the family business."

He looked up, searching, trying like hell to look the part.

"This your first assignment, Dutch?"

"First one for AP credit. I've gone on deliveries. Seven hours. Capiche?"

I snorted a laugh. "I get the picture. Get the hell out of here."

He took another step forward. I raised the pistol. He mouthed something I couldn't make out. I kept the gun trained in his direction.

"Seven hours," he said, and then looked me dead in the eye, "or he'll be swimming with the dolphins."

He looked quickly down. Out the window of the MINI, a Tarantula craned his neck. "Let's roll, Dutch." He looked at me. "Seven hours," he said.

"I did that already!" Dutch said to the Tarantula.

The Tarantula looked at me, then at Dutch. "Did you give him the survey?"

"Oh yeah." He reached into his back pocket.

"Don't even think about it, kid." Finger on the trigger.

"Take it easy."

"Don't talk to me that way, you little shithead."

"Easy," said the Tarantula in the car. "That's Deuce's firstborn you're talking to."

"Good for him. He tries anything and I'll blow a hole in his face and then yours." I almost laughed at my macho talk, but I was trying to make a show of it. Dutch had tried to send me a message—the dolphin thing—I was almost sure of it. If so, I didn't want him busted.

"If you got something for me, reach slowly into your pocket and take whatever it is and put it on the ground."

He did as I said. A moment later, he'd dropped a folded square of paper on the ground. He turned to go.

"Dutch"—the Tarantula leaned out—"give him the instructions."

The kid turned back to me. "It's a survey."

"What?"

"Your experience is important to us. The Tarantulas value your feedback. This short, one-page survey will help us learn how to improve the user experience."

"Get out of here, you little shitbag."

"Tell him 'bout the online thing," the Tarantula said.

Dutch rolled his eyes. "Of course, if you prefer, you can take the survey online. We're in the middle of a transition. Starting next year, we will be interacting with our users only online in an effort to save paper and respect the world's precious natural resources."

"You're drug dealers and killers."

The Tarantula yelled: "You can also scan that and e-mail it back if that's easier."

"Get the hell out of here."

"Let's go, kid," the Tarantula yelled. Then to me: "Seven hours! Six and change."

"I told him!" Dutch said.

He walked to the car and climbed inside. The MINI turned and exited, the other Tarantulas with it. I listened to my heartbeat and the voice inside my head: *swim with the dolphins.*

The kid was telling me something.

"Did you see that? Did you *see that shit*?" a voice said from behind me.

I turned to find a twentysomething dude with a bag slung over his shoulder. Behind him, the crowd dispersed. It occurred to me that he wasn't talking about the thing that had taken place with Dutch but was referring to whatever took place at the front of the parking lot. I eyed him. I didn't care what he was talking about, but he took the moment to keep talking. "You know that's been building, right? It was going to explode anytime and, boom, there it went. Are you with corporate? Nice ride."

"Just a bike messenger."

He looked skeptical, almost dangerously so. Like he might rat me out to someone or start spreading rumors about the weirdo in the parking lot. He was a purebred engineer, so unconcerned with appearances that he resented them, the way a homeowner resents a spider, the kind of guy who liked to show how smart he was even if it made him look awkward, maybe especially if it made him look awkward. I had to play along for a second, let him get his windbag out.

"What happened?"

"Brawl over the last Level Three charger. Guy from HR and the woman who heads direct marketing and they got to the last electric car charger at the same time. My friend in QA saw it from the beginning. At first, they were telling each other how much they liked the other person's car and how great it was for the environment, but then they just dove for the charger. They were rolling around on the ground and everyone was yelling "fight, fight, fight." And she leveled him. Leveled! Like the Black Widow from *Land Beyond*. Bloodied his nose. She hooked up her car and walked over to him and told him she really did like his car and she'd do a quick charge and text him when the charger was free. And you know what?"

"What?"

"This company is going places."

The dolphin, I thought. I knew how I could find out more.

"That's *exactly* the kind of people we need in marketing," he said. "If you want to make the move to a company with a big upside, I could introduce you to someone."

I had already revved the engine and started on my way.

TWENTY-FOUR

ON THE WAY to my destination, I drove by Floyd's. Still no presence I could detect. Still no answer on his phone. While I was paused, I called Lieutenant Gaberson. "Fitch," he answered. "This is fucked up."

"How's that?"

"Where are you at?"

"Around, Lieutenant. Why do you ask?"

"This is weird, that's all. We tracked the phone number—Terry's. It's . . . well, as far as we can tell . . . I'm not sure how to say this. It's off the grid."

"Like turned off?"

"Maybe. I guess. It's putting out a signal but from parts unknown."

"So Terry might've taken his phone with him and then the bad guys turned it off. Or they could've tossed it somewhere to throw off the scent."

"Fitch, I asked you where you are but I obviously know where you are: you're on the Peninsula, Menlo Park if I'm not mistaken," the lieutenant said.

"You're freaking me out."

"I'm not trying to. I'm trying to show you how easy this is. We've got this new phone surveillance technology. I put in the phone number and voilà. Of course, I wouldn't use it without the proper warrant. Nor would I ever, *ever*, intercept the contents of a conversation."

"What do you mean he's off the grid? What if the phone is turned off?"

"Could be. But before I go any further, we've got to clear something up."

"What's that?"

"This is our last conversation."

"Is that right?"

"Fitch, give me your word. I'm sticking my neck way out. I already warned you. We're facing a shit storm of legal trouble over the Adderall bust. Now you're dragging me into something with Deuce. They could sue us until we have to privatize. You hear me?"

"I hear you."

"I don't think you do. To the cops, you are persona non grata."

"Yes, Lieutenant, I'm signing on the dotted line. Now, for shit's sake, what have you got?"

"Okay, Terry's signal is down now, his phone probably off. But before it went dark, it went . . . I don't know. Like he's gone into the ether or a place with a different frequency. Only time I saw something like this was when we tracked a guy to North Korea, y'know, a totally different nation-state. He was importing counterfeit 'My Other Car Is a Tesla' bumper stickers."

"Like Terry's out of the country?"

"Maybe. Gone international." He paused. "Also weird. Same for the Deuce. You asked me to track him. He's in some international locale but I can't get a read on it."

"What the hell?"

"Fitch, can I ask you something?"

"Shoot."

"Did Terry leave a note?"

"What do you mean?"

"Do you think that Terry . . . is it possible that he . . ." Long pause. "How're things at home, is what I'm asking."

I figured what he was getting at—that Terry had picked up and left me. "Sure, Lieutenant. Maybe. I hadn't thought about it." There was no way. But it was in this moment that I realized I never 100 percent trusted the lieutenant and so he could think what he wanted.

"My old lady left me," he said. "Said I hogged our bandwidth."

"Is that all you got?" I asked. "On Terry."

"I'm sorry."

"I gotta run. Thank you, Lieutenant."

"What'd I say?"

"I gotta run."

I hung up.

One more quick call. After the second ring, Danny picked up.

"Hey, kid, you want to know who killed your grandfather?"

"Who is this?"

"Wrong day to be playing games, Danny."

I told him where to meet me.

I fired up the bike and headed back to the Palo Alto Hills. This was getting old but I was getting close, I sure hoped. Six hours and five minutes. I didn't doubt now that they'd kill him—Terry. Not if I was right about the scope of things. When billions of dollars are at stake, you don't leave any witnesses.

AS I NEARED the Donogue residence, I saw an old Volvo parked outside the gate. Danny sat inside, slunk down. I parked behind him on the dirt shoulder, walked over, and let myself in. I pulled the smaller of the guns from my left pocket and laid it across my lap.

"Howdy, Danny, or should I say David?"

"Who?"

"David. Skellow."

He reached for the door handle. I reached for the gun. He paused.

"This has nothing to do with my grandfather."

"Maybe it does and maybe it doesn't. I'll be the judge."

Lines creased Danny's forehead. He looked every bit the college freshman, razor burn from when he'd last shaved, sweat on his lip, fidgety, not yet three-quarters a man.

"It's not a crime to go to college," he said through his teeth.

"You took the words right out of my mouth."

He turned to me. "So what's the big deal?"

"That's my point, Danny. No one cares that you went to college."

He cleared his throat. "What happened with Grandpa?"

"I don't think so. Not until you answer my question."

"Which is what?"

"Who are you—Shirli? You heard the question: Did you go to college?"

From my phone came her voice: "This is Shirli. I can help you find a collage."

I flicked off the phone. I obviously knew the answer to the question I was asking Danny. But this served as confessional and test. Would he tell me what I knew from his transcript? How trustworthy was this canny kid?

The transcript held other interesting clues in that it had the words "pay dirt" and "Da Raj." And it was in the possession of a geek named Floyd, a guy who seemed desperate for seed capital. I was figuring I wasn't the first guy to figure out that Danny doubled as David Skellow and had attended Colester College.

But Danny wasn't giving an inch. He stared straight ahead.

"Maybe it wasn't you," I said. "David Skellow got a B-plus in computer science. I figure you're way better than that. You're a Donogue, after all."

Still nothing.

"Okay, kid. I'll let the cops sort it all out. You can go."

"Wait."

"I'm tired of waiting. A picture says you and David Skellow are the same guy."

"Just let me think for a second," he pleaded.

"What is there to think about? Good-bye, Danny."

"I have a lawyer. One of the best. She did the disclaimers for Gooble and every player in the virtual military-industrial complex."

"I thought you said there was nothing illegal about going to college."

No answer. The problem was that I didn't really want to turn

Danny over to the cops, at least not yet. I needed his help to find the Spirit Box.

"You went to Colester College for a semester."

"Yes," quietly. Then he looked up: "Yes. I went to Colester." He looked at me. "I thought it would be good to get a college education. Because my grandfather wanted me to get one and he was usually right about everything. Okay?"

"And you resented him for that."

"No, I don't know. Maybe."

"And so you came home and killed him."

"What? No. No!" He shook his head.

I realized I'd pressed too hard too fast. I could feel the clock ticking in my pocket, four hours and counting. But getting someone to spill took more than brute force.

"Why the fake name?"

He clenched his teeth together, every bit the adolescent. Then: "Did you ever hear of Priorit-E?"

Lord, another dot-com teaching moment. "I haven't had the pleasure."

He explained that Priorit-E was an app for your phone. It entailed programming in your top five priorities for the week. If by midweek you hadn't checked off at least two items, the phone started calling you names.

"What's your point?"

"Just listen. By the end of the week, if you hadn't completed at least four, the phone badgered the hell out of you. Shitbag, nowhere man, lazy bitch."

"Watch yourself."

"At its peak, Priorit-E had six-point-two million downloads. Pretty heady stuff for a high school sophomore."

"It was your app."

Yep, he said. He had come up with it, he said, and became, briefly, a darling of the can-do community. "Captain Don Jr., they called me. And Junior Don and Don Juan Don."

He accumulated millions of Twipper followers and took on the mantle he'd been given, touting school-of-hard-knocks homilies and linking to examples of other young studs innovating ahead of their time.

"You became the poster child for the who-needs-college movement. It would've looked awfully hypocritical to all those Twipper followers if they'd discovered that their man-child had logged some hours in an actual classroom."

"It was great."

"What was?"

"Colester. I was just another guy there. In the virtual world, as Danny, I was a big shot, the guy who'd done it by age fourteen and would surely do it again. But then, at college, I could just be anonymous. It's funny. You think of the virtual world as being the anonymous one. But no one knew me at Colester. I was just another funky kid from California, although one who kicked some absolute ass on Wife of Fugitive VI, the Legend of Fugitive, in dorm video-game tournaments."

"Dare to dream."

"I didn't want to be Captain Donogue's grandson and I didn't want to go against all the stuff I'd put out there on social media during high school."

"Respectfully, Priorit-E doesn't sound like great shakes."

"That's what Grandpa said." The kid looked at me. "He was right. Of course it wasn't great. It wasn't an innovation, no matter what *BusinessGeek* called it. It wasn't a time-saver or an efficiency maker or a niche or anything else. It was a nasty name-calling shit-bag. Though, seriously, Fitch, it is very funny to hear Shirli call someone a lazy bitch." He half smiled and I found myself laughing, almost connecting to this kid's awareness.

"So you had it both ways; to the kids at Colester, you were another Joe, and to the Twipper followers, you were the can-do kid."

"Something like that," he mumbled.

"But you came home."

"Grandpa got sick with something or other."

"Is that it?"

"You saw Grandpa's deathbed video yourself."

"And you figured you'd help him along into the afterlife?"

"What? No. I told you." He looked down and then up at me. "Anyhow, I was home and I got this idea for Froom. And I met some guys at Incubator Wednesday and one of them was Raj."

"Da Raj. What about him?"

He clenched his teeth hard. This next part didn't seem like it would come easy, or maybe he was making a show of it. "Da Raj wasn't satisfied with fifty/fifty on Froom, okay? So one day he shows up at the office and he shows me David Skellow's transcript." He sighed. "My transcript. He wanted to go seventy-five/twenty-five for him to keep his mouth shut about Colester. At first, I was like: 'Dude, you can't run this without me.' And he was like: 'Dude, watch me.' And then I was like: 'Dude, you're messing with the wrong guy,' and then he was like—"

"Slow down."

Danny told me that he agreed to give Da Raj sixty/forty and the title of Da Raj. But then, he said, Da Raj upped the ante. "He wanted the Spirit Box," Danny said. Sitting in the car, sun getting to noon above us on a dry Silicon Valley day, he looked like a pleading little boy. "I didn't have it. I told him. It wasn't done. Grandpa wasn't finished or, if he was, wouldn't tell anybody. It was just an idea, I told Raj."

"I can't figure how you got the Tarantulas to kill Da Raj."

"Oh yeah, I'm gonna kill a guy because he threatens to tell the world I went to college?" He looked at me. "Sure, I guess, some guys would do it. Not me. Hell, I could hardly butcher a cow."

"But you did."

"Anyone ever tell you you're a racist?"

"I really don't get that—calling somebody a racist. It's happened to me like five times in the last few days."

"You should hear Shirli say it." He half smiled again, winsome.

"So, Danny, I'll play along: Who do you figure killed Da Raj?"

He smirked. "You think you can protect me, Detective?"

"From whom?"

"From all of them. These guys are killers, whoever they are. I don't know all of them. I—"

"Danny, lemme make it plain: when I'm done, there won't be anyone left to be afraid of."

"You always talk like this?"

"Who killed Da Raj?"

"Hear me out. The way you talk, you'd have a huge Twipper following. Quippy, tough-guy stuff. Smart, concise. You should get a handle."

"I won't ask again: Who killed Da Raj?"

He sighed. "If I give you a name, will you, y'know, keep me out of it?"

"No."

"See, that stuff will kill on Twipper. Anyhow . . ." He looked out the window again. "My guess is a guy named Floyd Chiansky."

He turned to me and I knew now he was telling me the truth, laying it out.

"Who's that?"

"I'm guessing you know, dick. Guy from Colester. A fellow student of mine, freshman, total dud, I thought at first but cool in that he's half Chinese, half Polish, and half Thai, lucky bastard. One day, he comes to me after a late-night video-game and study session and accuses me of being Danny Donogue. Doesn't ask me, tells me. He was a few years older, a TA in computer science. I'd seen him before. I denied it, but that was hopeless."

"How'd he know?"

"Some facial recognition software he was working on. He uncovered like five secret identities in the freshman class. Me and four others who had told their parents they attended Yale."

It was coming together. Danny said that Floyd told him he'd keep Danny's secret. Then, little by little, Floyd started making demands. He wanted to meet a few people in the Valley, then he wanted some seed capital. Next thing Danny knew, he said, Floyd had showed up in the Valley, renting a house in Menlo Park.

It had the ring of truth. It also had some holes. I couldn't pinpoint them on the fly, but I sensed them.

"You loved your grandfather?"

He nodded.

"I love my husband."

"I don't see—"

"He's been kidnapped. He's going to be killed, Danny. I need your help to get him back."

"What can I—"

"Spirit Box. I need the Spirit Box. I need you to give it to me so I can trade it for Terry."

"I would if I could. It's not finished, as far as I know. Or if it is finished, I don't know where it is."

"Your grandfather is tweeping from beyond."

"Maybe he's got it. Maybe you should ask him." It was facetious, even deeply sarcastic. Then, "Or . . ." His face lit up.

"What?"

"Maybe I can ask him!" Far from sarcastic this time. He seemed genuinely enthusiastic, lacking entirely the adolescent show of ennui. He explained his idea: he could try to communicate with his grandfather. "You think he's out there?" he asked.

I shrugged. "I'm sure your mother has tried to reach him."

"I don't know. We're obviously not that close these days."

"You're about to be," I said. I held up the gun and pointed across the street to the Donogue estate.

"No . . ."

"Yep. Get in there and do everything you can to contact your grandfather, if he's . . ." Hell, what was I saying? I was grasping at straws. "You've got an hour. I'm going to make another stop and

I'll be back. Get me something or the cops hear what's been going on. Maybe your story about David Skellow checks out and maybe it doesn't. If not, the cops will get to the bottom of it."

"An hour. But . . ."

"Fifty-nine minutes. Get going."

TWENTY-FIVE

ALAN KLIPPER LOOKED like a mess when he met me at the invisible fence. "Nothing left for us to talk about," he said.

"My husband's been kidnapped."

This perked him up and he buzzed me in, though he stopped me in the foyer, crossed his arms, and made it clear through body language he'd prefer to keep this short. He wore a terrycloth bathrobe and slippers.

"I've got a boating question."

"I thought this was about your husband. Is he okay?" He peered over my shoulder, warily. He was nervous, but at the same time acting so nonchalant about my telling him Terry had been kidnapped. Not the kind of thing you hear every day. He stood two feet from a mirror hung on the wall behind him and I could see in his reflection how hunched and old he looked. I didn't remember his being this way yesterday—practically frail.

"No, not okay. Kidnapped. By bad guys. And you can help me find him."

"What?" This seemed to shake him and he fought to focus; he

looked like he'd been up all night. Maybe he hadn't heard me say the first time that Terry'd been kidnapped. "I don't understand. How can I help? I think maybe you should go."

I rocked forward on my toes, like I might step. It was a trick I learned in the ATF; a simple weight shift into a more aggressive stance could help me deduce the mind-set of the other person. A bad guy with ill intent, for instance, might move his hands to his belt to grab a weapon, while a less hostile bad guy might step back or put his hands over a cherished body part.

The Shipper practically fell into the mirror. "What do you want?"

"Say I'm in a boat, Alan, how do I connect to a cell phone?"

"Mr. Fitch, I don't see why this is so important that you'd barge in here. You're scaring me."

"Fitch. I didn't scare you yesterday."

"You weren't asking bizarre boating questions yesterday." His voice seemed to recover some dignity. He remembered that people *asked* for his time, pleaded for it, not demanded it. He smoothed out his bathrobe.

I leaned forward again. He stood his ground. "Get out."

"Or what?"

"Or I'll call the police."

"I'll wait," I said. "You have lemonade?"

He laughed, somewhat appreciatively—I wasn't intimidated and he sensed it. "When I'm on a cell phone on a boat, one of your boats, a gigantic yacht in the middle of the Pacific, can my phone be traced?"

"Not necessarily."

"Because the call comes from international waters."

"Depends on how the boat is registered and to whom and what kind of scrambler is used on the signal."

"Say your boat—the *Last Dolphin*."

"I don't—"

Now I took a full step forward and he lunged backward defensively. "You sure do. I saw the painting in your office. The *Last Dolphin*. I'll show you." Before he could respond, I walked through the dining hall to the right, leaving the pathetic man leaning against the wall. I passed the living room with the vegetable watching cat videos and wound up in his office. As I expected, the Shipper quickly was on my heels.

"Out!"

I looked at the painting that covered the safe. The *Last Dolphin*. I was thinking about what Dutch Abraham had said: Terry would swim with the dolphins. A message, it seemed to me. Had to be. And Lieutenant Gaberson had told me that he couldn't trace Terry's cell phone, if he even had his cell phone on him. It seemed to be somewhere international. So did the phone of the Deuce.

International waters. Or maybe a boat with its own damn zip code.

I grabbed Klipper by the lapels and I hoisted him in the air and slammed him on the desk. I had to be careful not to kill the frail technocrat but wanted him to think I might. "Where is it?"

"I don't know!"

"Where is the *Last Dolphin*?" I repeated.

"I don't know! I don't. Please believe me."

I loosened my grip a tad. "You have a boat called the *Last Dolphin*."

"Yes, of course. Everyone knows that. Did you read the piece in *Pacific Monthly*? I just want to say that those photos were taken before we redid the pet salon. So the experience has gone up orders of magnitude, especially if you're a dog. Where was I?"

"Where is the boat?"

"I don't know."

"I think you do."

"Let me up."

I let him up.

"It docks at the San Francisco Yacht Club, okay," he said. "It would be reasonable to assume that it's there."

"But you know it's not there. You just said that—five times . . . that you don't know where it is."

He grimaced. "Technically, I'm not contradicting myself. I don't *know* it's there or not there, but it would be reasonable to assume that it's there."

"Who did you give it to?"

"No one!"

"Was it someone from the Donogue family? Tess or Lester? Was is Danny?"

"Of course not, Danny's like a son to me."

"Interesting."

"What's interesting about that? Our families have known each other for years."

"It's interesting that you are pals with the grandson of a murdered man, and you all want the same thing—the Spirit Box. I count that as interesting."

He laughed. "You know what? You're just like the rest of us, Fitch."

"Meaning what?"

"Meaning you're trying to make connections between things, establish patterns, solve problems. But in your case, there's one big difference: You're doing it in a *way* less lucrative fashion. If I might speak freely, that's because you're doing it less ably than the rest of us. You're putting food on the table, sure, that's good enough. It won't win you any medals or patents or retirement money. If you can afford a house in the Bay Area, it's probably because you and your partner work crazy hours and squeeze into a box."

"Where's the boat?"

He moved five inches from my face, fighting distance. If this were a pickup basketball game, he was more than close enough to invite a shove and maybe a punch.

"It would be cliché to call you a dinosaur, Fitch. But I've earned the right to say any damned thing I want. You are a dinosaur—and a cliché. A tough guy cloaking himself in justice to push people around. But justice in my book is measured by market forces and innovation and shiny things that blink that, even if they don't bring eternal life, make you feel good and make this life worth living. I don't know where the *Last Dolphin* is and I don't care, and you know why? Because I have ten more yachts just like it and ten more under construction. One so small that you need a microscope to take a shit. Or, if you prefer a shorter version of this soliloquy, here it goes: go fuck yourself, dick."

Then he shoved me. Tried to. Gave me a push that I barely felt and I gently pushed him away, like swatting a child. On his way backward, his face contorted into fierce determination, and he snagged a paperweight shaped like a ship. I shook my head, urging him to think twice. With great effort, he lifted the paper-weight over his head and took a step forward and swung it at me. I ducked. Instinctively, I gave the guy a roundhouse. It was a whopper. The one that had been building up for days.

It sent the Shipper flying across the desk. He landed with a flop and tumble and crashed against the wall and I could see that he was knocked out cold and something else: he had a smile on his face. I knew right then that the Shipper had gotten what he wanted. He'd gotten himself knocked out so he wouldn't have to say another word. Hell if he hadn't out-negotiated me. Maybe he didn't know where the *Last Dolphin* was located. If he did, he wasn't going to tell me. He'd goaded me into giving him his escape route.

Exactly why he'd do that eluded me and, at the moment, didn't matter so much. What mattered was the *Last Dolphin* and the clock. Two hours and fifty-eight minutes until I faced a prospect I didn't want to think about. I did some searching around the desk, looking for clues or phone numbers, whereabouts, and what have you. Nothing.

On the way out, I passed the lady of the house drooling to the beat of cat videos. It put another beat in my step. I was planning to grow old with Terry, care for him as devotedly as the Shipper did his wife. If we both survived the next few hours.

TWENTY-SIX

I PULLED UP TO the gates of the Donogue residence and discovered Danny waiting there. I'd told him he had an hour to get what he could on the Spirit Box. I parked the bike next to him.

"Have you got something for me?"

"Maybe."

"Did you send a message to your grandfather?"

"I tried."

"Prove it."

He looked stricken. "How am I supposed to do that?"

"What did you say?"

"I said: 'Grandpa Don, are you out there?'"

He had tears in his eyes. Poor little chump didn't know which way was up. He couldn't tell what he was faking and what he was really feeling and neither could I.

"Yeah, so did you get a response?"

He let out a small sob. "'You can take it with you' and then an emoticon."

"What?"

"A note came back: 'You can take it with you' and then a smiley face."

"Your grandfather sent an emoticon from the grave?"

"I seriously doubt it, okay. My grandfather would've sooner sucked up to Steve Jobs than use an emoticon. I just don't think it's him. It's a fucking mind fuck."

I considered it. I asked myself whether I trusted this guy. I said: "Did you ask him about the Spirit Box?"

He nodded. A tear rolled down his cheek. "Same answer: 'You can take it with you,' and the smiley face."

"That's it?"

"That's it and then not another word, not a response, not a note."

"Danny, look at me."

He did.

"Do you think it's him—your grandfather?"

More tears, one on each cheek. It was my answer. I started the engine and left him standing in the dust. He was coming apart and I didn't want to be there for it, and besides, I had two hours and the most indistinct outline of a plan. A very bad plan but a plan.

ELRON DIDN'T SEEMED surprised to see me this time and Honey didn't even materialize. He asked me what I needed and we got right down to business. "Not a usual request," he said, "but none of yours are. I'll need forty-five minutes."

He finished in less than that while I paced in the green grass and silenced all my theories and the voices of people I'd encountered and focused on the plan. I didn't doubt that Deuce and his gang had Terry, and my gut told me they were on the *Last*

Dolphin. There was a reasonable chance that the yacht could be anywhere in the whole of the Pacific, which gave me zero chance of finding it in a million years, let alone two hours.

I had to start somewhere and that was at the San Francisco Yacht Club. After that, all I needed to do was sneak onto the boat, disarm the Adderall-fueled Tarantula crew, free Terry, and blast Deuce into his own hellfire afterlife.

That and $6.50 wouldn't even get me a latte. It didn't even qualify as a plan.

"Here ya go." Elron handed me the weapon. "You don't have any idea what you're doing, do you, Fitch?"

"I'm doing okay for a Thursday."

"It's Wednesday, Fitch."

Honey had emerged and the two of them stood arm in arm watching me speed off to parts unknown.

ANY OTHER TIME, I'd have loved this drive—weaving on the chopper among bumper-to-bumper vehicles on the 280. Even with the weight of the task ahead, I had to admit: it's no wonder people come here. Green hills rose on each side of the highway and to my left, the west, the ocean was less than an hour's drive away. And maybe the *Last Dolphin* and Terry in it.

I took Nineteenth Avenue through the city and crossed the Golden Gate Bridge. Midafternoon, sun totally blocked, wind sweeping the span. I stopped in the middle and pulled the bike to the right, to the chagrin of the cars behind me. Ignoring the honks, I looked for ships, big ones. There were three to the west of the bridge. One of them was clearly a container ship. Another too small to matter and a third was possibly the *Last Dolphin.*

No telling from here. To my right, in the bay, a mere handful of ships, none of them yacht size, then Alcatraz. Made me wonder: Could they have taken Terry to the prison island? Swim with the dolphins? Maybe the kid meant swim with the sharks—the mythological ones circling Alcatraz.

It wasn't lost on me that I was still so far from an answer. I was taking a flier. At least I was doing it at high revolutions per minute. I revved the engine and continued in the direction of the yacht club, which was located on the tip of Tiburon. So what if the plan was all wrong? What if there was no boat and no Terry? Deuce was bluffing. He'd give me another chance, right? Try as I might, I couldn't convince myself of that. I couldn't do anything but push forward and hope.

THE GUY IN the glass box at the gate looked at me like I *might* be suitable for chum. "I'm with Deuce," I said.

"This is a members-only club. Not that we discriminate against nonmembers." He had a black vest over a white shirt, a round face, an aggressive part in his hair, and glasses. "We very much value our nonmembers and people of all backgrounds and consider them our equals in every way except."

"Except they can't come in."

"They absolutely could come in—if they were members. That's how equal they are."

"Deuce," I repeated. "I'm here for him."

The guy pursed his lips. I read his name tag: *Dave.*

"Please, Dave. I won't cause any trouble."

"It's pronounced 'Dave,'" he said.

"Isn't that what I said?"

"It's a soft *a*. Erring more on the side of 'Dove.' My parents really were forward thinkers on vowels."

"Dove—"

"A tad harder on the *a*."

I was just about to bring out my gun when I noticed Dove or Dave or whatever studying me and then the bike. "What's the top speed on that thing?" he asked.

"I'd like to find out," I said, which was true but also this was my hitting the ball back over the net to keep this tiny spark of connection alive.

He looked at me and swallowed and then looked back at the bike. "Seat looks like it fits a pair." Dove or Dave bit his bottom lip. Uh-oh. He was flirting.

"I suppose it could, but I'm in a rush right now."

He looked at me like I'd promised him something and I could see the lonely in his exhale. I'd have to let him think what he wanted.

"You won't cause any trouble?"

"No, Dove, I won't. I promise."

"I'm working until nine," he said.

I half nodded and sped off and didn't get ten yards into the parking lot before my phone rang. Actually, I didn't hear it, but I felt the buzz against my leg. I thought I'd turned the damn thing off. The caller ID said: *Deuce McStein*.

And there was a text: *Your phone has been automatically turned on courtesy of Bono. U2 can feel safe that your battery is still working!*

I answered the phone. "What do you want, Deuce?"

"You know what I want. Do you have it?"

"Do you have Terry?"

"Do you have the Spirit Box?"

"You know how this works, Deuce. You give me my husband and you get what you want."

"So you have it."

"Put him on the phone."

I heard a muffled noise and then a slapping sound and then I heard a voice say: "You slap like my sister."

It was Terry.

"He's tougher than you are," Deuce said. "He barely flinched when I smacked him. Where are you?"

"Bite me, Deuce."

"Let me tell you how I'm feeling, Fitch. I'm feeling rotten and a little cheated. I let you listen to me slap your husband but you're not giving me anything. It's a one-way relationship, just the kind of thing that Dr. Simons said I shouldn't get involved in."

"Before you killed him in cold blood."

"I think that shows I was growing, not letting myself be taken advantage of—emotionally. So tell me where you are."

"Palo Alto. Around Alice's, where Captain Don bought it. We could meet in the Woodside Hills."

There was a pause. "Not so good for me." Another pause. "How soon can you be in Marin?"

I felt my chest thump. Marin. Not far from here. It made me think I was on target.

"I can be there in ninety minutes, give or take." I was lying but I wanted to buy some time, let him think I was farther away, get his defenses down.

"That should get you in under the clock, assuming you bring the Spirit Box."

"Where do you want to meet, specifically—I suggest some-place public."

"That makes me feel like you don't trust me, Fitch."

"I don't trust you. You're a lying, murdering drug dealer."

"Which makes me not trustworthy? It feels like you're name-calling instead of addressing the issues."

"You want the Spirit Box or not?"

"Give me five minutes and I'll call you back with a place."

I slipped the phone into my pocket. I felt my internal gears engage, a sensation I tended to get when my body took over from my brain. It was what Terry called his Fitch Action Model. Got a laugh out of me the first few times because he'd nailed it; in these moments, the barrier between brain and body dissolved. Thought was emotion was motion. I revved the engine and drove west in the parking lot past the handful of fancy cars and a catering van, left down a service ramp next to a spectacular white structure, doubtless a clubhouse and restaurant, and around the front to the right, where I almost lost my breath. The slips and yachts, even the small ones, magnificently carved and curved woods, sea scent wafting over the top. Enough to make a guy want to get filthy rich, whatever the cost.

I looked out at the boats, seeking a pattern or a sign of where the *Lost Dolphin* might park or signs of her whereabouts. But it just didn't compute. This place didn't seem big enough to ac-commodate the likes of what I imagined the Shipper would own. Maybe it wasn't as majestic as all that.

"Help you?"

The voice came from behind me.

I turned to find a codger, a sunbaked deckhand. I assumed he worked for the place. "Who you looking for?" He reeked of fish and cleaning fluid, his white jumpsuit streaked with oil. He held an empty bucket.

"I'm okay, thanks."

"You look a little lost."

"I'm okay, like I said."

"Suit yourself. World's gone mad if you ask me. You bring a bike down here and say you're not lost and some weirdo tried to drive down here earlier in one of those tiny little orange cars, looks like a VW bug knocked boots with a station wagon. I told the driver he'd run out of road but he was all hopped up on something and said his goddamn GPS told him where to go and I could talk to her if I didn't like it. Talk to a computer. Hell, what'll they think of next?" He looked at the sea. "Kids these days couldn't find north if you gave 'em a compass and a divining rod."

"Wait, go back. The guy was driving a MINI?"

"That what you call them? They look like the car version of those little tiny dogs that are good for nothin' but punting."

"When was this?"

"This morning, I told you."

"Did you tell me where he went?"

Now the guy studied me like I was getting too deep into it. "I've not seen you around before." It was as close as this yacht-club worker was going to get to risk telling me to take a hike.

"That guy, he's the one I'm looking for. Let me know where he went and I'll be out of your hair."

"When they first hired me here—that was sixty years ago—they told me there was one rule: people here value their privacy, so you don't see or hear anything and you don't say anything to anybody about what you've not seen nor heard. I made the mistake of telling them that that was more than one rule, which was the last time that I really listened to anything because, like the man told me at the time, they pay me not to."

Then he looked around and I could see that he could see there was no one in the vicinity but us and some birds.

"But I'm breaking that rule because I don't like a newbie coming down to my dock in a tiny dog car and then giving me the what-for. So I'll tell you that he took a skiff over to a beauty, the seventy-footer just beyond the span."

"The *Last Dolphin*."

He looked surprised. "Didn't hear that from me, son."

"Where do I get a skiff?"

"Getting choppy this time of day. Not what I'd be looking for in the way of fun. But maybe you go ask the guy."

"I thought you said he took a skiff."

"Brought it back too."

He pointed to the far end of the dock—in the direction of the farthest slip.

My phone rang.

"MEET YOU AT Sammy's in Tiburon," Deuce said. "Place with the outdoor tables."

"Ninety minutes."

"You'll have the Spirit Box."

"You'll have Terry."

"Nearby. See you there." Deuce clicked off.

THE TARANTULA SAT in the skiff, his back to me, facing the Golden Gate Bridge. The aging speedboat rocked gently with waves softened by the slip it occupied. Wind strong enough to skew my posture blew across the outer reaches of the dock. The noise covered my approach past one stunning craft after the next. When I got a slip away from Deuce's man on the ground, I stayed low behind a schooner called *You're My Beach*. I felt the big gun I'd strapped to my back to make sure it held steady. I pawed in my jacket front pocket for the Spirit Box and the little device Elron had made for me. I pulled out the pistol. Heavy, it nestled in my hand. A thing of substance in a world dominated by words.

A gust blew from the bay and the Tarantula turned away from it, shielding himself, and looked right at me.

TWENTY-SEVEN

DIDN'T BOTHER TO try to duck. It was coming to this anyway. I pointed the gun at the Tarantula and took two big strides forward. It put me on the edge of his boat, just to the right of the outboard. His eyes danced wide with double-synthetic Adderall and he reached for his belt and I nodded uh-uh, no way, and yanked myself into the skiff. I'd seen this gangster before and couldn't place where at first and then did: he'd leveled me outside the library. He gave a half smile, a tough-guy confidence grin, and I moved forward and hit him with a flash of backhand right across the jaw. My hand might've gotten the worst of it. Even his head was made of beefcake. It only inched to the side and returned to its place with a sadistic look.

"Lucky for you you've got a gun," he said while blood dribbled down his chin. He had braces, the kind that are supposed to be invisible. They must've cut the inside of his lip.

"Take me to the *Last Dolphin*."

"Yeah, I don't think so."

"Wind out here will muffle a gunshot sound pretty good."

"So kill me and you can drive yourself."

He had me with this chess move.

"I'm thinking kneecap, maybe Achilles." I took the gun, shoved it into the back of his knee so he could feel right where it would disable him. He grimaced but said: "We have great health care. Deuce is very forward thinking in that way. You get hurt on the job and you get three months of paid leave." He got lost in a thought and said: "We're still negotiating for paternity time."

"Shut your mouth."

"You don't believe in paternity leave? One of them, huh? I just can't get over the ignorance these days; men are supposed to do everything—bring home the bacon, take care of the kids, carry it all without a word and no support from the system."

He was obviously stalling. Smart one; I'd have to be careful. The boat looked empty. He sat in the middle of three benches. A gun would be stashed somewhere, most likely on his person. His blue windbreaker flapped in the wind and I couldn't get a read on any gun lumps beneath it. A tattoo ran up his neck, furry tarantula legs grasping at his chin. His phone sat on the bench next to him.

I grabbed it.

"Hey!"

"Nice screen. What is it, six inches?"

"Give it back."

"Take me to the big boat or this thing swims with the fishes."

"Put that down! It's got all my contacts."

"Let's go, shithead."

"I haven't backed it up in weeks!"

I made like I was going to toss it into the bay. The Tarantula didn't look so confident now.

I told him how it was going to go down.

WHILE HE PILOTED the skiff in the direction of the bridge and the *Last Dolphin,* I frisked him and found a long-barreled handgun that I tossed into the water. I turned off his phone. We skipped across the wind-irritated water and I looked at the tip of San Francisco, each eastward block of the city a littler sunnier than the last as the fog grew thicker toward the ocean. Hank Kane, the deceased columnist for the *Chronicle,* called it Berkshires by the Bay and I could see it, a village, really, at a distance, something quaint, even ancient, even though up close there could be few places on earth more dependent on and reflective of the new. One wave after the next of new people and modern ideas had come to define San Francisco, a gold-rush town to its core, the last stop before the Pacific on the manifest-destiny train.

My eye-level view didn't permit me to see the area in the Richmond where the Perns kept their rental house, the one with the supposedly suspicious tenant. Now I was all but sure of it; the Perns were the ones doing the dirty business, not their tenant. Flippers, the name of the company I'd seen painted on the van outside their house, was a company specializing in fixing up houses for sale. I didn't have proof yet, but I had a gut feeling: the Perns wanted to oust their tenant so they could sell the place and command a huge profit. They needed the money for Urban Ketchup, but ousting tenants in San Francisco was no small task with all the tenant-protection laws. So the Perns hired me to do the dirty work, dig up proof of the tenant's bad behavior, or something they could intimidate him with, so they'd have an excuse to send him packing.

"Deuce is a great guy to work for," the Tarantula said.

"Shut up and drive."

We were closing on the bridge. Cars had begun packing it, the precommute traffic. On the other side, a growing dot bounced—the yacht—which I assumed was our destination.

"You should think about working for him. He's in boomtown mode."

"What did I just tell you?"

"Suit yourself. I'm just saying. When I got out of community college, I sold servers for Cipco. Had a couple of huge years but it was totally cutthroat, no loyalty. No unions in Silicon Valley, you know that. One bad month and it was like I'd never closed a deal in my life. But Deuce, he cultivates his workforce. You know that I got two weeks last year to study French?"

"How do you say 'shut up' in French?"

"Fermez la bouche."

"Fermez la bouche."

"Not bad, roll your *r*'s if you can. I mean, it wasn't totally altruistic. We're opening a front in France. Brilliant sales pitch, if you ask me. Deuce is selling the Adderall to schools there with the idea that people need to stay alert to thwart the threat of hostile immigrants. Sure, marking against immigrants is totally out of line with our values as a company—half of us are immigrants—but sometimes you've got to let the market dictate. There is truth in economic forces, something undeniable. That's the lesson of the place."

I smacked him across the face.

"*Fanatique,*" he said. "Roughly translated: racist, or bigot."

The yacht, dead ahead, seemed to have suddenly taken on much clearer definition. It was a reality now, not a distant thing. I hoped to hell I knew what I was doing.

"Give me the throttle," I said. I told him to sit in front of me; he'd be what they would see if they were even paying any attention to us.

"I'm supposed to stay at the dock."

"You're a numbskull," I said. "They'll figure this is just another screw-up move and pay you no mind."

He shrugged.

"Keep your hands down."

I shoved my gun into his back.

"LOOKS LIKE A submarine," I muttered.

Streamlined, a thing emerging from the water, practically connected to it. White wings on the side, dark glass around the front and sides; not a submarine, maybe instead like a huge floating pair of wraparound sunglasses.

"What's the layout?"

He said something I couldn't hear given that he was pointed the other direction and his words were being swallowed by the wind. I poked the gun in his back again, repeated my question. He told me he'd only been on it once, in the captain's room up front. High-tech, he said, of course. Steps downstairs into what he assumed were bedrooms and a stateroom and all the rest.

"How many men?"

"Five at least," he said.

"Deuce?"

He shrugged. Was I him I wouldn't tell me either and he damn well knew I couldn't shoot him now.

The *Last Dolphin* pointed north and we were to its east. I told the Tarantula to wave. I put the jacket Honey had given me over my head.

The yacht slowed and we pulled up alongside it.

We stopped next to a steel ladder, bobbing in the whitecaps. I kept the gun poked into the Tarantula. I peeked out of the jacket. The wind and waves became an ally, making it hard for the guys on board to focus on what they were seeing, if they were even paying close attention. Without thinking much more about it, I whacked the Tarantula in the head with the gun to put him to sleep. I rushed forward to the ladder and scrambled up.

TWENTY-EIGHT

A TARANTULA AT THE top of the ladder had his shaggy face buried in his phone, clearly not expecting hostile company. He looked up at me just in time to take my head butt to the cartilage above his nose. Crack went the world and I followed with another pistol-whip, sending him crumpling to the damp deck. I struggled to keep my footing, gun drawn, glancing left and right and seeing myself in the clear on the seventy-foot gleaming walkway of the mouthwatering floating mansion.

I ducked below the darkened windows just in front of me, and crouch-walked to an opening midway through the boat. I gunled, entering a small area, a mudroom of sorts, coats hung and damp boots neatly arranged and a door opposite me with one of those classic portholes in it. Cautious steps forward put me to the side of the window, at the edge of the swinging door. I peered in at an angle. I got an eyeful: middle of the room, Terry, tied to a chair, next to a table. Dining room, I concluded, taking a more straight-on look, or stateroom, stairs leading up to the right to what must be the cabin. Next to Terry, another Tarantula. This one fingered an electronic tablet.

I swung the door open. Terry and the Tarantula looked up. Terry shook his head and grimaced. That's when I heard the jackboots behind me.

Trap.

Deuce walked down the stairs leading from the cabin, arms raised, less in surrender than victory. I pointed the gun at him, but I damn well knew this part of the battle was over.

"Howdy, Fitch."

I looked at Terry. I felt, perversely, relief. He was alive. A shiner colored his right eye and he looked tired. A hand landed on my shoulder from behind. I swung around and got slammed by metal and nearly saw the lights go out. I fell to my knees. A boot stepped on my right wrist, freeing the pistol.

"The codger at the dock tipped you off," I said.

"Yes, true, but after our phone signal told us your whereabouts," Deuce said. "Then we asked the aforementioned codger to concoct some nonsense about a MINI on the dock to get you heading this direction. You know, it's funny how predictable people are."

I eyed him.

He continued: "True to form, you followed all the bread crumbs. Anyhow, welcome. I'm glad you came. It's much easier for us to do our business out here in the great, white international waters of the *Last Dolphin*."

"Seized from Klipper or a gift?"

"Market forces at work. We promised him you'd help us find the Spirit Box." He looked, more than usual, like a complete imbecile. His blue suit was ill-fitting, the white boating scarf around his neck held together with a wooden yellow cinch monogrammed with his initials. "Let's have it."

"Screw you, Deuce."

A heavy foot slammed into my gut.

"William," Terry admonished me. "Go quietly."

I heaved for air. The room spun, the fine oak table turned upside down for a moment, the white leather chairs in the adjoining living room tumbling in my view, along with a big-screen television monitor hung on the wall. In a last-ditch effort, I rolled quickly and reached behind my shoulder blades to pull at the top part of my larger gun before a heavy boot put me back down on my stomach.

"I know that one of my guys talked to you about future employment possibilities," Deuce said. "I'm not sure. Were this an interview, it would be going very badly. You fell for an obvious trap and tried to pull a gun out under impossible circumstances. I do appreciate that you are currently motivated by love and we are a very family-friendly organization. We were well ahead of the Gripes and the Bleeds with dental and eye care. Full exam every eighteen months."

"What about paternity leave?" one of the Tarantulas mumbled.

"This is not the time!" Deuce said. He turned back to me: "You can't let affection cloud judgment. I myself am in the position of having to punish Dutch Abraham for warning you about the dolphin."

I looked down, not wanting to give him a tell.

"Yeah, of course he told me," Deuce said. "He's developing empathy, which is great. He felt for you and Terry. In the end, that's a quality that will work for him. In fact, in corporate America, empathy takes a very close second to loyalty."

"And loyalty takes a very distant second to greed."

"That's two seconds but I do take your point. Enough patter. Where is it—the Spirit Box?"

I looked at Terry and then back at Deuce and then at the Tarantulas, two behind me with guns, the one sitting at the table, and another at a white love seat in the living room area. All with guns except the one in the living room, who still had his head buried in his device.

"It's in my pocket," I said.

"Don't do this," Terry implored. "He's a madman."

"An immortal madman now," Deuce said. "Daryn, can you take it from his pocket? And Larry, can you get ready to shoot his husband if Fitch tries anything funny?"

The Tarantula at the table responded: "I'm almost done with Level Six, Mr. McStein."

"Do as I say or you'll have no screen time for a week."

"Whatever." He exhaled, looked up from his gadget, and pointed a gun at Terry.

The Tarantula called Daryn, the one who had tortured me, shoved a hand into my jacket pocket and pulled out the black box I'd been given by Alan Klipper. The gangster held it up to Deuce, who smiled. "Give me that!"

He stepped forward and in the ensuing gleeful pause, I reached into my pocket and flicked the switch on the jury-rigged device Elron had made for me. My last hope. Desperation at its most desperate.

"Fitch, thank you. I knew you could do it."

"So we're free to go," I said.

"What?"

"You told me we were making an exchange."

"Didn't you read the disclaimer? Doing business with me can have serious side effects, including a horrible, painful death."

"Also disfigurement," said Daryn.

"Daryn, thank you," said Deuce, "but I sort of think that pales in comparison to death."

"It's my area," the Tarantula thug said. "You told me we'd put more emphasis on that this year."

"Suck-up," another Tarantula said.

"You weren't really expecting us to let you go," Deuce said.

I didn't answer.

He cradled the box. "Someone," he said, "get me a laptop."

TERRY PUT HIS hand on my arm and the Tarantula allowed it. My husband gave me a searching look that I didn't return. "Sorry," I mumbled.

"We'll always have Montana," he said.

"That's enough," said the Tarantula.

Terry and I had spent two weeks in Butte a few summers ago while Terry ran the tax numbers on a farming estate and we spent the hot afternoons fishing and swimming. Daryn returned with a laptop. He set it down in the living room. Deuce, hopped up on greed and who could guess what else, shoved the USB cord into the laptop and stared at the monitor, waiting for something to happen.

I turned my attention to the Tarantula sitting on the love seat. He looked quizzically at his phone, then pushed the buttons on it. "My frickin' signal," he said. He looked up. "Anybody else having trouble getting service?"

I watched Daryn pull out his phone. "Had five bars a few

minutes ago. There's an extender in the cabin. You should be fine unless you have T-Noble." He chuckled.

"Nice one," said the Tarantula at the table. He looked at his device too.

"Zero bars," said the Tarantula near Deuce, who watched the screen materialize.

"It's happening," the leader said. "This is it."

"What the heck?" said Daryn, looking at his big-screened device, tapping it. "Did you try turning it off?" The Tarantula next to him, the other one who'd had a gun trained on me from behind, pawed frantically at his phone. "Someone try texting me," he said.

"I just did," said the guy at the table.

Terry looked at me and I looked away, not wanting to make a show of it. The Tarantulas were freaking out. Three gathered beside the table, texting back and forth and having nothing happen. No messages going through. One tried to bring up his browser. "It's working! Wait, no, it's just cached. Check the extender? Can we reset the modem?"

In the chaos and panic, I stood up calmly. I walked to Terry to untie him.

"I think it's in the cabin," one of the Tarantulas said. "Hit the little button on the top for twenty seconds."

"You don't think I know how to reset a modem!"

"Fuck you!"

"Calm down, we'll get this fixed."

Deuce seemed not to notice. His face was entranced by the laptop screen.

Terry nodded at me: *nice work,* it seemed to say. I got the last knot undone behind his back and, so entranced were the Tarantulas, that I picked up the gun of the one sitting next to us. We walked to the door, five feet from our captors but millions of miles away. They couldn't peel their faces from their paralyzed phones. I pictured Maslow's hierarchy of needs and wondered where electronic connectivity would fall in relation to food and oxygen. Clearly, above stopping the escaping hostage and detective.

I felt Terry tug my arm from behind. As in: *stop admiring your handiwork*. I turned to follow him. Deuce yelled: "What is going on?! Stop them!"

The door with the porthole swung behind us.

"We have no coverage," a voice yelled back as a shot shattered the door and whizzed past us and we leaped onto the deck.

TWENTY-NINE

I GAVE TERRY AN unnecessary push from behind to urge him on, then fired a shot to hold the bad guys behind the swinging door. I pointed Terry down the silver ladder, followed him, sent two more bullets screaming toward the door, mindful I might not have many more. As I reached the ladder myself, I caught sight of a Tarantula moving around the front of the boat, cabin-side. The bad guys, awakened, were coming strategically and in force.

A shot buzzed over my head. I jumped onto the skiff and unlatched us. Terry had already found the motor. The first Tarantula appeared over the edge of the *Last Dolphin,* shooting indiscriminately. There was nowhere to hide. So I shot back, giving enough cover for Terry to rev the outboard. Two more Tarantulas appeared. On the skiff, the bad guy I'd gun-swiped remained unconscious but gurgling. I propped myself behind him, a human shield that left me feeling some instant guilt, but it was him or us and I hoped it would at least give pause to the bad guys amassing in view on deck. It did that — gave them pause. But only for a second. Three shots rang out, one of them slamming into the arm of the Tarantula I held up between us and the yacht. This shocked the stupor out of our captive, blood spurting from his forearm.

Deuce appeared at the yacht's edge, laptop in hand.

"Hold it," I said to Terry.

"What?" He didn't understand.

Twenty yards separated us from the boat. Not much by munitions distance but the shooting conditions were nearly impossible with wind and surf. Bullets flew around us. I poked my gun out from the bleeding Tarantula and fired two rounds. I couldn't be sure but it looked like I'd hit my marks: one bullet speared the Spirit Box and the other pierced the laptop and then exploded into Deuce standing behind it.

"Nice shooting," I thought I heard Terry say. And he throttled the skiff across the choppy waters.

NO MATCH FOR the yacht, but more maneuverable and well ahead of it, we headed into the crowded San Francisco side of the marina. As we neared shore, I pulled out my phone to call Lieutenant Gaberson. I discovered a text from Veruca Sap. It contained a revelation: she'd broken the code on the papers I'd found in *The Selfish Gene*. She gave me an address for where to meet her. She added: *Come ASAP. It's complicated.*

I dialed the lieutenant. I told him where he could pick up a bleeding Tarantula and tied the poor sap to the skiff. I tossed my phone into the ocean.

We hailed a cab.

"THAT WAS SLICK," Terry said. "The thing you did turning off their phones."

"Are you okay?"

"Never better. You know, these guys, killers, yes, but they take their hospitality seriously. They asked me which eye I preferred to have bloodied and the frozen steak they put on it was grass-fed."

"You're kidding."

"Grass-fed is true. But, yes, largely I'm kidding. You can dress up a killer in locally sourced hemp but he's still a killer. This is a world gone mad, William."

"Fitch." I half smiled.

He kissed me on the cheek. I felt relief flood me, water in my eyes. I wanted to say, *I thought I'd lost you,* but I managed: "How does a guy like you get kidnapped?"

"You thought you'd lost me, didn't you?"

I smiled. "How did you get kidnapped?"

He pursed his lips. "Gun malfunction. I heard them come in, sat up, gun over my lap, and when the bedroom door opened, I made sure it wasn't you and then shot for the eyeball. And, *click.* The Winchester let me down."

"Ouch."

"Where are we headed?" he asked.

"Later, to dinner. First, we have to finish the job so we get paid."

"I don't see why that is really necessary at this point," my husband protested. "You smell of fish."

I didn't answer. I was sure he didn't. I wasn't sure I saw the point either. But just because you love someone and marry him doesn't mean you have to see eye to eye.

"How'd you do it?"

"What?"

"Shut down their phones?"

"Simple thing Elron came up with. Killed the signal in the immediate area."

"Elron. Good man. His idea?"

"Bono."

He studied me. "The U2 guy? You met him?"

No, I explained. Bono's song had started showing up on everyone's phone to make sure the ringer was going. The more I saw of it, the more I realized people couldn't handle being disconnected for even a second. I pulled Elron's device from my pocket. "This thing is more dangerous than an AK."

"I bet those liberal kooks will try to get it banned," Terry said. "I'm kidding, mostly."

"It is banned."

"There you go."

"WHERE ARE WE?" Terry asked.

I shrugged. It was the address sent by Veruca Sap—in a strip mall in Redwood City, a few towns north of Palo Alto. Same general area as the video-game training center but less fancy, really an old-school place, decidedly not gentrified. I let the cabbie go with a healthy tip, stuffed the gun in the back of my pants, and looked around for something that was supposed to be here.

"Over there?" Terry asked. He pointed to the right corner of this semicircular outdoor commercial development. A handful of people stood outside, a veritable standoff it looked like. I couldn't quite make them out, but at the distance guessed I might be looking at Veruca and someone alongside her and, facing her, Floyd Chiansky.

"You want to wait here?" I asked Terry.

"Not if there's a chance I get to see you exercise your Second Amendment rights."

"This is no time for foreplay."

He laughed. It was great to hear. Wasn't much else that got me up and out of bed in this world.

Yep, I could see as we neared, Veruca, the world-beating lawyer, alongside someone I didn't recognize. Opposite them stood Floyd. They eyed each other like wrestling combatants. Behind them a small retail establishment, looked to me like it said: *PAST Office.*

"Is that supposed to say 'Post Office'?" Terry said.

"Not sure. It might be the Captain at work," I mumbled.

"Who?"

Before I could answer, Veruca said: "Hello, Mr. Fitch, we've got company."

If Veruca looked like a million bucks—and commanded it—Floyd looked like a wooden nickel. Sweatpants and sweat-stained T-shirt advertising the band Golden Hamlet. Even the other geeks would notice the rancid smell.

I said: "Anyone want to tell me what we're all doing here—other than waiting for the cops to come arrest Floyd for murder?"

"Murder? I—"

"Right, Floyd, I should be more specific. And blackmail and other assorted sordid acts."

"You've got the wrong guy!"

I held up the gun. "Keep talking, Floyd, by all means. Who is the right guy? Near as I can tell, you blackmailed Danny at Colester. Accused him of masquerading as David Skellow. Tried to get seed money for some nonsense project you were working on."

"It's not nonsense! Facial recognition is . . ." He paused, realized he was damning himself.

"Then you got out here to Silicon town and your eyes got wider and dreams bigger."

"That's not—"

Veruca interrupted him. "Can this wait? I've got a six thirty. I'd like to settle the matter at hand."

Floyd wasn't going anywhere.

"What's the matter at hand?" I asked.

Veruca pointed to the small storefront with the sign *PAST Office*. It was little bigger than one of those boutique candy stores or a small corner flower shop. On one side, a gym and on the other, a vacant storefront. Inside the PAST Office, a very old man stood behind a counter reading a magazine. Behind him, the man, a post office box. Just one.

"I'll bring you up to speed," Veruca said, "while we wait for the others."

"What others?" I asked. "Who is this guy?" I looked at the lackey behind her.

"First-year. Princeton, then Duke. He carries my devices. I'm pretty sure he has a name."

"Phillip," he said.

"You can talk after you've made junior partner." She looked at me. "We're waiting for the Donogue family. Should be here any moment." She looked at the loose-leaf notebook pages in her hand. "So this paper you gave me, the pages that Captain Don allegedly wrote—"

"Allegedly?"

"I'll stipulate for now that he wrote it. The pages give some instructions. The first instruction is to come here, to this address."

"I was here first," Floyd said. "But I think I should go."

"Shut up and don't move," I said.

Veruca continued. She explained that the code described a mechanism for sending and receiving messages, just as she'd posited earlier.

"The system involves having users write messages in pen—"

"Or pencil would work," Floyd said.

"Shut up!" Veruca and I both said. She continued: "And then sealing the message in another piece of paper using glue—"

"Or tape," Floyd said.

"Shut up!"

"I'm just saying: it's an open system."

"I'm going to sue you for no reason," Veruca said. "I've done it before. Anyhow, the message gets sealed up, and then—here's the ingenious part—it gets handed to a courier or dropped in a sealed box and then hand-delivered to the recipient."

I gave her the you've-got-to-be-crazy look.

"It's the post office," Terry said, exasperated. He looked at me: "For this you went to detective school?"

I watched Veruca closely. I could definitely see that she thought this was nonsense but she wasn't going to say it aloud. Of course not: a client is a client is a client. In fact, she said: "It's the PAST Office. Might be something new here. But we can't really tell. Some details are left out, I think. We won't know until we get inside."

"So let's go inside."

"That's what I say!" Floyd exclaimed.

"As I've explained," the lawyer said, "the final instruction is that the Donogue family must be present. And, well, here they are!"

She was looking over my shoulder and I followed her gaze, and lo and behold: Tess and Lester and, walking from a separate direction, Danny.

THIRTY

"CAN WE GO inside?" Floyd said.

"We can go inside," Veruca said.

"What's going on?" Tess screeched. She looked at her son: "What's he doing here?" Then at Floyd: "Who is that?"

"Floyd Chiansky."

"Thank you for coming," Veruca said.

"Floyd Chianksy. Is that supposed to mean something to me?" Tess asked. "Were you on one of the InEf missions? My God, you smell. I can tell from here. Are you in one of those video-game detox programs? You poor boy. Is this an intervention?"

Hard to get a read on this woman and her hysteria and non sequiturs, feigned or otherwise.

Veruca put her hands down in a calming manner, hushed the woman. Then, to the startled assemblage, explained that Captain Don had allegedly left a note for people to come to this place, and once so assembled, a security box would be unlocked with a final message.

"Final?" Lester said. "Like *final* final?"

Veruca shrugged. She told the rest of the story, just as she'd explained it to us, and I filled in with the piece about finding the message in *The Selfish Gene* and endured hateful looks from Tess Donogue. And we all packed inside.

STANDING ROOM ONLY, especially since there were no chairs. We looked at the man behind the counter, who hadn't even glanced up when we all walked in. Never once did this gray-hair take his bespectacled eyes from a copy of a fishing magazine. Tall and lanky, he looked like he'd go over in a gust of wind.

"Ahem." Veruca cleared her throat.

Nothing. No response.

After another minute, Floyd said: "This is ridiculous! The wait here is incredible. I've got half a mind to Yolp this thing and tell the world."

No reaction from the codger.

"It really *is* the post office," Terry whispered to me.

Veruca walked to the counter and rang a little silver bell. Still no movement from the old guy, and, then, about a minute after she rang it, he said: "Next!"

Everyone scurried to the counter.

"Who was next in line?" the man said. "We'll be closing shortly."

"I'll handle this," Veruca said. "I'm here to pick up a . . . to . . ." She looked at the piece of paper. "I think there's a package or message for me."

"Name?"

"Veruca Sap."

"ID?"

She handed it over. The man studied it. "Nothing for you here," he said. "Next!"

Everyone looked baffled. I said: "Let's try another way at this. Do you have a package for anyone?"

"Who are you?"

Rather than answer, I said: "Do you have a package for the Donogue family?"

He squinted. "Are they all here?"

Murmurs and nods.

"IDs, please!"

Tess and Danny stepped up. So did Lester. They put their IDs on the counter. The old man scrutinized them, first on the counter, then lifting them and comparing them to the faces. Like the post office, as Terry kept reminding me with prods to the ribs, or perhaps like a none-too-quick security checker at the airport making a good show of his power. He put the IDs down, turned, put a key into the little box on the wall behind him, and pulled out an envelope.

He started to put it on the counter and then, as all the hands scrambled for it, he pulled it back.

"Sign here, please," he said, and pointed to a ledger.

All three signed.

I bullied forward and took the envelope before anyone else could grab it.

"Hey!"

"Hey!"

"Hey!"

"I'm the only disinterested party here," I said. Without further ado, I opened the envelope and discovered a piece of paper and a tiny box with a button on it. "Step back and I'll read this aloud." They looked skeptical and ticked off to the point of being

.murderous. So I added: "Or step forward and try to take it from my hands."

"Read, then!" Tess said.

> *Dear Family and Ms. Sap (and your overpaid lackey),*
>
> *I'm glad you found my little note. I'm sorry I had to take precautions but I had an inkling that this whole will and testament thing could be manipulated and then I had an even more jarring inkling that at least someone out there wanted to kill me—and has possibly succeeded. More on that in a bit.*
>
> *Isn't this great? All of you together? Can you feel the love?*

"I think he's being sarcastic," Lester said.

"'Be quiet, Lester,'" I read from the letter.

"How could he tell I would say that?" Lester asked.

> *Because we're all so predictable. Let me finish. I have some good news and some other news. Let me start with the other news. To learn more about it, please press the button.*

I looked at Veruca. She shrugged. I eyed Danny. Pale, shrunken, he stood near the counter at the far left. I felt myself glance suspiciously at his pockets, looking for signs of trouble—a weapon, I didn't know what. Tess stepped forward, a look in her eye that said, *May I press the button?* Another shrug from Veruca.

She pressed the button.

From behind the counter there was a sound like POOF. And we all looked and noticed a bit of smoke rising from a cabinet.

"HI, EVERYONE," THE Captain's voice rang out from the little gadget in my hand. "Where was I? Right. Good news and other news. First, the other news. I am officially dead!"

"Daddy!"

"Shh, Tess. It's for the best. Some people may even consider this to be the *good* news," the Captain's recording continued. "Regardless. I am dead. The second you hit that button, it sent a wireless signal that imploded whatever was left of me and the Spirit Box. I kept a program on a server at the PAST Office and loaded it with explosives and now it's all gone. Speaking of which, did the Spirit Box work? I've no idea. I'm obviously not there to revel in the success or failure. I did think I had it figured out there, right at the end, just about the time I realized it was very possibly the worst idea that I'd ever had. I mean, first of all, let go. It's time to let go. Me, all of us. Forgive me if I droned on about this before in the video . . ."

"BOOORING," said Lester.

"You're right, Lester, and you know how much I hate saying that. I am, though, deadly curious about whether it worked. Get it, *deadly* curious? I put the Spirit Box in place, a test run, one and done, to see if I'd send anything from beyond. Did it embody my essence, extrapolate from my previous statements, and adjust based on current conditions of the world to offer a digital version of yours truly? It really is a remarkable program in that it mixes me, or someone else, with all the data in the world so that my digital self can react to current events even though my body has passed on. Did I offer any insights or did I just drone on about how bad traffic has gotten? It has gotten very bad." He cleared his throat.

"Now, let us move on to a related matter and some unfortunate business: my murder. This would be a good time for each of you to look around the room and leer at each other suspiciously. I'll give you a moment."

I watched as everyone did a seemingly impossible task: looked at each other while also trying to look at the ground.

"Did anyone blink?" the Captain asked. "Truth is, I don't know who did it, if anyone did. And I'm not sure it matters. I had something or other and I was going to die anyway. It was imminent and I was done seeking treatment. If I was ever good at anything in my blessed life, it was pattern recognition. I saw a few things in my day and I could just feel the hostility building around me in those last days. It was easy to explain: I was headed for the beyond and everyone wanted the part of me that would live on, the money."

"No matter where this is going, the landline is mine," Lester said.

"Let him finish!" said his wife.

"You two really are meant for each other. Weirdly, I do hope you'll work it out," the Captain continued. "Anyhow, see, I can kind of feel the rhythm of life. So I could feel that someone wanted to kill me, or threaten me, and I can tell you exactly why. Before I go on, though, I should tell you that this part gets complicated. Is everyone ready?"

Nods all around.

"Someone wanted to kill me because they wanted to use the Spirit Box to keep me alive. They wanted to take it over."

"That makes no sense!" Lester said. "I'm taking a nap."

"If you're wondering why someone would want me alive, there is a simple reason. When I'm dead, my patents go with me. Or rather, I no longer control the royalties and licenses. I'm sure Veruca told you all this. I am mortal and so are my innovations, and when we both die, so goes an income stream that could keep many people doing whatever you people do with money, which I never did care about or pay attention to. As an aside, do you realize the entire economy of Silicon Valley is built on patents? Oh sure, those patents represent innovation, but not nearly as often or as profound as the paper they are written on. Now, paper: that was an innovation. So in my genetic line, it ends with me."

I looked over and saw tears running down Danny's face.

"I could be wrong about motive here. I mean, after all, someone might've wanted to kill me just to get the Spirit Box technology and promise the world an afterlife. But, well, I clearly have made sure that didn't happen. The Spirit Box is no more."

This must've been the smoke coming from the cabinet behind the codger. The server had imploded with the push of the button. I looked at Floyd, who stared at the ground.

"Now for the good news!" The Captain's voice sounded whimsical, to me at least. Tess looked earnest, her husband (-ish) sound asleep on her shoulder. "This place, where you are standing, is the future: the PAST Office. That's right, this is the way to send secure messages. As the kids say: Do you feel me? It is yours, all of it, the concept, the design, the patents, and Melvin!" He paused.

"I can stay on?" asked the man behind the counter.

Captain Don continued: "Electronic mail, who needs it?! Too easy to manipulate, steal, imitate. This is going to be our greatest innovation, my legacy, a system for face-to-face verification of missives. You can send something to whomever you want. You write it on paper and then leave it in a box and it gets picked up by a courier—real human person—who will deliver it by hand to a physical address of the recipient."

"He is so fucking with them," Terry whispered to me, right at the moment Tess said: "Daddy, it's brilliant!"

I couldn't get a read on Danny.

"There is one caveat, one critical caveat," Captain Don said. "This is for Veruca Sap, who, fairly or not, is the center of the known universe."

I looked at Veruca, who I discovered was doing push-ups but lifted her head and mouthed, *I can listen.*

"Counselor, please make sure that my daughter and my grandson mend their relationship. There is only family. Should these two continue to act like children, I will ask you to put the PAST Office into the public domain, where all my other patents have now found their final resting place. Veruca, recognizing your fee might not be covered by a twenty-year expected negative revenue stream from the PAST Office, I have left you several million dollars. You were going to figure out how to get it anyway."

She smiled thinly. "Well, if that's it, I'll do some chin-ups and go."

"That is about it," the Captain said.

"William," my husband whispered.

"Huh?"

"William!"

The audiotape continued: "This has been Captain Don, saying—"

"Fitch!" Terry implored. I followed his gaze out the window and there stood none other than Dutch Abraham. The muzzle of an automatic weapon pointed into the tiny shop. Then time slowed down as bullets screamed from the muzzle, the glass shattered, Terry dove to tackle me out of harm's way, and everything went black.

THIRTY-ONE

F ITCH?"

I forced my eyes open and saw Lieutenant Gaberson standing next to me, upright, which I decidedly was not. Bedridden, more like. Colors and lights blurred. Didn't take but a moment to make sense of it: hospital. Blue and white colors, a TV in the distance, regular beeps, a tank of oxygen and a mask beside my head.

Terry.

I couldn't get the word out. My head hurt something fierce. Gaberson looked concerned. "Just a concussion, pal, but a whopper. They sedated and cooled you to make sure that you didn't suffer any spinal damage."

"Terry," I whispered.

Gaberson shook his head. "You've got one tough husband."

"He's okay?"

"Okay?" Gaberson laughed. "He decked you so hard your head slammed into the counter. Knocked you out cold."

"This gets you out of dishwashing duty for no more than a week," a voice said, and I saw it was Terry walking out of the bathroom. "Frankly, I think the problem is yours for being so big. Velocity equals force plus . . ." He shrugged. "No clue how that goes. Maybe: force equals MC squared."

"Floyd Chiansky wasn't so lucky," Gaberson said. "No longer with us."

"You're at Stanford Hospital," Terry said. "It's freaking me out. All the doctors talk to holograms of the patients rather than the patients themselves, who sit idly by looking at holograms of doctors."

He could see this baffled me.

"The theory is that it's easier to express your true emotions if you're not looking a real person in the eye. A doctor told your hologram an hour ago that this technology makes for a better human experience. Your hologram didn't respond, on account of the concussion, but it looked irritated."

"My hologram and I need a burger and fries." But my mind was elsewhere: Floyd didn't make it. "Anyone else hit?"

"Glass shards injured Tess and Lester, but they'll be okay."

"Danny?"

"Fine," Gaberson said.

"Dutch Abraham?"

"Clean getaway. People say it was the fastest MINI they'd ever seen."

Terry sat by the bed and put his hand on my shoulder. He pointed to the oxygen mask beside my head. "You get a little woozy," he said, "take a puff."

"Lieutenant, I thought I was persona non grata?"

"Yes. It's complicated now that Jorge McStein is no longer with us."

I looked at him for confirmation: Deuce? Dead?

He nodded. "The world is a better place. But your life might get worse in the short term: he had the best lawyers in the world and they are that much more effective when jacked up on double-synthetic Adderall. They'll make a dandy civil case—wrongful death of upstanding citizen."

I let it sink in. Deuce was gone. Good riddance. His son, evidently, had come seeking vengeance on me and put a bullet into Floyd instead. Dutch Abraham was just a kid. Hell, he'd helped me find Terry. But maybe he realized he'd sent me on the mission that would kill his father; of course he would want vengeance. Another enemy out there in the world.

"I might have a secret weapon to help you out in court," Gaberson said. He looked down to the edge of the hospital bed at the black box that I'd seen him toting around. He patted it, the way Terry was patting my shoulder.

"Thanks for not asking, Fitch," Gaberson said. He looked down. He felt guilty. "This is OTR." Off the record.

I gave him a halfhearted okay with my eyebrows.

"As you know, we would never violate anyone's, um . . . which is the amendment to the, um, Constitution, about the privacy thing?"

"Fourth?" Terry said.

"Right. We'd never violate anyone's Fourth Amendment rights or their, um, due process-y thingies."

"Cut the shit, Lieutenant," I managed.

"'Nuff said. So this little beauty lets us capture every conversation that ever takes place."

"That's not a privacy violation?" Terry said.

"Not if you get the proper warrant. It's just we're still trying to understand the paperwork."

"What? You've been getting warrants for decades."

"Right, well, y'know, Terry, the forms change and the print is very small. Anyhow, you're missing the point. This is all about protecting the public. See, what we do is we record conversations and then we wind up with a massive database of how people talk."

"What . . ." Before Terry could finish his question, Gaberson put his hand up, like: *don't worry and let me finish.* "You know about fingerprints and how valuable those are in terms of getting bad guys. This is the digital version of the same thing." He paused for effect: "Voiceprints."

He explained that individuals have individual voice patterns, subtly different ways of using language that make them different from everyone else. So if we could create a database of people's voices, their manner of speech, we could know if they were in a particular place. "Say, the scene of the crime," he said.

"But to know that, you'd have to be listening in to every conversation," Terry said. "So you could match each person at a place against your database. It would be like having the entire world under surveillance at all times."

"Which we'd never do without a warrant," Gaberson vowed. Over his forehead, he held up three fingers in the shape of a *W*: whatever.

"What does this have to do with Deuce?"

"Officially, I'm to have nothing to do with you. Unofficially, I kept tabs on you—pointed this powerful thingy in the direction of the area I suspected you were in and scooped up all the conversations. I think Deuce's attorneys will find it hard to pin anything on you."

"That's absurd and inadmissible," I said.

"We'll be okay. Our lawyers are smart too and they have access to their own medications that enhance focus. Which they'd never use without a prescription."

"Or a warrant," I said dryly.

"Yes. Wait, what?" Gaberson looked flummoxed and then recovered. He was a pal, sure, but he was one of them too. And I realized just how closely the good and bad guys had become aligned, how little the difference—and where all this technology was taking all of us. The Spirit Box preyed on the predictability of humans to want to create a digital afterlife; Gaberson's new surveillance technology relied on the predictability of humans in order to create a digital voiceprint.

"Y'know," I said, "there's a difference between fingerprints and this box you're using to capture everyone's language."

Gaberson stared at me.

"People give their fingerprints willingly. You're capturing people's voices without their knowledge."

"No one is making people speak," Gaberson said. "Besides, talking is sometimes an admission of guilt."

Terry said: "I think you've got that wrong. The cliché is that refusing to talk is an admission of guilt. And even that is wrong."

"Well, then, see, we may have it right this time."

Another no-win situation with the law. My ATF trainer was right. I existed as a private dick, outside the system, standing on the sidelines, sometimes yelling foul.

"You did some good," Gaberson said. "Evidently, Floyd gave a deathbed confession."

I perked up.

"In his last moments, he said that Captain Don had died of an—"

"Oxygen shot!" I shot upward, causing a surge of headache.

"Jinx," Terry said. "Look at my man go."

"How'd you know?" Gaberson asked.

I didn't answer but it made sense. No sign of foul play when they found Captain Don. Just a little extra oxygen. "How would he have gotten close enough to . . ." I didn't finish.

"Let it go," Gaberson said. "He confessed. Said he'd wanted the Spirit Box and worried that Captain Don would destroy it."

"He confessed to whom?"

"Everyone there testified to the same thing, except an old man named Melvin. He said that generally he couldn't hear anything at all and that his poor hearing was considered a job requirement. Case closed, Fitch, go back to your day job."

Gaberson took off after a bit and I thought it over, head back, eyes opened and closed, snoozing, then waking up every few minutes and taking in the oxygen port. Oxygen.

I signed my release papers. "So it's over?" Terry asked as we headed out.

Over?

I had to guess so—it was over. Best I could figure it, Floyd and Da Raj had conspired to blackmail Danny about Colester College. Floyd was the main man, a real bright kid, Da Raj his goofy sidekick. Then they got even greedier and pushed Danny to give up the Spirit Box. When it became clear that Danny wasn't giving it up and neither was Captain Don, they got threatening and they put the old man down with an oxygen shot. Then I got involved and the Tarantulas got onto me, and Floyd, who seemed to follow everything—know every move—made a quick decision to bring them into the mix. He promised them the Spirit Box in exchange for taking out Da Raj, his weak link.

Weak, just like my theory. It was all I had. And now Floyd was dead.

THIRTY-TWO

C LYDE!"

"Whaaaat?" His singsongy voice came from outside my office.

"Can you show Fred Pern in?"

Clyde appeared at the door. Dapper-looking, a totally different façade; three-piece suit, top hat. "Can I help you, sir?"

"Clyde, can you show Fred Pern into my office?"

Clyde looked at me, and then at Fred Pern, who was sitting in the chair opposite me. "He's already in your office."

"Very good, Clyde."

"So why are you bothering me?"

"Because it's your job to show people into my office."

"Well, then, frankly, Fitch, I'd like to ask you to not do my job for me. It's very emasculating."

"He walked right by you, Clyde. Because you were lost in your *Them* magazine. He couldn't get your attention."

Clyde looked at Fred Pern, a squat fellow in his forties, prematurely gray. "I apologize, Mr. Pern."

"No problem—"

"I just don't know why Mr. Fitzgerald gets like this," Clyde continued. "It's not like I try to do his job, whatever that is. Do you realize that the other day, he took over the expense reports—just commandeered them? How am I supposed to have any feeling of authorship?" He shook his head. "Fitch." He looked at me. "I'm going to be taking the afternoon off."

"Is that right?"

"If you insist." He tipped his top hat and left.

"Interesting character," Mr. Pern said.

"I actually asked him here for a reason, Mr. Pern." I leaned back in my chair. It had been a good morning. Slept in a bit, had Terry's French toast, the subway free of Phippies, and I was about to stick it to Fred Pern. "He's guileless."

"How's that?"

"You know the word?"

"Sure, I don't—"

"No, you don't. You don't understand it. It wouldn't surprise me if you can't even pronounce it."

"I'm not paying you to shout at me."

"I'm not shouting and you're not paying me at all. Your money is no good here. You told me that your tenant was up to no good. But it was you, all along. You wanted me to dig up dirt on him so you could find a way to evict him, get around the tenant protection laws. You wanted to flip the property and make a killing and pour it into your trendy restaurant."

"So?"

"So you admit it."

"Sure, whatever. Why can't I evict my tenant and flip my house and make some money? Everyone else is making money. How am I supposed to survive in this town?"

So there it was, his admission. It hadn't been hard to put together. The van parked outside his tenant's house belonged to Flippers, the company that fixed up houses that were for sale. The lawyer that the tenant had contacted was a tenant advocate, as I discovered after a few phone calls.

"Mr. Pern, get out."

"You're a child, Mr. Fitzgerald."

"Fitch."

He stood.

"Fitch, listen to me."

"Out."

"Just listen. I . . . I got caught up in terrible debt. It was one of those horrible upgrade cycles. You heard about this?"

"No."

"I bought a new phone, a great one, and I tried to use the Bluetooth function to pair it with my car, y'know, so I could talk when I drove. But my car was too outdated to pair with my phone, see?"

"No, I don't s—"

"So, obviously, I got a new car."

"Obviously."

"But by then, my phone was outdated, so I had to upgrade that. Three phones and four cars later I couldn't afford anything. And this deadbeat is living in my house and I can't oust him with all these pro-tenant rules in San Francisco. I need the money and this town is moving way too fast."

"My heart bleeds."

"How am I supposed to survive?" he repeated. "What about *me*?"

I didn't answer him. What was the point? This one had succumbed to the whole filthy idea that you said what you needed to say, and did what you needed to do, to get yours.

Anyhow, I had something else on my mind. This upgrade cycle. I realized it had been the boy all along.

THIRTY-THREE

"SHEESH. THIS KID should pack it in," Danny said. He sat in the balcony of the Video Game Olympic Training Center. On the theater screen in the distance, a gorilla repeatedly slammed a hammer down on an animated baby that was screaming: "Uncle."

A voice came over the intercom into our little booth: "Danny, I'm sorry, I missed the trapdoor."

"Hit the showers, kid," Danny said. He turned to me: "I'm going to have to tell him he's got no future and he should resign himself to the college route. Maybe he'll get a job at Starbacks or become a doctor."

"You're just a kid yourself."

"Age is in the eye of the beholder."

"Let's talk about *your* college days."

"You're still humming that tune, dick?"

"No one talks like that, I told you. I think things went down at Colester a little differently than you've told me."

He turned to me and looked incredulous, like: *Are we really rehashing this?*

"Want to hear my version? Actually, strike that, Danny, I'll tell you my version and you can sit here and pretend to look uncomfortable."

"Suit yourself, Detective."

"You went to Colester because you weren't sure about your abilities and you wanted to grow up and learn—and your granddad liked the idea. No shame in that. Then you got pulled aside one day by Floyd, who had discovered your real identity."

"This sounds a lot like my version of events . . ."

"Here's the twist. He didn't really threaten you. In fact, you were thrilled to meet Floyd because you realized he was a brainy dude. He could program and figure things out and code in ways you couldn't. He seemed like he had genius potential. You two started talking—about business ideas, concepts. You told him about the Spirit Box. Sound familiar?"

"Whatever."

"I can see it, Danny—late-night bull sessions drinking energy drinks with immune boost, getting existential, just like everyone does at college, asking the big questions: Is there life after death? What's the point of being here? What if we could live forever?"

I stared at Danny. He tried to roll his eyes but couldn't quite pull it off.

"The Captain was getting sicker—he told you. You came back and you invited Floyd with you to Silicon Valley, right? He had a reasonable cover story with his facial recognition software. But the reality is that you were going to pair up and put together the final pieces of the Spirit Box, take it out from under the Captain. Get there before he did."

"You're crazy." Now he wasn't looking me in the eye. He was

looking at the distant screen, where a bullfighter with a flame-thrower was holding a cape and being charged by a lamb with a nuclear warhead attached to its back.

"Here's what I think, Danny. I think you were terrified. I think you hated the idea you wouldn't be Captain Don or live up to his legacy. I think you were terrified that you'd become like . . ." Christ, it hit me. "Alan Klipper. You didn't want to be the sidekick, the guy in the shadow of the great innovator. Or a faux innovator, revered for money but not ideas."

"He had a stroke, you know. Alan Klipper."

I didn't say: *couldn't have happened to a nicer guy.*

"You needed your own thing, right, Danny? You wanted to have a real innovation of your own."

"Froom," he said weakly.

"Oh yeah, wonderful. About as innovative as pictures on cash registers or cat videos."

"Heretic," he mumbled.

"You can't even sell your emotion right now. With Froom, you looked like the big man on campus, at least relative to Da Raj. But it was just a stupid idea. You know it, in your heart. In fact, my guess is it was just a ruse, a cover so you and Floyd could work on the Spirit Box.

"You suckered Da Raj into it. Made believers out of a few gullible saps, but little by little Da Raj got wind of your sinister side and so did Floyd. They saw the madman behind the boy wonder."

On the distant screen, a lamb exploded into a billion little pixels and words appeared: *Gold Medal Contender.*

"It took me a while to understand why you wanted the Spirit Box so badly."

He didn't answer.

"You knew your grandfather like no one else. You knew he wouldn't leave you or your family anything. You had to put the finishing touches on the Spirit Box before he got there. You had to figure it out."

"Oh, I get it, so I was competing against him."

"In a way, yes. But the Best and the Brightest—you and Floyd—you couldn't crack it, even after you got some inside looks from Klipper. He loved you like his own grandson. Even though you resented his second-class status, compared, at least, to the Captain."

"You've got no proof of this."

"None."

"So you're going on what exactly?"

"Instinct. It's what drove your grandfather, by the way. He made money and changed the world, of course. I'm just a hack taking on little misfortunes. Captain of the minimum wage. In this case, I kept getting nagged by something you told me when we were sitting outside your parents' house. We were talking and you told me that you knew I'd already seen Captain Don's video, the one where he talks about fearing death. It's the video that your mom showed me in that weird wooden house."

He shrugged. "So?"

"So I'd never told you that I'd seen that video. How did you know I'd seen it? Here's my guess: you'd been listening to everything your mother did and said. Everything. Her initial visit to my office, the activity in the house."

"You should write fiction."

"My guess is that you put a bug on her brief-back-case."

"This is laughable."

"I don't think so. I think you realized something else when she came to me: you realized that your grandfather was sending messages about his own murder. Am I right?"

No answer.

"She came and told me that he was warning about his murder. And now the whole story turned. Now you had to destroy the very technology you'd hoped to complete. It was working too well. From the grave, your grandfather was outing his murderer—you!"

"No." This time it was halfhearted, a denial, sure, but only in language. The white in his face told me otherwise.

"You had to shut this thing down before Captain Don turned in his own grandson. It was that good—too good. It was everything Captain Don had hoped for. You got the Tarantulas on board with the promise that they'd get a piece of the Spirit Box. But the reality was that you needed to find it, shut it down fast, before you got outed as a murderer."

Danny had tears in his eyes.

"I loved him—more than any of those people did!"

"He loved you, Danny. He believed in you."

He didn't speak.

"He knew you could do it on your own, that you could be great and create and that you just needed to wait. You didn't need to accelerate your life with a bunch of money from his innovation."

"He was suffering, Detective."

"The trouble is: you didn't believe in yourself. So you had to lay down a financial future. You got Floyd on board. You were young guys picturing yourselves as the Beatles of the afterlife."

"The who?"

"Not the Who? The Beatles."

"Sorry, who?"

"Bruce Springsteen?"

"The guy who built the car-sharing service?"

"Never mind. Look . . ." I waited until he did look, right at me. "I think you'll do better if you confess. You'll be free."

He shook his head. His jaw hardened. The moment had been lost, his mask was back on.

I let out a deep exhale. "It's one thing to take out your dying grandfather," I said. "Maybe it was merciful, though it feels to me like murder. Even harder for me to digest, though, is killing Da Raj. I realize you thought he was the weak link, that you thought he might crack and tell me everything. But he also was only twenty years old."

"You mean practically twenty."

"That's what I said."

"Over the hill. Past his prime, Detective. Whoever killed him was doing him a favor," Danny said.

He'd taken on a look of pure evil. In this moment, he wasn't like his grandfather at all; he was a sociopath.

"Now can I tell *you* something, Detective?"

"Knock yourself out."

"Guys like me and Dutch Abraham, we're the future," Danny said, and smiled.

Holy hell. It hit me. He'd gotten Dutch to drive by the PAST Office and take out Floyd. The last remaining witness. And everyone else who heard Floyd's deathbed confession had reason to want to keep Danny out of trouble—Tess and Lester, Veruca Sap, who needed the family's business.

"I'm sorry you had to waste your time coming down today, Detective."

I shook my head. "No waste, Danny. You've taught me more about the world than I thought any teenager could."

"Say hi to your husband for me."

I walked outside, my gut tight with recognition: Truth, what did it even mean anymore?

THIRTY-FOUR

TERRY AND I were on the last bites of a homemade casserole when justice was served. The local news said there had been a near tragedy in Palo Alto. Danny Donogue had been found in his garage.

He locked himself in there and turned on the car.

Unfortunately, he'd failed to realize that he had an all-electric vehicle, which would not suffocate him with carbon monoxide. After a couple of hours, he fell asleep, then awakened, thinking maybe he'd died. Then, as he gathered his senses, he thought maybe he was just delirious or hurt. He had second thoughts about killing himself and started to drive himself to the hospital. But he ran right into the garage door, which he'd forgotten to open. He'd been badly injured. Another garage start-up tragedy.

Terry put his arm around my shoulder.

"Maybe he's learned his lesson."

Maybe.

I leaned against Terry's shoulder. Goddamn if it didn't feel good to be old.

ACKNOWLEDGMENTS

THE USUAL NODS (but never mailed-in nods) of eternal gratitude to the gang at William Morrow, led by Liate Stehlik (publisher), Peter Hubbard (world-class editor), Lynn Grady (best publishing-industry dual threat marketing executive/tennis player), Nick Amphlett (secret brains of the operation), and the entire sales and publicity team. I'll single out here Kristen Bowers because she is so talented and also because she has some kind of magical hold on the Internet and might reverse witch me if I didn't give her the rightful honors.

My main message to this talented and gracious group is: How many genres will you permit me to stain? Really, you should all seek psychological assistance.

My heartfelt thanks to Vicki Yates, a natural-born copyeditor who came from the blue to scour my many lapses and redundancies.

To my agent, Laurie Liss, you are complicit. Can you live with that? Love you.

To my wife, thank you for letting us get a dog. To my children, thank you for saying you'll walk the dog. To the dog, Uncle Mort, you cannot read. Love you all.

Finally, the idea for this book sprung, as so many ideas do, from a conversation with a barber. I was getting my hair cut by Tom, and he told me about his badass husband, who works for the ATF, and carries heavy artillery and busts up bad guys, and I thought: "Hey, that sounds like a good character," and, also, "I should probably leave a good tip." Thank you, Tom!